"Where a

His tone was flat, his jaw tensed as if he were still fighting a temper. His blue gaze shot past her to watch the children.

"I don't know." Her throat went dry. Her tongue felt thick as she answered. She trembled not from fear of him, she truly didn't believe he would strike her, but from the unknown.

"You can't keep living out of a wagon," he said. "I have an empty shanty out back of my house that no one's living in. You and your children can stay there for the night."

"*What?*" She stumbled back. "But—"

"There will be no argument," he bit out, interrupting her. "None at all. I buried a wife and son years ago, and to see you and them neglected like this—with no one to care—" His jaw ground again, and his eyes were no longer cold.

Joanna didn't think she'd ever seen anything sadder than Aiden McKaslin as the sun went down on him.

Without another word, he turned on his heels and walked away, melting into the thick shadows of the summer evening.

Books by Jillian Hart

Love Inspired Historical

Homespun Bride
High Country Bride

Love Inspired

Heaven Sent #143
**His Hometown Girl* #180
A Love Worth Waiting For #203
Heaven Knows #212
**The Sweetest Gift* #243
**Heart and Soul* #251
**Almost Heaven* #260
**Holiday Homecoming* #272
**Sweet Blessings* #295
For the Twins' Sake #308
**Heaven's Touch* #315
**Blessed Vows* #327
**A Handful of Heaven* #335
**A Soldier for Christmas* #367
**Precious Blessings* #383
**Every Kind of Heaven* #387
**Everyday Blessings* #400
**A McKaslin Homecoming* #403
***A Holiday to Remember* #425
**Her Wedding Wish* #447

*The McKaslin Clan
**A Tiny Blessings Tale

JILLIAN HART

makes her home in Washington State, where she has lived most of her life. When Jillian is not hard at work on her next story, she loves to read, go to lunch with her friends and spend quiet evenings with her family.

JILLIAN HART

High Country Bride

Published by Steeple Hill Books™

STEEPLE HILL BOOKS

ISBN-13: 978-0-373-82791-6
ISBN-10: 0-373-82791-1

HIGH COUNTRY BRIDE

This edition published by arrangement with Steeple Hill Books.

www.SteepleHill.com

Printed in U.S.A.

I wait quietly before God, for my hope is in Him.
He alone is my rock and my salvation, my fortress
where I will not be shaken.

—*Psalms* 62:5–6

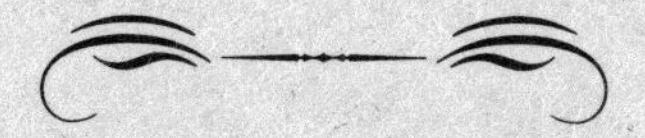

Chapter One

Angel County, Montana Territory
June, 1883

It was a hot day for a wake. Joanna Nelson swiped the dampness from her forehead, closed the oven door with her foot and slid the sheet of biscuits onto the wooden cutting board. The kitchen window was open wide to let in the sweltering wind. It gave her a clear view of the horse and buggy lumbering along the road, kicking up chalky dust.

Few mourners had shown up for her pa's brief funeral in the graveyard behind the church. None had yet made their way to the house. Just this lone horse and buggy ambling tiredly through the heat waves on the dirt road. When the vehicle was near enough, she recognized the driver. Not a mourner, but one of the bankers from town, dressed up in his fancy work suit.

This was not a social call, she suspected. No, Edwin Wessox had been a regular visitor over the last year, because of the bank's worry over Pa's debt. With her father gone, this visit did not necessarily mean good news. Without a doubt, it concerned the mortgage on the farm. She knew, because this had happened to her once before—after her husband died, one year and three months ago. The banker had paid a visit to her not three hours after she'd laid her husband to rest.

Would they be allowed to continue on with the payments? Her stomach twisted in a nervous knot. Don't expect the worst, she told herself. She slid the biscuits from the baking sheet into a cloth-lined bowl. Her half brother had come to stay when the doctor had given Pa the diagnosis. Lee said he wanted to keep farming the land, although he didn't like farming.

It will be all right, Joanna. She took a deep breath and poked her head into the parlor. Lee sat by the open window with a hand to his forehead, looking as shocked as she felt. He didn't so much as blink an eye, much less look in her direction. He clearly had a lot on his mind.

"The banker's coming," she said, then went back to her kitchen work.

She didn't know if that news would make her brother stir. They were not close; he'd only come after she'd telegraphed him. As she hefted the pot of beans from the oven, she tried to keep hopeful. Heaven knew, hard times had rained down on her before like the worst kind of storm. Things had started to get a little easier, finally, while she'd been staying here with her pa.

Please, Lord, she prayed, *don't let things get worse for us.* Praying these days was more habit than belief. She set the bean pot down on the battered wooden table and feared the Lord and all his angels had forgotten her.

Upstairs, she heard the patter of her young son's bare feet, as if to remind her of all she had to protect. Her little girl trailed after him. The two of them sounded like a stampeding herd barreling down the steps.

"Ma! Ma!" James burst into the kitchen and ran straight to her skirts, burying his face in her waist.

Daisy raced after him. She was too young to remember the consequences of her father's death, but was upset because her older brother was. She fisted her hands in the extra material of Joanna's skirt and held on tight.

Since she was as good as hobbled, Joanna left the potatoes to their boiling and scooped her little girl into her arms. Poor baby. Joanna kissed her daughter's brow and snuggled her close. "Why are you crying, little one?"

"I don't wanna live in the wagon. James said."

"Is that true? Did you say that to your sister?"

James held on tighter and didn't answer.

Too many losses, too many upheavals, too much uncertainty. Joanna hated how it had marked her children. "I have dinner on the table. Let me take a look at you. However did you two get so dirty?"

"In the attic, Ma." James tipped his head back to look at her, his sweaty brown hair sticking straight up.

She smoothed it down, wishing she could smooth

away bigger troubles as easily. "It will be all right. Now, go wash your hands and faces while I see to our company."

The worry did not leave James's features when he released his hold on her, or when he took his sister's hand and led her to the washbasin by the back door. Joanna straightened, her skirts sticking to her as she left the hot kitchen for the front door.

Mr. Wessox was tipping his hat to her on the other side of the screen. "Ma'am, I'm sorry for your loss."

"Thank you." Dread quickened her heartbeat and made her hand tremble as she unlatched the door. "Please, come in. Can I get you something to drink?"

"No, I've come to speak with Lee."

Of course. It was a man's world, and Lee was to inherit the ranch. She knew that. But the nerves jumped in her stomach like oil on a hot pan as she hurried back to the kitchen. Her gaze went first to her little ones in the sunny corner. James was holding the towel for his sister as she splashed her hands in the basin.

What is going to happen to us, Lord? To them? She tried to believe—she had to believe—that Lee would be able to stall the banker as handily as their father always had. She and her children would keep this solid roof over their heads. The garden was flourishing, the cow was giving good milk and the chickens were laying so well there would be plenty of food on their table.

Harvest season was coming up, and although Lee hadn't wanted to talk about it, he would clearly need her help when it came to threshing time. Joanna knew there would be harvest workers to feed—that was a large task he could not do without help—and then they had the canning and preserves to do and the garden to put up. Come winter, perhaps she could get some kind of job in town, cooking or cleaning for part of the day to bring in a wage.

All this had kept her up the last few nights, and it all—her future and her children's—depended on Lee and the banker. She couldn't help peering through the doorway, but the men were sitting in the corner, out of her sight. She heard the drone of their voices, too low for her to make out a single word.

"Ma, we're all washed up." James held the towel while Daisy dried her little hands.

"We're real clean, Ma." Daisy's flyaway blond hair stood out at all angles in the dry air. She looked like the precious blessing she was in the little calico frock and white apron Joanna had finished sewing last week, cut down from one of her own dresses. She wished they had money enough for a new piece of fabric, but Daisy looked dear, anyway.

"I'll dish up your supper for you, and you two can eat on the back porch in the shade." At their enthusiastic response, she took a couple of clean plates from the drainer and filled them from the stove.

When she carried the full plates to the back door, she noticed a team pulling a wagon down their driveway. Well, good, at least someone had come. She couldn't make out the driver through the blistering glare of the sun. The big dark draft horses looked familiar, however. Then she recognized the man on the seat. It was their neighbor to the north, Aiden McKaslin. The dour, disagreeable man had come to pay his respects? That surprised her. He and Pa had not gotten along at all, even though they attended the same church.

"Sit down right here, you two." She set both plates on the small wooden table she'd brought out from the kitchen earlier. The chairs scraped as the little ones climbed up and settled in. "James, say the blessing, please."

"Yes, Ma." The little boy scootched forward in his seat and gave his sister a serious look. "Are your hands folded, Daisy?"

"Yes." She blew out a sigh of frustration, stirring the long platinum-blond strands of her hair. "He's bein' bossy again, Ma."

Joanna pressed a kiss to the crown of her daughter's head. It was hard being little. She remembered it well. "I need to go greet Mr. McKaslin, so you two mind your manners, all right?"

"Yes, Ma," they both said gravely.

She left them to the sound of James's serious prayer, trying to keep them in her sight through the window as she headed through the house toward the front door. She was surprised to see the banker and Lee in the front yard already, shaking hands. They were both smiling, and her brother seemed relieved.

Apparently their business was over. Their smiles had to be a good sign—the bank must be willing to let her brother continue on with the payments. The burden of worry slid right off her shoulders like rain from a tin roof. Her children would have a solid, good home. It was a lot to be thankful for.

Aiden McKaslin pulled his draft horses to a stop and stared straight at her. "I've come to take back the cow I didn't receive full payment for."

"What? You're not here for the wake?"

"I'm busy, ma'am. I've only got time to take the cow."

"The milk cow?" Her children needed the milk. She looked to Lee, but he stopped chatting with the banker to shrug in a careless way.

"Let him take the cow, Joanna. We can't keep her."

"We c-can't?" She hadn't considered they might be that bad off. Her brother turned his back and continued walking the banker to his horse and buggy, which were parked in the shade.

Well, they could get along without a cow. Heaven knew they had been much worse off before and managed well enough. What mattered was that they could keep the house and land. This thought bolstered her as she hurried across the crackling dried lawn.

Aiden McKaslin stopped to face her. "I'll return the payments your father already made."

He tugged some folded twenty dollar bills from his muslin shirt pocket and held them out with a steady, sun-brown hand. A capable hand, she noticed, not quite able to meet his gaze. Shyness seized her, for he was a big man, tall and physically intimidating. She felt very small as she took the bills.

"Thank you, that's awful decent of you. I—" She

blushed, realizing how sorry she must look. She smoothed the grease spackles on her patched apron. "The cow is picketed out in the field. You can't see her from here, but she's just behind the barn in the shade by the creek."

"I brought my own rope, so I'll leave you her halter, picket rope and pin. You may be able to get another cow later on, and those will come in handy."

It felt as if a rock had settled in her throat, and she couldn't seem to answer him. She could only nod as she slipped the two twenty dollar bills into her pocket.

"I'm sorry for your loss, ma'am." He tipped his hat. She could see his shadow on the ground at her feet before he whipped around and strode away toward the barn.

"Ma?" Little Daisy stared at her through the slatted porch rails, clutching the weathered wood with her small hands. Tears stood in her eyes. "My plate slid off the t-table. It's all in the d-dirt."

From around the corner, just out of sight, James called out, "Weren't my fault, Ma!"

One tear trickled down Daisy's cheek. "I real s-sorry."

Joanna remembered to count to ten and then took a deep breath of the hot, dusty air. She reached between the boards and caught the wetness on her fingertip. "It's all right. Go help your brother clean up, then come around to the kitchen door and meet me."

"Y-yes, Ma." Her daughter hiccuped once, spun in a swirl of pink calico and padded off on bare feet.

Poor baby. Joanna watched to make sure no more tears fell as Daisy hopped down the step to kneel beside her brother. Their hands worked quickly. The mess couldn't have been very much. After she filled a second plate for Daisy, Joanna would see to the rest of the cleaning up.

She felt an odd tingling at the back of her neck. It wasn't a good feeling. She peered around, but Mr. Aiden McKaslin had already cut behind the barn and was out of sight and earshot—and quickly, too. A staid bachelor like him, close to thirty years old, probably had an unpleasant opinion of children and their messes. She'd married a man just like that.

The last thing she intended to do was pay him any mind. The banker was driving away, kicking up more chalky dust into the heavy air. Lee headed off to the barn. Most likely to talk with Mr. McKaslin, who was likely tying the cow to the back of his wagon now.

If only they had enough money in hand. Joanna wistfully glanced into the blinding shafts of June sunlight. She would have liked to have milk for the children. But beggars could not be choosers, and she was glad for what they did have. As she hurried around to the door, she spied the garden beginning to crisp beneath the harsh sun. She'd have to remember to give the vegetables an extra watering after she was through in the kitchen.

While she dished up another plate, she caught sight of Mr. McKaslin returning from behind the barn with their Jersey cow on a lead rope. Something about the man caught her eye. She'd seen him in church, of course, but he was the type of worshipper who arrived at the last moment, kept to the back and slipped out before the final hymn. There was a sadness to him that hung over him like a storm cloud. It was that melancholy that kept him from being truly frightening.

Had she offered him a meal? She couldn't remember. Her mind was a muddle and she felt frayed to the last thread. She put more fuel in the stove and more water to heat. She went to the back door, but Mr. McKaslin was already in his wagon and driving off, the cow trailing behind. Before she'd blinked twice, there was only a dust cloud where he had been.

Daisy stood leaning at the rail with those wide blue eyes of hers even wider. "Why's Uncle Lee all packed up on the horse?"

"Packed up? No, he's probably out back in the fields, gone to chat with Mr. McKaslin. Don't you worry about it, honey." She set the plate on the table. "Here, sit down and eat your dinner."

"O*kay*..." Daisy said in one long, drawn-out sigh.

As Joanna brushed a comforting hand over her daughter's head, a movement caught her eye. There, against the background of the growing wheat fields and the fading patches of red on the barn, was Lee astride Pa's horse. Daisy was right. There were two bulging packs behind his saddle and a satchel hung over the saddle horn. Lee had his black hat drawn low and didn't look her way.

James glanced nervously over his shoulder. "Ma, where's he goin'?"

"I'm sure to settle a few business matters in town,

is all." A punch of apprehension hit her square in the stomach. Something was very wrong. She forced a smile into her voice for the children's sake. "Stay right here on the porch, eat your dinner, and I'll get you a surprise for dessert."

"There's dessert?" James swiveled toward her, his uncle forgotten. "Honest?"

"Is it cake?" Daisy asked with a fork halfway to her mouth.

"You'll have to wait and see."

Lee rode out of sight behind the house, and it was hard to keep her step natural as she headed straight to the kitchen. The moment the door slapped shut behind her she rushed through to the front yard. Lee didn't look behind him, but his back stiffened, so he had to know she was hurrying after him.

"Lee?" She had to keep her voice low so the children would not be able to overhear this. "Lee? Where are you going?"

"Away." He bit out the word, then appeared annoyed as he reined in the horse. "Truth is, I sold the place."

"You *what?*" She couldn't be hearing him right. Maybe it was the lack of sleep last night and the emotional upset over the funeral. It was all the hard kitchen work in this stifling heat. Yes, that's what it was. "For a moment there, I thought you said you'd sold out, but there's still the crop in the fields."

"I sold it, too. The banker said you've got until nightfall to get out."

"Get out?" There was something wrong with her

mind. She could hear Lee's words, but her brain was not making sense of them. Surely he didn't say— "You want me to get out of the house?"

"You can't live in it if it belongs to someone else. The banker bought the place for his sister. She'd like to get settled tonight."

"Tonight?" The earth began to spin. "Lee, what about the children? You aren't putting us out, are you?"

"You aren't my lookout. They're your ragamuffins, not mine. I'm not beholden to them or to you. Pa left me this place fair and square. It's mine to sell."

"But before Pa died, you said…" Not only was the earth spinning, but it was tilting, too.

No, this can't be happening. This cannot be right. She had to be ill from the heat, that was it. Her mind was fuddled from too little sleep and too much worry. "Y-you said we could live here."

"I know what I said." Lee glared down at her. "I came to help you take care of the old man. The crops are still doing well in the fields because of me. The banker met my price and I took it. Leave the pigs and the chickens when you go. They're part of the sale, too."

"But—" Her brain seemed stuck on that word like her feet to the dirt. "It's not right. You just can't—"

"Sure I can. I only came back here for the money. You know I never held much regard for our old man. He was a louse."

"But you said—"

"In this world, you've got to look out for yourself and no one else. It's the only way to survive." Lee gazed down on her with pity. He pulled his billfold from his shirt pocket. "Here."

She stared at the twenty dollar bill he held out, the end flapping in the brisk scorching wind. The truth hit her like dry lightning. "You really sold the land and you're keeping all the money."

"It's legal. Pa left everything to me. You know that."

"But you said you would stay to farm. You promised. You gave your word."

"Yeah, well, I hardly expected you to help me out if you knew." Since she didn't take the money, Lee tossed it at her. The wind snatched it and blew it away like a dry leaf. It stuck to the wall of sticker bushes growing along the road and flapped there, helplessly trapped.

Joanna gulped hard. She fisted her hands, fighting to stay calm. Getting upset would not make this easier. "You lied to me. Lee, you're my brother."

"Half brother. Take my advice and start packing. That banker's not a nice man. He'll put you and your young ones out by force. Do you want that?"

A bead of sweat rolled down her spine. She shook her head once, but the horse was already trotting away, kicking up bits of earth and small rocks. In the matter of a few heartbeats, all that she could see of her brother was a thick cloud of dust.

He'll put you and your young ones out by force. The image of that tore through her and, without thought, she moved forward. She snatched the twenty dollar bill from the bush, ignoring the bite of scratches across her knuckles. She added the bill to the money Mr. McKaslin had given her. The sun was already sinking in the sky, the day more than half over. She had a lot to do if she wanted to spare her children any unpleasantness.

Woodenly, she stumbled into the kitchen, checking through the open window to see them seated at the little battered wooden table, comfortably finishing their meals. The wind puffed James's dark hair straight up like one big cowlick. Daisy sat as dainty and as dear as a princess.

Lord, please help me to manage this well. For their sake. She might have prayed further for shelter and work and somewhere to go, but she'd learned from experience that the good Lord did not hear many of her prayers. So she kept them simple.

"What's for dessert, Ma?" James had hopped off his chair and stood at the window, happily watching her through the mesh screen.

"You sit down and watch your sister, handsome, and I'll bring you both big pieces of cake."

"Cake! I knew it." Delight rounded his sweet face and he dashed the short distance back to his chair.

That's my answer, she realized as she found a knife and went to work on the cake hidden in the cellar to keep cool and fresh. This will be an adventure, a special trip. Not a scary life living out of the wagon. They would be explorers, like in the book she was reading to them, a few pages at a time, at night.

She swallowed all her fears and worries, put a smile on her face and cut two huge slices of cake. Her mind was busy making plans of how to pack and what they would take as she pushed her way through the screen door.

Two darling faces turned toward her in sheer delight. "Cake!"

She knew from sad experience that the Lord might not provide for them, but she would find a way.

Chapter Two

If it wasn't one problem to deal with, it was another. Aiden McKaslin drew his horse to a halt and squinted into the long rays of the setting sun.

Sure enough, there at the edge of his property, just inside the boundary fence, was a squatter. A covered wagon huddled in the shelter of an old maple. Judging by the fraying cover, it had seen better days. The smoke from a newly lit fire rose thick and unsteady from a tidy circle of stones.

What with the glare of the sun, and the shadows the tree made on the ground, he couldn't see a living soul. Just two horses nipping at the growing grass.

He yanked his Winchester from the saddle holster by its barrel and cocked it with one hand. Aiden carried the weapon mostly for the wild predators that got to eyeing his livestock for dinner now and again. But when he ran into trouble of the human sort, he was doubly glad he always rode armed. He'd had trouble like this before, and experience taught him that squatters were mostly criminals.

He hated trouble, but the law was a good five miles away, so he approached the camp with caution, studying the lay of things with a careful eye. There was wearing of the earth around the stubborn tufts of grass at the creek bank. The careful sweeping of footprints out of the dirt seemed to be a clue that whoever was staying here might not want to leave a sign of how many of them there were. The trampled grass around the wagon was another hint—still fresh, but with significant usage.

What if the men were dangerous? Aiden drew his horse to a stop and considered. He was out in the open now. Too late to retreat. Trouble like this had occurred early last year, and a ranch hand had been shot and left for dead by squatters. They'd never been caught. Thankfully, the hired man had survived.

Aiden would rather deal with dangerous wildlife anyday than a pack of armed criminals.

Then he saw something in the dust by the right rear wagon wheel. He leaned forward in the saddle, squinted a bit and realized it was a small, crudely carved wooden horse—a child's toy. A child's toy? Not what he'd figured on finding here in a squatter's camp. Then he heard a rustle, and a puff of dust rose from beneath the wagon.

He lowered the hammer and the rifle. "Is your pa around?"

A round face peered between the spokes of the wheel. "Nah. He rode away to heaven."

Aiden studied the wide brown eyes and dark hair sticking straight up, recognizing the child. The widow's kid who had lived on the neighboring ranch for a spell. Probably another sad story, he figured as he dismounted. He was learning that life was full of sad stories. Even though he'd lost his heart long ago, and there was nothing but an empty hole where it had been, he steeled himself. He didn't want to feel a thing, and he knew this situation was going to be full of sadness. "Your ma then?"

"She said not to talk to nobody. Shh, Daisy." There was more rustling and the boy drew back.

To his surprise, a little girl with white-blond hair held back with a bright pink ribbon crawled out from beneath the wagon bed. She brushed the dust off her skirt primly. "Ma didn't say *I* couldn't talk to nobody."

Aiden couldn't rightly say that he wasn't affected by that cute little girl. Such a wee thing, not much to her at all, and living out of a covered wagon. The little boy crawled out, too, looking annoyed with his younger sister. He drew himself up tall—he couldn't be more than seven or eight years old—and scolded his sister for not minding.

They hadn't been living here long, Aiden decided as he glanced around. Everything was neat and tidy, and a woman's presence might explain the swept dirt. While he didn't have the best opinion of most women, he'd learned even the worst of them liked to dust and sweep with a vengeance.

The little boy was shaking his finger at his sister.

"Ma said to stay hid. You oughtn't to be talking to strangers."

"Are you a stranger?" The little girl gazed past her brother and straight into Aiden's eyes.

He choked a little, feeling a gnawing of something in his chest. He didn't like it. He didn't like feelings. Life was too hard for them. A smart man didn't give in to them. He set his jaw tight and answered between clenched teeth. "Your brother is right. You ought to mind him."

"Oh." The little girl wilted like a new seedling in a late freeze. "Do you know where Ma is?"

"No. She's not here? Did she go off and leave you?" There it was. Fury. It roared through him unbidden and with a power that he hadn't felt since—

"Excuse me." A woman's voice carried like a gunshot on the wind. "Step away from my children."

He did as she asked, so as not to startle her. But as he pivoted on his boot heel to face her, he steeled himself a tad more. He still wasn't prepared for what he saw. Exhaustion was a mask obscuring her young face. Her dress was clean and proper and pressed, and her soft blond hair braided casually in one long tail that fell over her shoulder. The air of her, the feel that hung over her like a cloud, was pure hardship.

His emotions weren't ironclad enough, because he felt the tug of pity. And more. The fury remained, digging deep. "This is my land, ma'am. You can't go leaving your children alone here."

"I didn't leave them alone. I was down at the creek."

As she strode to the crest of the rise, he could clearly see the two five-gallon buckets she carried, one in each hand. She was a tiny thing, and water was heavy. He was striding toward her before he realized he was moving at all.

There was fear in her eyes—fear of him, he realized, as he yanked the first bucket out of her hand. She drew back fiercely, sloshing water over the rim and onto her faded skirts, clutching the remaining bucket's handle with a death grip.

"Give me the water." He tucked his rifle against his forearm and held out his free hand.

Her eyes widened at the sight of his rifle, pointed downward at an angle toward the grass.

Women. He ought to have remembered what they were like, having once been married. He did his best to keep his annoyance out of his voice. "I use my rifle for defense, nothing more, ma'am. Now, give me the bucket."

She swallowed visibly, as if she were about to hand over a potful of money. He had frightened her more than he'd realized.

Shame filled him and he took care when he lifted the heavy bucket from her small hand. He cleared his throat, not at all sure how to say what he had meant to say. Talking had never been his strong suit. He hefted the heavy water buckets and lugged them toward the camp, where both little children watched him wide-eyed. Anyone could see they were well-behaved, that their ma was doing a good job raising them up.

"Where you want these?" He glanced over his shoulder, but the woman seemed frozen in place on the rise. Mrs. Nelson looked like a sensible sort. Her pink calico dress might be faded, but it was simple and clean, void of frippery.

She came across as a decent lady down on her luck. And she was staring at him with fear on her face. Not the terrified sort of run-and-hide fear. No, the fear he saw on her delicate features was the kind that made him even angrier. The kind that spoke of ill-treatment.

"Where do you want me to put the water?" he repeated in as clear of a voice as he could manage.

Mrs. Nelson visibly swallowed. "Under the tailgate."

Without a word he turned and marched angrily on, his boots clumping against the hard-packed earth. He hauled the buckets to the back of the wagon and dropped them with a small puff of dust. When he straightened, he realized both children had followed him, single file, and were staring up at him with dust-smudged faces. Mrs. Nelson's skirts snapped as she hurried to stand between him and the young ones.

That only made him madder. "What are you doing here?"

"I'll not have you using that tone in front of my children." Her dainty chin came up, and she was all protective fire, though the old, worn fear was still there.

He hated that fear. It was all he could do to keep his tone low and his voice calm. "This being my land, ma'am, I'll use whatever tone suits me. Now, answer my question."

That chin lifted another notch before she turned to speak to her little ones. "You two go on and wash up for supper, while I speak to Mr. McKaslin."

They nodded and politely went straight to it. The little boy fetched a bar of lye soap and a worn but clean towel from the back of the wagon, and took charge of seeing to the hands and face washing of his little sister.

With the children busy, Aiden followed Mrs. Nelson out into the grass. She turned to face him with her arms crossed over her chest and her spine straight. "We had no place to go, Mr. McKaslin."

"You have family."

"Family? I have no one and you know it." She held herself very still. "If you'll excuse me, I'll get my children into the wagon and we'll be off your property by sundown. That is what you want, isn't it?"

"You just said you have no place to go."

"And a man like you cares?" She heard the heartlessness in her own voice and stopped, took a breath and a moment to compose herself. She might be homeless, but she had her dignity. "I cannot reimburse you for our stay on your land. I am sorry for that."

"Sorry?" A muscle worked in his granite jaw. He repeated the word as if he'd bitten into something sour. "Sorry?"

"There's no need to be so angry." She took a step back and drew in a gulp of air. "We hardly did any harm."

"Any harm?"

"We wore away some of your grass, and the horses

grazed on the bunchgrass, but it wasn't as if you were using—"

"This is unacceptable." A vein throbbed out at his temple. *"You've been living here for how long?"*

"Since Mr. Wessox found us camped out at the edge of his farm on the other side of the creek." She curled her hands into fists, keeping her chin set and her tone even. This was not the first irate man she'd ever had to manage.

"How long?" Tendons stood out in his muscled, sun-browned neck.

"We were only there a few weeks." She felt very small. "We've been on your land for a little longer."

"And you have no family?" A tick started in the corded muscles of his jaw.

"You already know the answer." She took a few slow steps in retreat. She could not get to her wagon—or her children—without going past Mr. McKaslin. "My half brother has no interest in helping us. There is no one else."

"What of your husband's side of the family?"

"As he's passed away, and his family did not approve of me, they want nothing to do with us. Not even for the children's sake." She didn't know how it could possibly be, but her words seemed to make the man towering over her even angrier. He appeared to be restraining his fury, but it was a terrible sight. He was more than twice her size and strength, and as he began to breathe heavily with his anger, he seemed invincible.

A thin thread of fear shivered through her, but she firmly clutched her skirts, lifting them so she would not trip. Her first wobbly step took her closer to him. Closer to his rage. "Excuse me."

To her surprise, he let her walk by. She did her best to ignore the stone pillar he seemed as she hurried past him, adrenaline kicking up with every step she took. Her children were waiting, sweet and good, with their faces and hands washed. They were carefully wiping up their water splashes. Her heart warmed toward them as it always did, and she hoped she could keep them safe.

"Ma?" James leaned close, all brightness gone from his face. "That man's gonna make us leave again, ain't he?"

Before she could answer, Daisy fisted her little hands in the folds of Joanna's skirts and looked up with frightened eyes. "I don't wanna go."

"Why ever not?" She did her best to put a smile on her face and soothing love in her voice. She knelt down so they could look into her eyes and clearly see they should not be worried. "We always knew this was just a stopping off place. Why, we're ready to go and start our next adventure. Doesn't that sound fun?"

"No." James would not be fooled, her poor little boy. "Do we gotta go now? Before supper?"

Aware of Daisy's lower lip trembling and how intently the little girl watched her, Joanna tried to weigh her next words carefully. She did not want to make promises she could not keep. But neither did she want to be so truthful it shattered her children. She was out of options, and her prayers had simply gone unanswered for so long, they might never be again.

All she could do was the best she knew how. "All right, you two, start rounding up your toys. Be sure to get them all. We don't want to leave any behind."

"Okay, Ma." James sighed with sadness, his shoulders weighed down as he went to bring in his wooden horses.

"Yes, Ma." Daisy sniffed, her head down, and trudged away.

The wild grasses crunched beneath Mr. McKaslin's boots. She dreaded facing him again. He strode toward her through the waving stalks, his work clothes rippling slightly in the strong westerly breeze and hinting at his steely strength. Vulnerable, she braced herself for whatever wrath he'd come to inflict on her.

He had some right, she admitted, for they *were* squatters. They *were* illegally using the land he worked hard to pay for and to maintain. She was, essentially, stealing from him. That shamed her.

Silence stretched between them, and she felt the rake of his gaze, taking her in from the top of her windblown hair, where escaped tendrils snapped in the wind, to the toes of her scuffed, patched shoes. She watched him fist his big, work-roughened hands, and expected the worst.

"You never told me, Mrs. Nelson. Where are you going to go?" His tone was flat, his jaw tensed, as if he was still fighting his temper. His blue eyes glanced past her to where the children were going about their chore.

"I don't know." Her throat went dry. Her tongue felt thick as she answered. "When I find employment, I could wire a payment to you. Rent. Y-you aren't thinking of—of bringing the sheriff in?"

"You think I want *payment?*" Aiden's voice boomed like winter thunder. "You think I want *rent money?*"

"Frankly, I don't know what you want."

"I'll tell you what I *don't* want. I don't want..." His words echoed like cannon fire as he paused, and a passing pair of geese overhead honked in flat-noted tones. He grimaced, and it was impossible to guess what he would say or do.

She trembled not from fear of him—she truly didn't believe he would strike her—but from the unknown. Of being forced to take the frightening step off the only safe spot she'd found since she'd lost Pa's house.

When you were homeless, everything seemed so fragile, so easily off balance. It was a big, unkind world for a woman alone with her children. She had no one to protect her. No one to care. The truth was, Joanna had never had those things in her husband. How could she expect them from any stranger? Especially this man she hardly knew, who seemed harsh, cold and hard-hearted?

And, worse, what if he brought in the law?

"You can't keep living out of a wagon," he said, still angry, the cords straining in his neck. "Animals have enough sense to keep their young cared for and safe."

Yes, it was as she'd thought. He intended to be as cruel as he could be. She spun on her heels, pulling up all her defenses, determined to let his hurtful words roll off her. She grabbed the towel the children had neatly folded and tossed it into the laundry box in the back of the wagon.

"Mrs. Nelson. I'm talking to you."

"Yes, I know. If you expect me to stand there while you tongue-lash me, you're mistaken. I have packing to get to." Her fingers were clumsy as she hefted the bucket of water she'd brought for washing—she wouldn't need that now—and heaved.

His hand clasped the handle beside hers, and she could feel the life and power of him vibrate along the thin metal. "Give it to me."

Her fingers let go. She felt stunned as he walked away, easily carrying the bucket, which had been so heavy for her. Quietly, methodically, he put out the small cooking fire. He did not seem as ominous or as intimidating—somehow—as he stood in the shadows, bent to his task, although she couldn't say why. Perhaps it was because he wasn't acting the way she was used to men acting. She was quite accustomed to doing all the work.

James scurried over, clutching his wooden horse, to watch. Daisy hung back, eyes wide and still, taking in the mysterious goings-on.

He was different when he was near to them, she realized. He didn't seem harsh, and there was no hint of anger—or, come to think of it, any other emotion—as he shook out the empty bucket, nodded once to the children and then retraced his path to her.

"Let me guess." He dropped the bucket onto the tailgate, and his anger appeared to be back. Cords strained in his neck and jaw again as he growled at her. "If you leave here, you don't know where you're going and you have no money to get there with?"

She nodded. "Yes, sir."

"Then get you and your kids into the wagon. I'll hitch up your horses for you." His eyes were cold and yet not unfeeling as he fastened his gaze on hers. "I have a shanty out back of my house that no one's living in. You can stay there for the night."

"What?" She stumbled back, and the solid wood of the tailgate bit into the small of her back. "But—"

"There will be no argument," he snapped, interrupting her. "None at all. I buried a wife and son years ago, what was most precious to me, and to see you and them neglected like this—with no one to care…" His jaw clenched again, and his eyes were no longer cold.

Joanna didn't think she'd ever seen anything sadder than Aiden McKaslin standing there in the slanting rays of the setting sun.

Without another word, he turned on his heels and walked away, melting into the thick shadows of the summer evening.

Chapter Three

As he led the way across his land, it was all Aiden could do not to look behind him. He knew the covered wagon was following him across the rolling prairie, but he steeled his resolve. He would not turn around and see that woman alone, thin from hunger and pale with strain. He could not take any more, so he contented himself with listening to the plod of the tired horses' hooves on the sun-baked earth, and the rhythmic squeak of the wagon's rear axel.

Yep, he didn't like this one bit, but he hated even worse the notion of sitting home tonight, comfortable and safe and fed, knowing that a nice woman and her children were unprotected and uncherished and alone.

No, it just wasn't right. Emotion clogged his throat, making it hard to swallow, making it hard to breathe. He refused to let his gaze wander to the east, where the family cemetery lay in shadow, the headstones tall enough to see from his saddle. That's what got him all stirred up. Seeing this woman alone, and her small children homeless, rubbed at the break in his soul that had never healed properly.

He didn't see how it ever could. A loss like that was too much for a man to take.

It was a long ride home through the low rays of the sun. A cooling breeze kicked up, and he drew in the fresh air until it settled in his lungs. He let his chest empty of all the feelings in there. By the time he spotted the sun winking on the windows of home, he was safe from his wounds again.

The young boy's voice rose above the call of a quail and the rustling wind in the grass. "Ma! Ma! Is that where we're gonna live?"

Aiden tried not to be affected by the young'un's excitement, nor by his mother's gentle response.

"No, sweetheart, that's where Mr. McKaslin lives."

"But it's so *big,* Ma. Are you sure?"

"Yes. We're going to live in his shanty."

"Oh."

Aiden steeled himself to the sound of the small boy's disappointment, too. He told himself the shanty was snug and would do just fine for them all, but the truth was, he couldn't stomach the notion of having another woman in the house he'd built for Kate.

He followed the fork in the road that skirted the barn and led south from the main house to the small dark structure of wood and plaster. He heard the children's quiet questions to their mother and tried not to hear the soothing lull of her answers as he dismounted.

Opening the door and finding the nearest lantern kept his mind off the ragged family climbing down from their wagon in the front yard. By the time he'd lit the second lantern, the boy stood in the open doorway, looking smaller for the darkness and shadows cast over him.

The child's serious eyes were unblinking as he watched Aiden cross the one-room house to the cookstove in the corner. If his guess was right about Mrs. Nelson, she would want tea with supper and wash water for cleaning up. He knelt down and began to build a fire with the bucket of kindling and sticks of wood left over from when his middle brother had been living here.

The boy said nothing, just watched with wide eyes. Aiden tried not to think much about the child. Not out of heartlessness—no, never that.

By the time he got the fire lit and flames licked greedily at the tinder-dry wood, the woman arrived at the door with her littlest on her hip. Without a word she glanced around the shanty. Her face was gaunt in the half darkness, her feelings masked. He couldn't tell if she was disappointed in the shelter or relieved.

After closing the stove door, he rose to his feet. "I'll bring in some water for you, ma'am. I'll send my brother out with supper."

"No. Thank you, but no." She looked stricken. "I've already been so much trouble to you. I can't be—I won't be—more beholden to you. I—"

"You shoulda thought of that when you decided to

live on a piece of my property." He watched her rear back—just a step, just a small movement, but somehow it felt like a larger motion. As if he'd truly insulted her. It was not what he'd meant.

Tread softly, man. He checked his voice, gentling it as much as he was able. "Just put aside your worries for tonight. I'll sleep easier knowing you and your young ones are safe instead of sleeping out there alone on the prairie. Do you understand?"

"Fine. Then we'll speak again tomorrow. I am grateful." Tension still tightened her face, and the flickering light seemed to emphasize the hollows and lines there, in those lovely features that ought to be soft with happiness and contentment.

It was not a fair world, and he knew it as much as anyone. He jammed the match tin onto the shelf with a little too much force. Watching the way Mrs. Nelson's gaze moved with relief and pleasure around the shanty shamed him. The place wasn't much. He wasn't sure what his Christian duty was, but he hoped he was doing his share. He touched his hat brim. "'Scuse me, ma'am, I'll say good night, then."

"Thank you for your kindness." She moved from the doorway with a rustle of petticoats and a hush of skirts, careful to keep her distance from him. "Good night, Mr. McKaslin."

When he crossed the threshold, he could feel her sigh of relief. He made her uneasy, and it troubled him as he hiked through the growing grasses, for he was uneasy, too. He'd never thought there would be another woman on his land—even for just the night and even in the shanty.

He kept going until the shanty was nothing more than a faint black outline against the shadowed sky. Kindness, Mrs. Nelson had called it, but it was nothing of the sort. He was only doing the right thing, and that did not come without cost.

"Ma, that was a mighty fine supper!" James's grin was so wide it was likely to split his face. "I cleaned my whole plate."

"Yes, you did." Joanna lifted the kettle of water steaming on the back of the stove. "You be sure and thank Mr. McKaslin the next time you see him."

"Yes'm. I'm puttin' him in my prayers tonight. I was gettin' mighty tired of creek fish." The little boy slid his plate and steel fork next to the washbasin on the table. "Are you sure we can't stay here forever?"

"Yes, I'm sure. This is only for tonight." Holding her heart still, Joanna carefully poured the steaming water into the basin and returned the half-full kettle to the stove. Mr. McKaslin. Now, there was a puzzle. She could not figure that man out. In the field, when she'd come up with water from the creek, she'd been afraid of him. He'd been so angry. Now she realized it wasn't anger at all. No, not if he'd brought them here.

She reached for the bar of lye soap she'd brought in from the wagon earlier, and began to pare off shavings, which fell into the hot water to curl and melt. She felt a little like those shavings, wilting a bit. She wasn't used to taking charity, but as she watched her children move about contentedly, she was grateful to Mr. McKaslin. Somehow she would find a way to repay him for his kindness.

Daisy sidled close with her plate and yawned hugely.

"Is it time for bed already?" Joanna glanced at the shelf clock, which sat mute, the motionless hands frozen at ten minutes after one, clearly the wrong time. "Go on, you two, wash up and get changed."

"Ma." Daisy tugged on a fold of Joanna's skirt, looking up with big blue eyes full of worry. "What about the angels?"

Joanna's heart twisted hard. The first night they'd slept in the wagon, she had told them that the wagon cover was better than a roof because it made it easier for the angels to watch over them. "The angels will be able to keep an eye on you just fine, baby. Now, you wash up and we'll read more from our book. How's that?"

Daisy's smile showed the perfect dimples in her cheeks.

"That'd be mighty fine!" James, listening in, looked as if he could not believe his luck.

As they scampered to finish their washing up, Joanna left the dishes to soak in the water and plucked a sheet from the small box she'd brought in earlier. There, in the small mirror above the washbasin, her face was staring back at her.

That's me? She froze, gazing at the strange woman in the mirror. She'd never been pretty, and she knew it. Her husband had always taken pains to point out her plainness. But she could never remember looking this poorly. Her hair—her only vanity—was dry and fly-away instead of glossy and sleek. Her face was ashen and the hollows beneath her eyes were as dark as day-old bruises. Her cheeks were gaunt and her eyes too big. Sadness had dug lines that had not been there before.

That was not her, she thought, ashamed. That was not the face of a twenty-eight-year-old woman. No wonder Aiden McKaslin had barely glanced at her, and, when he did, it was with that shuttered look of annoyance. What must he see? What must he think of her? And why was she remembering how kind and strong he'd seemed, too? And how changed he'd been around the children?

It didn't matter. After tomorrow she would never see him again.

Tomorrow. That was one thought she wanted to avoid. As hard as she tried not to admit it, she and her children were now covered-wagon people—the homeless people of the West—and she could no longer deny it.

Should they stay in the area? Find another forgotten piece of prairie to park their wagon on? It was too early for harvest work in the fields. And where would she leave her children while she was working?

Should they leave Angel Falls? The horses were in no condition, as old as they were, to pull the wagon a long distance. She did not have the money to stay—particularly come morning, after she squared up what she owed to Aiden McKaslin.

"Ma!" Daisy's sweet voice broke into her thoughts. "I can't reach."

She blinked, realizing her daughter was waiting for her to unbutton her little dress. Joanna banished her worries with a shake of her head—there would be enough time to dwell on them later, when she was unable to fall to sleep—and tackled the tiny buttons marching down the back of Daisy's pink calico dress. "There, now. Go get your nightgown and I'll have your bed nice and ready."

"Yes, Ma." Daisy scampered off to where their satchel of clothes sat on the floor. She knelt, all sweetness, to peer inside the bag and search for her nightie.

Yes, Joanna had some decisions to make. She shook out the worn muslin over the straw tick with a snap. The fabric fluttered into place, and she bent to smooth and tuck quickly. Her troubled thoughts turned to Aiden McKaslin. Funny, her pa had lived next door to the McKaslins for the last five years, and he'd never said much about Aiden except that he was highly disagreeable. Then again, Pa had been highly disagreeable himself.

Joanna had seen Mr. McKaslin in church since she'd come to stay with her father, but didn't know anything about him at all. Certainly not what he'd said. His words came back to her. *I buried a wife and son years ago, what was most precious to me, and to see you and them neglected like this—with no one to care—*

Not only was she sad for this man who had lost so much, but she admired him, too. He was a good man—

rare, in her opinion—or at least good enough to care about someone not his concern. There were men who would have thrown her off the land without blinking. Some would have threatened her with the sheriff.

But Aiden McKaslin had brought her here. She looked around the structure, so solidly built, and clean, except for a little dust here and there. There was a stout roof overhead and not a single crack in a wall. Real glass windows stared out at the gathering darkness and showed a round moon hanging low over the valley. Yes, she would remember Aiden McKaslin in her prayers tonight.

By the time she'd added a top sheet to the straw tick and the quilts from the wagon, the children had said their prayers and were ready for bed. She tucked them in, kissed their brows and told them what a good job they'd done today. When she turned out the lantern by the bedside, after reading to them as she'd promised, she left them sound asleep. She finished the dishes in the meager light of a single lantern, listening to the sounds of the night. Thinking of her problems and her limited choices to solve them overwhelmed her.

When the dishes were done and put away into the crate, she sat down with her mending. She worked while the fire burned down and moonlight moved across the floor of the shanty. Midnight came and she was still sitting with a needle in her hand, wondering what the morning would bring.

She hoped she would be strong enough to face it.

* * *

Aiden looked up from his newspaper when he heard Finn's boot steps pounding into the kitchen. Sure enough, there was his little brother—twenty years old—worked up into a fever. No surprise there. Aiden took a sip of his tea, assessing the boy's mood over the rim of his cup. Finn could surprise you, but it was best to try to at least figure out his state before attempting to deal with him. As much as Aiden loved his youngest brother, he had to be honest about his flaws and weaknesses—there were many of those. Judging by the disgruntled frown, the crease of annoyance in Finn's forehead and the angry way he tossed the harness strap across the back of one of the chairs, Aiden figured his brother was working himself up into a temper.

Best not to react to it or encourage it. "I see you had trouble fixing that harness. Why don't you get a cup of tea? We'll tackle it tomorrow."

"Trouble? I didn't have any trouble." Finn took off his battered work hat and plucked his newer, going-to-town hat from the wall peg. "What I have is a problem sewing that up for her."

"It's what I asked you to do. Technically, you would be doing it for me."

Finn cursed. "Do you think having a woman live out there is a good idea?"

"No, but what else would you have me do with her?"

"I could name a few things, all of which would involve her moving on to take advantage of someone else. She's trouble, Aiden."

"Oh? Do you know the Widow Nelson?"

"I know her type. Whatever she's offering you, beware. She's just trying to get her hooks into you."

"I'll keep that in mind." Wryly, Aiden finished the dregs of tea in his cup, trying to imagine quiet, proper Joanna Nelson as Finn was attempting to paint her.

It was impossible. When he thought of her, he recalled how gentle she was, how diligent and kind to her children, and of all the work she must have been forced to do for her father. That old man was the type who wouldn't give shelter to his daughter and grandchildren without expecting a good amount of profit from it.

No, when Aiden thought of Joanna Nelson, he thought of hard work and that simple beauty of hers. The good kind of beauty that was more than appearances. She was the brand of woman who would face down a man twice her size if she thought her children needed protection.

That was the type of woman he could understand. He folded the newspaper in half, then in half again, watching Finn exchange his work shirt for one of the clean ones folded in the basket near the door, where the laundry lady had left it. It appeared that Finn was heading to town. Would it do any good to forbid him to go?

Finn had that belligerent look to him, the one he got when he was in no mind to be told what to do. "Fine, don't mind what I'm saying. You'll see I'm right when she's got you standing up in church wearing your wedding ring."

An arrow to the heart, that's what Finn's words

were to Aiden. Finn was thinking he was so smart, as he always did when he got up a full head of steam. He was just talking to impress himself. What did he know about real life? Not one thing. He spent most of his time dreaming about the bottom of a whiskey bottle.

Finn had never loved so hard that his breath and heartbeat were nothing, nothing at all, compared to a woman's breath and heartbeat. He had never sat the night through, bargaining with God every second of every minute of every long, long hour to take his life—to just take it—and to please let her live.

A wife? That was far more than a wedding ring and a minister's words. A marriage was more than something a woman hoodwinked a man into. Anything short of that was a falsehood and an affront to God, whose love was a great gift. Pressure gathered at Aiden's temples, and he dropped the paper. He was in no mood to read now.

Finn grabbed his Sunday coat from the wall peg.

Yep, Aiden could see exactly what his brother was up to. "I don't want you going out."

"You're not my lord and master, are you?" Finn had the audacity to wink. "C'mon. I worked hard today. I deserve a little fun."

"No you don't. What you deserve is to work harder tomorrow." Yep, he knew exactly what Finn meant by fun. He meant trouble. "We're getting up an hour earlier tomorrow and hitting the fields."

"Aw, Aiden. It's all we do around here."

"If I find out you went to town and drank even a

drop of whiskey, you're off this property. Out of this house. There'll be no more roof over your head. No food in your belly. You'll leave with exactly what you came with, which was the clothes on your back."

Aiden braced himself for the coming wrath. He regretted his current headache because it would only pound more when Finn slammed the door on his way out.

"Whoa there." His brother's chin shot up. For the briefest moment there was the hint of the good boy he'd been—honest and sensitive and a little afraid—but in a flash it was gone. Replaced by the easier emotions of anger and bluster. "We agreed before I got out of prison and stepped foot on this land—*our* land—"

My land, Aiden thought, but he let it pass. He wasn't a greedy man, but he figured more than twenty years of blood and sweat and backbreaking work made the place his. He'd worked harder than their drunkard of a father to clear and build this place from a wild quarter section of prairie. And it was his name on the deed. His name on the mortgage.

"—that I just had to stay out of trouble and do my work around here. No one said I couldn't have a little fun on my own time."

"No one's debating that, Finn. What I am saying is that you show up half-drunk or hungover for repairing the north field fencing, and your free ride is over."

"What free ride?"

That did it; he'd pushed too hard. Aiden shrugged. His head throbbed. His burden was heavy. Seeing Widow Nelson's troubles today had cinched it for him.

He was heartsick thinking of the way some men could be. He didn't need to look at it in his own house, in the house where he'd once been happy. He squeezed out the memories that hurt too much. He blotted out the images of her here, of the feminine scent of her lotions and soaps, of her cinnamon rolls baking in the oven just for him, where her laughter and sweetness had made life—his life—better for a time.

"No man tells me what to do." Finn's tirade broke into his thoughts. "Yes, even you, Aiden. You might be my brother, but you are not my keeper."

Aiden waited for the door to slam, and Finn didn't disappoint. On his way out, he slammed it so hard the sound echoed in the kitchen like summer thunder. The windowpanes rattled. The cups swung on their hooks beneath the cupboard. Pain sliced through Aiden's skull. Great. Exactly what he needed on his plate right now: more worries about Finn. The boy was going to make a terrible mistake sooner or later; Aiden knew it. He didn't like that sad fact, but there was nothing he or their other brother, Thad, could do about it. Finn would either pull himself up by the bootstraps and make a man of himself, or he'd keep going on their father's sad path. Only he could make that choice. No one could do it for him.

I sure wish I could. Aiden rubbed his temples, but that didn't stop the pain. No, the real pain was deeper than worries, broader than a physical hurt. His spirit felt heavy with troubles that could not be healed. He pushed himself from the chair and put out the light on his way to the window. He didn't want Finn to see him standing there, filled with regret, watching him stalk to the barn.

The round moon hung over the prairie valley like a watchful guardian, a platinum glow over the growing fields. The night looked mysterious, as if touched by grace, as if solemn with possibility. Aiden leaned his aching head against the window frame and wished he could feel hope again. Wished he could feel even the faintest hint of it.

What he could see was the shanty's faint roofline, as dark and as quiet as the night.

She's just trying to get her hooks into you. Finn's words came back to him. Hooks? Joanna Nelson didn't have any hooks. Not a woman who wore her heart and her love for her children on her sleeve. Not a woman who was so thin, the hard lines of her bones were visible through her summer dress. She'd gone without eating in order to give more to her children, so their bellies would be full while she went hungry.

The void where his heart had been was suddenly filled with an unbearable pain. *That* was love.

Chapter Four

Daybreak was her favorite time of day. Joanna drank in the peaceful quiet of the morning, savoring it like a rare treat. Every sunrise brought its own unique beauty. As she breathed in the hush that seemed to spread across the still land before the first hint of dawn, she could almost pretend that today would be full of promise, too. While the songbirds fell silent and the mountains seemed to sigh in reverence, she could almost feel the grace of God's presence, and hope—how she hoped—that she was not forgotten by him.

The cow grazing in the yard lowed quietly, the only sound in the entire world. The serenity of the morning seemed to swell as the first trails of gold flared above the deep blue mountains. She squeezed her eyes shut and let the soft warmth wash over her, willing the pure first light to cleanse away her fears and her doubts. She prayed that it would give her courage and insight for the hard morning ahead.

The cow mooed again, impatient this time. Joanna opened her eyes to see the animal Aiden had taken back from Pa's farm gazing at her with pleading eyes. The cow must have scented the small portion of grain in the bottom of the feed bucket, and was straining against her picket rope to get at it.

"I'm sorry, Rosebud. Here you are." She set the bucket down at the cow's front hooves. Instantly, the animal dived into her breakfast, tail swishing with contentment.

At least she looked better fed here on the lush grasses of Aiden's land. Pa had always been stingy with the livestock's feed, although Joanna had always sneaked grain and treats to Rosebud. She set the three-legged stool on the cow's left side and placed the milk pail between her feet. Holding it steady in case Rosebud lurched suddenly, Joanna stroked the cow's flank, talking to her for a few moments before starting to milk.

She could no longer see the rising sun breaking over the mountains, but the light was changing, the darkness turning to long blue shadows. A golden hue crept across the land to crown Aiden's two-story house. Painted yellow, it seemed to absorb the slanted gold rays and glow.

I buried a wife and son years ago, what was most precious to me. Again, his words came back to her like a haunting refrain. His wife had chosen that soft buttery color. Joanna didn't need to know anything about Aiden or his past to know that. No Montana rancher would choose that feminine, comforting color for his house. Just like the carved wooden curlicues decorating the top pillars of the porch fronts. Or the carefully carved rail posts. Such workmanship must have been done out of love for his wife.

Joanna felt in awe of such devotion. What a deep bond Aiden must have known. Respect for him filled her like the rising sun, and suddenly, there he was, as if her thoughts had brought him to life, striding down the porch steps with a milk pail in hand. She didn't know if it was just her lofty opinion of the man, but he looked wholly masculine. With light outlining the impressive width of his shoulders, he strode through the long shadows.

Not even those shadows were enough to hide the set of his frown and the tension straining his jaw as he marched toward her. "Who said you could milk my cow?"

"Sorry, I guess I've helped myself to your morning chores. I wanted to make your load easier, for doing the same for me last night." She spoke over the hissing stream of milk into the pail. "It's a fair turn. Surely you're not angry with me for that?"

Was it her imagination, or was there a weakening of that grimace in the corners of his mouth? "You are a surprising woman, Mrs. Nelson."

"You can call me Joanna." She could not resist saying it, even though she knew he would refuse to. "I gathered the eggs in the henhouse, too."

"There was no need to do my chores."

"How else am I to pay you what I owe?"

Aiden came closer, casting her in his long shadow. "Who said you owe me anything?"

"Please don't try that tact, Mr. McKaslin."

"What tact?" He knelt beside her, bringing with him the fresh scent of soap. "And you can call me Aiden."

"You're a decent man, Aiden. I'll not take advantage of that."

His hand, so very large, reached out and covered her wrist, stopping her. His fingers, so very warm, squeezed gently. "I'll finish up here. You had best go see to your little ones."

"They'll be fine enough until I finish."

"Please." It was the plea in his eyes that moved her, that revealed a man of great heart. "I'm not comfortable letting a woman do my work. I'll bring you some of the milk after I strain it."

How could she say no to the man who had given her one night of safe harbor? One night of peaceful sleep? He was like a reminder of hope on this perfect, golden morning, even with the shadows that seemed to cling to him.

"Go on." It was softly said, and surprising, coming from such a hard-looking man. "You have done enough for now."

She swallowed, lost in his midnight-blue eyes. They were shielded from her, and as guarded as the peaks of the Rocky Mountains towering over the long stretch of prairie. Curiosity filled her, but he wasn't hers to wonder about, so she pulled away and rose from the stool. With the first step she took, she felt a pang of lonesomeness. Her hand, warm from his touch, was cold in the temperate morning.

He watched her with his penetrating gaze, unmoving. Behind him on the porch, another man came to a sudden halt, yanked down the wide brim of his hat to shield his eyes from the sun without bothering to disguise his disdainful frown in her direction.

Last night Aiden had mentioned a brother. A brother who made him look even kinder and ten times more mature and masculine by comparison. The intensity of this man's scowl made Joanna shiver.

"Don't mind Finn." Aiden's comment carried on the breeze. "He's got a lot to learn about life and manners."

Across the yard, Finn muttered a terse answer that was drowned out by the harsh clatter of his boots on the steps. Anger emanated from him like heat from a stove. Joanna took one look at him and stayed where she was.

"Don't blame you for not wanting to cross his path." Aiden had hunkered down on the stool beside the cow. "When Finn's got his dander up, he's meaner than a rattler trapped in a brush fire. I apologize for him."

"There's no need. I'm the trespasser here."

"You've gone pale. He upset you."

"No, he reminded me of someone. M-my husband."

That explained it. Aiden didn't need to know anything more to see how her life had been. Sourness filled his stomach. Life was hard enough without such people in it. "Finn would make a poor husband."

She didn't comment, but the way she tensed up, as if she were holding too much inside, let him know more than her answer ever could. "Come by in, say, thirty minutes and I'll have breakfast on the table. Your young ones might as well eat while we figure out what you and I are going to do."

"About what I owe you?"

"No." Tied up inside, he said the word with all the patience he had. "You have to go somewhere, Joanna. You can't keep living out of your wagon."

He could see her face beneath the shadow of her bonnet. Really, she was very lovely; her forehead and nose, cheekbones and chin were so fine they could have been sculpted of porcelain. Her big blue eyes were as pretty as cornflowers and her mouth looked soft and cozy, as if she had spent a lot of her life smiling. Once upon a time.

Her brows knit and her chin shot up. "Plenty of folks live out of their wagons when times get hard."

Pride. He knew something about that. "I wasn't criticizing. Only saying that eventually winter is going to come. Maybe I can help you with that."

Her throat worked at the word *help.* Pain shot across her face. Whether she suspected his motives or wanted nothing to do with his help, he couldn't know. She gave a nod of acknowledgment—not of agreement—and went on her way through the growing, seed-topped grasses.

Painted with dawn's soft golden light like that, framed as she was by the crisp lush green of the prairie, Aiden felt he was seeing her for the first time. She was a truly lovely woman. He might even say beautiful.

He wasn't proud of himself for noticing.

* * *

Joanna kept swallowing against the painful burn in her throat as she whisked a dollop of milk into the egg batter. *Eventually winter is going to come.* Aiden McKaslin's remembered words made that pain worse. *Maybe I can help you with that.* Charity. That's what he saw when he looked at her. A woman to be pitied.

Shame filled her, because it was the worst sort of criticism. She stopped whisking to flip the thick-cut bacon sizzling in one of the frying pans. Charity was all pretty and tidy and wrapped up real nice when you were the one giving it. It was different when you were on the other end. She'd been able to keep her chin up before, because she had been doing her best. There had been solace in that.

Now he thought she expected his help, that she would accept it. He meant well, but she was afraid of being in a man's debt. Even in a *good* man's debt. Anyone could see that Aiden McKaslin was a good man.

"Ma." Daisy gave her rag doll a squeeze where she sat on a chair at the round oak table. "Can I get a drink of water?"

"You just had one, baby." Joanna knew the child wasn't asking for water, but to be able to get down from the chair and move around. "This isn't our home, so we have to mind our manners. I want you to please sit there a little while longer."

"Oh. Okay." The little girl sighed and squeezed her doll harder.

"Ma?" James fidgeted in his chair and swung his

feet back and forth. "I'm awful hungry. Especially for some of that bacon."

There was no missing the hope on his face. Real bacon. They'd had such a luxury when they had their own little plot of land and their own pig to butcher. Joanna sighed, remembering those times, harder in some ways, better in others. "This is Mr. McKaslin's breakfast. We ate in the shanty before we came here."

"I know, but I was hopin'..." He left the sentence dangling, as if afraid to ask the question he already knew the answer to, but wanting to hold on to that hope.

She couldn't blame him for that. "Maybe there will be a surprise for two good children later on. How about that?"

"Yes, ma'am!" James stopped fidgeting and sat up soldier straight, eager at the thought of a surprise.

"Oh, yes." Daisy offered a dimpled smile.

It took so little to please them. Joanna's heart ached as she poured the eggs into the waiting skillet. If only there was something more than another few pieces of saved candy for them. They deserved more than she could give them—at least now, anyway. In a month's time, there would be fieldwork to do. It was hard labor, and she still didn't know what to do with her babies while she worked, but at least she could hope for real wages. Hope for a betterment of her children's lives.

The eggs sizzled and she whisked them around the pan, reaching for the salt and pepper. She surveyed her work in progress. The bacon was crisping up real nice, the tea was steeping and the buttermilk biscuits in the oven were smelling close to done. Cooking for the man wasn't much of a repayment, but it was all she had to offer.

The back door swung open and there was Aiden, leaving his boots behind in the lean-to and staring at her with shock on his stony face. The kindness she'd come to see there vanished, replaced by a cold blast of anger.

"What are you doing?" His voice was loud enough to echo around the room. He came swiftly toward her, with raw fury and full power. "Get out of my kitchen."

She'd expected him to be happy that she'd cooked for him, saving him the chore. She kept stirring the eggs so they wouldn't congeal. "In a moment. I'm nearly done here. I didn't mean to intrude. I know it was forward of me, but—"

"I want you out." He drew himself up as if ready for a fight.

Yet she was not afraid of him. She heard Daisy crying quietly at the table and James hop off his chair to come to her aid.

"Outside, both of you." She laid down the whisk. "Aiden, the biscuits are ready. Let me take them out of the oven."

"Now, Joanna." The words came out strangled.

He was not angry at her, she realized. There, behind his granite face, she thought she caught something terrible—grief and sorrow—before that glimmer of emotion faded from his eyes. He stared at her, cold and imposing. He did not have to say another word. His face said it for him. She was not welcome here. Coming had been a mistake. An enormous mistake.

Miserable, she turned away. She had to detour widely to avoid bumping his arm with her shoulder, for he'd planted himself in the middle of the kitchen. Shame made her feel small as she hustled to the door, where her children waited, wide-eyed and silent, in the lean-to.

So much for her brainy ideas. She took James with one hand and Daisy with the other. They tumbled into the blinding sunshine together. Dust kicked up beneath their shoes as they hopped off the last step and into the dry dirt. To the right lay a garden, the vegetables small and stunted, wilting in the morning sun. Duty cried out to Joanna to water those poor plants, for their sake as much as for Aiden's. She glanced over her shoulder, remembering the awful look on his face.

She could see him in the shadows of the kitchen, standing where she'd left him, his shoulders slumped, his hands covering his face.

She'd never seen a man look so sad. Her feet became rooted to the ground, even though James was tugging at her hand. Something held her back. Something deep in her heart that would not let her leave the man behind.

He'd loved his wife. He really had. Joanna stared at him, transfixed by the shadows that seemed to surround him, by the slump of defeat of his invincible shoulders and the hurt rolling off him like dust in a newly tilled field.

She could see as plain as day what she'd done. Had there been another woman in this lovely house he'd built for her since her death? Probably not. He'd simply walked with no warning into the kitchen from his work in the barn to see a woman standing where his wife had once stood, cooking his breakfast.

Sympathy flooded her. Joanna hung her head, staring at her scuffed and patched shoes dusty from the dry Montana dirt. What she'd done with the best of intentions must have cut him to the soul.

How did she make this right? Would it be cruel to try to stay and work off what she owed him, and put him through this kind of remembering? Or was it better to pack up the children and leave? Which would be the best thing to do? There had been a time in her life when she would have turned to the Lord through prayer for an answer.

Now, she merely felt the puff of the hot breeze against her face and the muddle of agony in her middle. It was strange that Aiden's hurt was so strong she could feel it as easily as the ground beneath her feet.

"Why's he so mad, Ma?" James asked quietly, his hand tight in hers.

"He's had a great loss."

"Oh. Does that mean he had a funeral?"

"Yes."

"He's sad. Like I was when Pa died." James's breathing caught in a half sob, and he fell silent.

Joanna had never known that kind of sorrow, one

that was deep and strong enough to have broken a person in two. Out of respect for Aiden's privacy, she turned away. She made her feet carry her forward, past the garden and those tender parched plants, and she did not look back. Although not looking made no difference. She could feel the powerful image of him standing motionless while the bacon popped and the eggs cooked in that lovely kitchen he'd no doubt built with love and his own two hands.

As Aiden set several biscuits on a platter, Finn banged in from the lean-to wearing his barn clothes and a scowl. His brother took one look at the buttery biscuits and the fluffy eggs on the table and shook his head.

"What did I tell you?" he grumbled as he poured himself a cup of tea. "Hooks."

Guess there was no need to mention who had cooked breakfast. And a mighty fine one, too, judging by the smell of things. He'd loved Kate dearly, but she was not a good cook—not even a passable one. But Joanna, why, she could put his ma to shame in a cooking contest.

"I'm just glad not to have to fix breakfast," he told his brother. It was partly the truth—close enough—but not the whole truth. It still hurt to remember how she'd been standing at the fancy range he'd ordered in to surprise his wife.

"This is how it starts." Finn's scowl turned to a grimace as he drew a chair back with his boot and slumped into it. "She's gettin' into your good graces.

Treating you to a meal so you can see what a good wife she'd make."

"I suppose the fact that she's been living without paying rent on the back pasture, and wanted to do something in return, has little to do with it." Now that Aiden's mind had cleared, and the agony was gone from the empty place in his chest where his heart used to be, he could see what she might have been doing. For some reason he didn't want to think too hard on, he could understand Joanna Nelson pretty easily.

He slid the platter into the warmer—food he intended to take over to the children later. "She's just doing what she can. Heaven knows I could use having my load lightened a bit."

Finn, as usual, either ignored the comment or didn't figure it applied to him. "See? That's how it'll go. Next thing you know, she'll have this house spick-and-span and her brats—"

"That's enough, Finn." Aiden reached for the teapot. "Mind your manners. Those are good kids."

"—living in the upstairs bedrooms. Watch." Finn took a loud slurp from his cup. "Open your eyes now and smarten up, Aiden. Stop her while you can, otherwise you won't know what hit you. You'll have a wedding ring on your finger and three more mouths to feed, and she'll be gettin' a free ride."

If there was something he couldn't imagine, it was a woman like Joanna behaving in such a way. No, she was quality—simple as that. A real good, hardworking, God-fearing woman. Aiden rolled his eyes and carried his steaming cup to the table. "I don't want you talking about her like that."

"Sure, don't listen." Finn was already crunching on the bacon Joanna had fried up. "You'll see that I'm right."

"Aren't you forgetting something? How about grace?"

"Why bother?"

Aiden shook his head. The boy was never going to learn. "You might not want to believe in God, but that doesn't keep Him from believing in you. Sit up straight, stop chewing and bow your head."

Finn's grimace darkened but he did as he was told.

"Dear Father," Aiden began, bowing his own head and folding his hands. "Please bless this meal we are about to receive. Thank you for your bounty and keep us mindful of our blessings—"

"Amen," Finn interrupted, with the intent to end the blessing, as if that was about all the religion he could take on an empty stomach.

One day, Finn was going to learn, but in the meanwhile, Aiden added a silent prayer. *Lord, please watch over Joanna Nelson and her children. Show me the right way to manage this.* "Amen."

He opened his eyes, and saw Finn already biting into one of the biscuits, moaning because it was so good. Aiden didn't need to take a bite to know that for himself. The buttery fragrance was making his stomach rumble. He reached for one and broke it open. Light and fluffy, better than even Ma could make.

There, out the window, he could see Joanna crossing the lawn toward the barn. She was walking with a fast stride, her head down, her shoulders set. She looked like one determined woman. One who always did the best she could.

Odd how he could see her so clearly. He slathered butter on the biscuit and took a bite—sheer perfection. No doubt about that. Finn was already digging into the scrambled eggs, and so Aiden did, too. They were light and fluffy, with plenty of flavor. Saying she had a gift for cooking would have been an understatement.

He chewed and chased it down with a gulp of tea, watching as Joanna disappeared into the barn. He stood up, wishing he could take his plate with him.

"Don't you do it, Aiden," Finn warned, as if he were about to take a plunge headfirst off a cliff. "Don't you ask her to stay and cook for you."

"Mind your own business." Aiden didn't look back. He was in no mood to put up with his slacker of a brother, who did the least he could get by with. "I expect you to take a page from her book and work harder at earning your keep around here."

Finn grumbled something, but Aiden gave the lean-to door a slam so he wouldn't hear it. That boy could get his dander up in three seconds flat. Maybe because there wasn't an ounce of appreciation for the roof over his head.

"Joanna?" He wasn't surprised to find her at the end stall, where he'd stabled her two horses. "Don't trouble yourself with the team. I'll bring them out after I'm through with breakfast."

"I would like to get a good start on the day." She gave

the lead rope a twist to release it, and tried to back the old work horse into the aisle. "I have the wagon packed, so ten more minutes and we will be on our way."

"To where, Joanna?"

"I shall figure that out on the way there." She gave the gelding's halter a gentle tug. "C'mon, boy. Back up. C'mon."

Aiden laid the flat of his hand on the horse's rump, stopping him before he could move. "I didn't mean to run you off. I never should have spoken to you like that. I was surprised to see you there. Unprepared."

"I understand." She still wouldn't look at him. "I overstepped my welcome. I only meant to do you a kindness, to pay back how you've been kind to us."

"I know that. I've been a widower a long time. Maybe too long." Pressure built in his chest, directly behind his sternum, making it hard to talk. Hard to feel. Hard to do anything. "I didn't mean to be so harsh."

"I said I understand." She sounded a little firm herself.

He hated that he'd done that to her. "That was Kate's kitchen. I wasn't prepared to see—" His throat closed up. The rest of him did, too.

"Another woman standing in her place." Joanna finished for him.

Amazing that she could know that. Amazing that she could see what no one—not even his family—could understand.

"Don't worry, Aiden. I didn't mean to make you remember something that brings you so much pain. I intended to be leaving, anyway. I have a debt to you, and

I will pay it. One way or another, you can be sure of that. Now, if you'd let me take my horse, I'll be on my way."

She was such a little bit of a thing, frail for all her strength. There was a world of fortitude in the set of her chin and the steel of her spine, but it wasn't right to send her off just because it would be best for him.

No, that wouldn't be right at all. He squeezed his eyes shut for just a moment, trying to listen to common sense, or maybe to that voice from heaven giving him a little direction. Just one word came to mind. "Stay."

Chapter Five

Had she heard him right? Joanna's fingers slipped from the halter. Dancer stared at her, patiently swishing his tail, as if there was no explanation in his mind to her behavior.

In truth, she couldn't explain why Aiden's kind request turned her to stone. Or why the feeling was worse than the fear gathered up inside her like a hive of angry bees. Being alone in this wide world was not a comfort. But neither was accepting a good man's charity. All she had to remember was the look of horror and hurt on his handsome face to know the right thing to do. "I'd best take the children and move along. You don't truly want me here."

"No," he agreed. "You're right about that. But you owe me, Joanna. I expect us to be squared up before you head off. I don't think I'll get what you owe me otherwise."

"You're worried that I won't keep my word?" Her throat felt tight, her eyes hot.

"Absolutely. You might be the kind of woman who means to keep her promises, but there's no saying what will happen to you once you're off this land. Hardships come along, as both of us well know."

Kindness rang in his voice like the toll of a church bell. Like salvation on Sunday morning. "Yes," she said quietly. "There is no telling what's up ahead of any of us."

"You might get in a worse situation. Or can't find a job, like you haven't found one in these parts. Then where will I be?" Aiden came close, close enough so that she could see the goodness in the man. Down deep and all the way to his soul.

Oh, she could see what he was up to, finding a way to keep her here without her pride getting in the way. Making it seem as if it was her duty to stay. When the truth was this had to be costing him something terrible.

She swallowed hard against the pride building in her throat. "So this is about money."

"It is." The softness in his eyes—and the sadness—said something different.

So did the twist of her soul. She was awestruck by this man's generosity. She was touched by the chance he was offering her. "What will it take for me to pay back what I owe you?"

"I'd expect meals cooked or at least made up ahead. Maybe some cleaning and laundry. Heaven knows the garden needs someone interested enough to tend to it every morning."

"Heaven knows," she agreed, understanding a deeper meaning. He was offering a hand to a drowning woman. She thought of the hot dusty miles, the crack in Dancer's left front hoof, the weeks—maybe months—on the road and how hard that would be on the children. She would have to travel until she found work. Who knew how long or how far away that would be? Times were hard in Montana, true, but the drought had stretched beyond the territory's borders.

"At harvest's end, you and I will talk. If we can find you a paying job for a few hours a week, which I think I can do, then you ought to be set to move on then, wherever you have a mind to." His jaw tensed, betraying him.

This wasn't easy for him. Nor was it for her. She took a ragged breath. The gelding lipped her bonnet brim, and she rubbed her hand along his warm, sleek neck. How could she say no? She'd be able to work off what she owed Aiden. She'd have a real roof over the children's heads and a stable for the horses. The crack in Dancer's hoof might have time to grow out. She might have the chance to work for cash in her pocket. Money for good meals and new shoes for the little ones. A little savings to put by for a trip.

He was offering her so much. But saying nothing about himself, about how hard this would be for him. That meant staying was not the right answer, either. Yet it was best for her children. She thought of James and the unspoken sadness in his eyes at having to leave another house. She thought of Daisy, too little to understand, but needing security and comfort all the same. Joanna thought of how hard she had wished for just one chance to improve her life. This was certainly a chance she had to take.

Then she studied the man in front of her. His eyes were dark and bleak. His presence like stone, cold and remote.

"How can I say yes?" she said into the silence that had grown between them. "My being here upsets you."

"I know." His hands curled into fists. "But I have my sense of duty."

"You pity me. That's not reason enough." Everything within her longed to stay. To repay him for his kindness at giving them lodging and supper. To have the chance to provide better for her children. But at what cost to him? "I saw you in the kitchen after we left you. I've never seen that kind of emotion."

His knuckles turned white as he clenched his fists. It was as if his sorrow began to bleed. "What I lost is in the past. Perhaps God has put you in my path to teach me."

"That sounds harsh." She hated to think that life—and God—were so brutal. That love lost was like love never felt. That hardships and loss were only meant to teach lessons. Maybe that was why she'd stopped hoping prayer could help her. Why she didn't believe God would.

Aiden shrugged one brawny shoulder. "What if I had been the one to die? What if I had left Kate widowed? I want to believe there would be someone out there man enough to help her and protect her. To make sure she and my boy would be safe and fed."

His words were like a knife to Joanna's heart. She

blinked away the tears from her eyes, feeling pain take over. The poor man.

A muscle worked in his neck, perhaps his attempt at controlling his emotions. "Will you allow me to help you, Joanna?"

"I'll allow you to help my children." It took all her dignity to keep her chin up. "I appreciate your offer, Aiden."

"Good." His fists loosened. "Your gelding needs care. The balm you're using is what most folks use, but I've got something better."

"I noticed that you had done something different to it. Thank you for that."

"It was no trouble. You'd best be leaving the gelding here, as you're staying. I'll be by after I'm done in the fields to help you unpack your wagon."

"I hate to trouble you, Aiden. I suppose you have fence work to do, and haying?" She said the last like a question.

"You were a farmer's wife."

"And a farmer's daughter. If you need an extra hand, I can drive horses, turn hay and I'm good at pitching."

"I never would have guessed that." He had his opinion about women working in the field—he had never wanted his wife to labor that hard—but Joanna spoke of her experience with a hint of pride. He had to admire a good work ethic.

"I have a certain knack with topping haystacks. I'd be happy to help. I have the children, but..." She stopped, leaving the question unasked.

He had his beliefs, but he wasn't about to deny her the chance to make her life right again. "I reckon we will figure something out. Perhaps my ma wouldn't mind keeping an eye on them. We'll see."

"That would be wonderful." Tension rolled off her. She smiled up at him, and in the dappled stripes of sunlight coming through the plank walls, she seemed transformed. Young and dainty and softly beautiful.

Aiden felt his throat tighten up with too many emotions—too much feeling for a man who'd lost his heart—and looked away. "Where are your children?"

"Playing in the yard by the wagon. I can see them..." She glanced through the slatted walls. "James is watching his sister."

Aiden managed to nod and to keep his eyes down on the straw at his boots. It was easy to hear the affection soften her voice. He figured love would do the same to her face. Best not to be noticing that. He took a step back. "Why don't you bring your children up to the house? There's a platter in the warmer for them."

"We ate."

Toasted bread, or oatmeal, was his guess. "Treat them to the food you fixed. There's plenty, and make sure you feed yourself, too. I mean that, Joanna. Then clean up the kitchen when you're done."

He winced inside at the sound of his hard tone. He didn't have much of a choice. He couldn't allow himself to soften toward her. He ignored the ache in the hollows of his chest and took the gelding by the rope.

He could feel her gaze searching his face as he

turned to the horse, pretending she was already gone from the barn and on her way to follow his orders. But she wasn't. She stood in the aisle, her presence as sweet as morning light. He could feel the radiance of her smile, sweeter than spun sugar, before she turned and hurried away.

"Ma! Ma! Look at me!" Daisy sang out as she climbed a boulder at the edge of the field, her little blue dress snapping in the breeze. Sunshine glinted like gold in her hair as she followed her brother to the flat top of the large rock. "Look, Ma!"

"I'm looking, sweet girl." Joanna laughed as she hefted the crate off the wagon's tailgate. She had already put in a hard day in Aiden's kitchen, first cleaning up the breakfast dishes and then baking and cooking and cleaning up after that. Then there had been the shanty to scrub clean—it was surprisingly dusty, with a thick layer of dirt in the corners. Now there was the wagon to unload, and she wasn't about to wait for Aiden to come in from his work. He'd done more than enough for her already.

"Ma! I'm gonna jump!" Daisy crept to the edge of the rock, afraid but determined. She grasped her brother's shirtsleeve with fisted hands.

James looked burdened. "Ma! She's on my fort."

"I see that. You're a good boy to let her play with you."

James didn't say anything to that, but the look on his face was one of adorable resignation. He clutched a wooden horse, as if he'd been about to set up his horse corral on part of that boulder top.

Joanna carried the crate across the ripening grasses, keeping a watchful eye for Daisy's courageous jump. It was good to see them so happy. James had been such a good boy, watching his sister play with her doll by the shanty door all the while Joanna had been cleaning. Her son looked more secure as he leaned close to whisper something in his sister's ear. Daisy lit up with a huge smile and then bunched up before leaping off the rock. She landed on both feet, squealing.

"Ma! Did you see? I jumped!"

"I saw. That was the best jump I ever saw." Joanna loved knowing that her children would have the security of home. That for now, for a while, they could play in this field and jump from that rock like normal kids. They were no longer homeless. It hurt to accept Aiden's charity, but looking at her little ones, she had no other choice.

"Ma!" Daisy came racing through the grass, hardly visible, it was so high. "Watch. I'm gonna do it again. James! James! Are you gonna jump, too?"

James had that put-upon look again, but good boy that he was, he merely blew out a breath. "Yes, Daisy. Now, stand back."

Joanna stepped into the shanty's shadow and suddenly felt that she wasn't alone.

"That looks heavy. Let me get it." Aiden stepped into sight in his work clothes and heavy boots, dusted with bits of cut grass. He smelled sweet with it. "I thought I asked you to wait for me."

"I'm not so good at following orders, as my former husband learned to his great dissatisfaction."

"Did he now? I did not have the best success with my Kate." Aiden took the crate out of Joanna's hands. "Why don't we make a bargain? If you don't mind fetching me some cold well water, I'll empty out your wagon."

"You're trying to keep me busy and out of the way."

"I'm thirsty," he corrected, and it was hard to tell if he was unhappy with her or simply being his stoic, reserved self. "And I don't take to women doing heavy lifting. Next you'll be telling me you're capable. I don't doubt it. But a man ought to make a woman's load lighter, even if they're strangers to one another."

Joanna took a step back to study the man before her, damp with a hard day's sweat in high temperatures. He did look intimidating. But there was kindness on his face. It was an attractive combination. She shook her head. "You have some mighty strange notions, Aiden McKaslin, but I do happen to like them."

"What's mighty strange about them?"

He didn't seem to know, she marveled, wondering how on earth he could be real. But he was a flesh and blood man standing before her, of that there was no doubt. She headed for the shanty. "I'm used to men trying to get out of work, not stepping up to do it."

"I'm not afraid of a little hard work." He didn't crack a smile, but he sounded slightly amused, although it was hard to tell with his deep, wry baritone. "I see that you watered the garden, so I know you found the well."

"I did. Don't worry. I'll fetch your water."

"I had to wonder, since you were heading in the opposite direction from the well."

"To grab the water pail." She snatched the bucket from just inside the shanty door, and took off toward the main house. On the rising slope of land, she had a better view of her children. James had turned to watch her with careful, inquisitive eyes, just making sure. She hated that he worried so. One small change—her stepping away to fetch water—and he went from a carefree little boy to a burdened one. She lifted her hand in a wave to show him everything was fine. After a moment he went back to play, paying attention to Daisy, who tugged on his hand.

When Joanna knelt at the well to hook the bucket onto the end of the pulley, Aiden had emerged from the shanty, his arms empty of the crate. He was a big man, even from a distance. He had a long gait, steady and strong, and did not swing his arms when he walked but kept them at his sides. His wide-brimmed hat shaded his face as he hauled a straw tick from the wagon bed. He easily carried the awkward mattress, quickly disappearing into the house.

What I lost is in the past. Perhaps God has put you in my path to teach me. She could hear again his words and see again the look of desolation on his face. She ached for him. He'd shown her kindness when she had been sure there was no more of it left in the world. He was a good man, and in her experience, those were rare. She intended to do the best possible job for him. She was going to work harder than she ever had. He deserved nothing less.

"Ma!" Daisy ran ahead of James, who had come

close to watch the unloading of the wagon. "Can I have a drink of water, too, please?"

It was impossible to look into those pretty eyes and say no. Joanna unhooked the bucket of crystal-clear water and held the full dipper for her daughter. Smelling of fresh grass and sunshine, Daisy leaned close and sipped daintily. Joanna smoothed the fine tangle of platinum hair that had escaped from her daughter's twin braids. It would need a good brushing later.

A movement blurred at the edges of her vision. It was Aiden reappearing from the shanty, bringing the shadows with him. He cut a dark figure across the lush green prairie. His wide hat shaded his face, but she could feel his gaze on her like the tangible rays of the sun.

"Come on, baby." Daisy was done, so Joanna took the dipper and dropped it into the bucket. "Let's take this to Mr. McKaslin."

"Okay." Her daughter bobbed to her feet and skipped through the tall grasses. Her happy gait lifted Joanna's heart another notch.

Aiden had already hefted the second straw tick from the wagon box and was halfway to the shanty. This time James trailed after him and hesitated on the front step, peering in. Joanna set the small pail on the open tailgate. "James? Don't pester Mr. McKaslin, honey."

"But I gotta thank him for the bacon!" Earnestly, the little boy planted both dusty feet.

"No need, little man." Aiden filled the shaded doorway.

James hopped back, his head tilted to gaze up at the tall man. "I can help. I'm real strong."

"I see that."

Aiden's tone might be gentle, but she could see his white-knuckled fists and the cords tight in his throat as he marched back to the wagon. She didn't get the feeling that he disliked children—no, not that. She thought of what he'd told her, and wondered if her children were a reminder, too. Her spirit ached for him, and she laid a hand on Daisy's little shoulder, pulling her close to her skirts.

"James," she said softly. "Keep out of Mr. McKaslin's way."

"But I'm helpin'." James proudly climbed into the wagon box.

"James." She loved him for his good heart, but the last thing she wanted to do was cause Aiden more pain.

"It's all right, Joanna." He swept off his hat, stopping to take a long cold drink. "Thank you kindly, for I've been thirsty. I see you already carried in what you could. I'll finish up bringing in the furniture, if you want to help yourself to my kitchen and start on dinner. Finn and I will be in the field until dark. If you don't mind, if you could bring our meals out to us."

"And water, too," she said with a nod.

"That would be greatly appreciated, ma'am." He dropped the dipper back into the bucket and the hat onto his head. He had a fair piece of work ahead of him if he wanted the last of the south field cut before the Sabbath. "I'd best get crackin'."

"Come help me in the kitchen, James." Joanna held out her hand. The boy gave a sigh but did as he was told, and followed his ma and sister through the whispering grasses.

This wasn't going to be an easy thing, having her here. Aiden steeled himself and held his feelings still. This was going to be tough on him. He'd learned that the right thing rarely was the easy thing. God was surely handing him a challenge when he'd put Joanna Nelson in his path.

I hope I don't let you down, Lord. Aiden slung a wooden rocking chair over his shoulder, rockers skyward, and lumbered back to the shanty.

Already she had changed it. He set the chair down by the window. There was something different about a house with a woman in it. It smelled pretty, looked tidy, felt peaceful. The old tick on the bed was made up as neat as a pin with a colorful ringed quilt. A tiny crate of blue dishes sat on the floor next to the table. A towel embroidered with roses at the hem hung on the bar next to the water basin.

The sound of children's laughter drifted on the wind. Why that picked his spirits up, he couldn't quite say. He stacked Joanna's straw ticks and laid them flat next to the bed. She would be more comfortable with the second mattress between her and the hard dirt floor.

The shanty wasn't much, but it had housed his family just fine when he was a boy. The roof needed a bit of work, he thought as he stepped outside, but he would get to it before the next heavy rain. As he hiked up the rise, he caught sight of the children running in the grass outside the main house's back door. The little girl gave a musical giggle and the boy let out a whoop as he carried his wooden horse high.

Aiden tried not to think of the son he'd buried. The little boy he had never gotten to know. He swallowed his emotions, skirted the house and cut behind the barn. The sounds of the children seemed to follow him, those carefree, innocent sounds, teasing at the lost places within him.

What was he going to tell his family? They were bound to find out come church tomorrow. This was only the start of speculation, he knew. His ma and middle brother, Thad, thought he ought to get married again. His mother would especially start quoting Scripture on the subject. Now, he wasn't objecting to the Scripture as much as to his ma getting her hopes up. Ever since Thad and his wife, Noelle, had gotten married earlier in the year, she had hopes for grandchildren again.

Hopes Aiden could never see clear to fulfilling. Love could put softness into a man's life, and that was nice. Real nice. But it left him wide-open and vulnerable, without a single defense. He'd been broken clear to the quick. There had been no way to prevent it. When Kate and his son died, it had cost him too much. There was no color in Aiden's world, no gentleness, no music. There would never be again. His ma wouldn't understand, nor Thad, either.

But perhaps Joanna did.

If he glanced over his shoulder, he could see the

kitchen windows clearly. Sun streamed into the room, backlighting the woman there. She was searching through the cabinets for something…she went up on tiptoe and brought down a large mixing bowl.

He could not say why he lingered to watch her as she set the bowl on the counter. Her long skirt swished around her ankles as she headed to the pantry. She stopped by the door, disappearing from his sight, perhaps to check on the children. Sure enough, both the girl and boy stopped playing and called out to her in reassurance that they were staying close by, before she swept back into his sight with a small sack of sugar.

He could not say when it happened. He only knew the sunshine felt warmer on his face and the hollow where his heart used to be felt less cold.

Work was waiting, so he turned and headed back to the south field.

Chapter Six

It was a beautiful morning, Joanna decided as she wiped the last ironstone plate dry and stowed it on the shelf. She laid the dish towel over the top rung of the ladder-back chair and carried the washbasin to the doorway.

The children were playing outside in the sun. Their innocent laughter brought joy to her heart. They were her greatest blessings. The best things that had ever happened to her. Since it was Sunday, it was a good day to make a list of her blessings. It had once been a short list, but now it was much longer. Because of Aiden.

She sent a sparkling arc of water flying into the brilliant sunshine beside the path to the door. There was Aiden McKaslin driving a wagon behind his matched set of black Clydesdales. He was dressed in his Sunday best, a tan hat, a blue shirt and tan trousers. He was a fine-looking man.

He reined the horses in and studied her a moment from the high seat, his gaze stony.

She felt plain in her best sprigged calico and with her braids pinned up in a simple coil. "Mr. McKaslin. I was just about to come find you."

"Guess I saved you the trouble." The brim of his hat shaded his face, and so his expression remained a mystery. "I wasn't sure, but I thought you were a churchgoing woman. Wanted to ask if you and your children wanted a ride in to town."

A ride? With him? She gripped the ironware basin so hard the rim bit into her fingers. In the background, her children had stopped playing, to watch the man with guarded interest. "We planned on walking."

"That's a mighty long distance for your wee one."

"I was going to carry her."

"Carry her? That's a far way." His jaw snapped shut and tension bunched in the corners. He looked out at the prairie stretching off toward the mountains, toward town. "I know you want to save your horse's hoof. I suppose the other one doesn't drive well alone?"

"That's right." Joanna wondered what was troubling him. "I did not accept your offer to cause you more trouble, Mr. McKaslin. I can see what you're about to ask. I know you feel your Christian duty deeply, and I respect you for it, but not if it causes you pain. I'm not here to bring you more trouble."

His midnight-blue eyes snapped to her, studying her bare head—she'd not put on her bonnet yet—and her feet peeping out from beneath her skirt ruffle. Again, she felt oddly plain, and that made no sense. She knew she'd always been a plain woman. But now watching Aiden up on that high seat, looking handsome and powerful with that backdrop of rich blue sky and pure white clouds, her breath hitched in her chest a tad. Soft feelings—kind feelings—rushed into her heart for this man.

"I don't mind a little trouble, Joanna." Aiden knuckled back his hat.

She remembered the image of him in the kitchen with his hands to his face. Surely the feelings swirling to life within her were deep admiration and respect for him. Surely that was all and nothing more.

"As I'm already here and we're both going the same way, you may as well come along. Is that all right with you?" He leaned forward in the seat, his gaze on hers, his strong frame tensed.

Realizing she had been staring at him for too long, she blushed and ripped her eyes away. She glanced down at the basin she was gripping with white-knuckled fingers. "Y-yes. It would be better for the children."

"Fine, then." He leaned back against the seat and crossed his ankles, as if setting in for a pleasant wait.

I've never met a man like him before. Her eyes found him like sunlight found the earth. The feelings within her sweetened. Surely it was impossible not to admire him. There was nothing wrong with a little admiration for the man who had done so much for them, right?

Right. She whirled around and hurried into the shade of the shanty. Every step she took, she remained aware of Aiden high up on his wagon seat behind her. She thought of his brother, who usually accompanied him to town. Where was Finn? Had she caused trouble between them? Worry curled in her stomach as she buttoned up her shoes. And what were folks in town going to think when she walked into the church vestibule with him?

People were bound to talk; it was simply human nature. And without a doubt, that talk, that speculation, would hurt Aiden. As if a man who had loved and lost as deeply as he had could simply start courting again. No one in his or her right senses would ever mistake his sense of kindness for romantic interest.

Joanna set the sunbonnet on her head and tied the ribbons beneath her chin, glancing in the small mirror. She was too thin, too peaked, too ordinary. No man was going to love her. She'd learned that the hard way.

"Ready?" Aiden called from the wagon seat.

"Yes." She closed the shanty door, turning to call for the children, but they were already close, standing at the edge of the grass with quiet, solemn expressions. Bits of grass clung to Daisy's pink gingham skirt, and dust streaked James's cheek, but they still looked presentable.

She held out her hands. "Isn't this a treat? We get a ride to church."

Daisy galloped forward and grabbed her mother's fingers. James looked up wistfully at Aiden and took her other hand. She was surprised to hear the seat springs squeak faintly. Aiden's shadow fell across her as he descended. She felt a shiver at his closeness, for he brought the shadows with him.

"Let me help them up." He spoke to her, not the

children. He lifted Daisy into the back, where two board seats had been carefully anchored, and then James.

Such thoughtfulness. He took care with them. Joanna felt the wedge of gratitude take a bigger piece of her soul.

"Your turn." Aiden held out his hand, palm up. "I reckon you want to sit with your kids?"

"Yes." She felt like a lady at his kindness. She reached out to place her hand in his. Her fingertips grazed his palm, and it was like touching winter's frozen ground. Sympathy filled her as he helped her up over the board side of the wagon. Her shoes thudded on the wooden box and her skirts swirled around her ankles, but she was only aware of Aiden's lost heart.

He released her hand without a word and turned his back, as if he were unaware of the moment. The lark song came again to her ears and the blinding glare of sunlight to her eyes, and yet still she felt cold as she settled with the children onto one of the seats.

He's without hope, she realized. She knew that place of darkness. It was like being in a blizzard, pummeled by the wind and battered by the ice-sharp snow, unable to see. Perhaps that was why her soul recognized his.

Looking at him, you would not know it. Her gaze caressed the strong straight lines of his shoulders and back, the determined set of his hat and the purposeful way he held the reins. The wagon bounced and jostled through the grass, perhaps following a road that once had been there, to the main driveway, where wild rabbits darted out of sight and gophers popped up out of their holes to watch the travelers rolling by.

Joanna thought she heard something in the whisper of the wind, like a voice just out of reach. The sunshine blazed, the seed-topped grasses stretched like a long ocean of green around them and the music of the birds filled the morning like the sweetest hymn. She knew, impossibly, that Aiden needed far more help than she did.

Aiden halted the horses along the tree-shaded town street, hardly having the room in his thoughts to be glad for the handy parking spot because he felt the weight of so many eyes. He felt the curious looks as surely as he did the hot wind puffing at the back of his neck. This wasn't the first time he'd been a source of speculation. He gritted his teeth, told himself he didn't much care and set the brake.

"Those are mighty good horses you got."

The little boy was standing right behind him, chest up, hands fisted. Aiden swallowed hard, forcing himself to answer. "Clyde and Dale are getting along in years, but right you are. They're good horses."

"Clydesdales." The little boy's serious eyes lit up with excitement. "My pa used to have one once, but we had to sell him."

Little boys liked horses, Aiden told himself as he knotted up the reins. That was all it was. No need to look at the fatherless boy. No need to think the lad was needing something in return.

"James, come." Joanna laid her hand on her son's

shoulder, speaking in that soft way of hers. "Goodness, you're as windblown as a tumbleweed. I can't have you going into church like this."

Aiden swung down, not wanting to see the motherly way she dug a comb out of her reticule and smoothed down the boy's hair. Nor did he want to see the snap of her skirts in the breeze, or the way she smiled as she worked, or the love on her face making her beautiful.

He swiped his hand down Clyde's neck, concentrating on the horses. Over the angled line of their manes he could see a buggy roll to a stop and the delight on his ma's face as she hopped to the ground, hoopskirts swaying. Delight. That hit him deep. Yep, this was going just as he figured. His ma, wearing a grin twice as big as the Montana sky, was hurrying across the street.

"Aiden!" Ida McKaslin had had a hard life, and the worry and a lifetime of troubles had etched deep into her face, but she was still lovely. Smiling, she raised her arms and pressed her hands to the sides of his face. "Look at you. I can't get over how much I miss seeing you every day."

Aiden's chest knotted up with failure, with emotion he could not let himself feel. "Ma, you look as if Thad and his wife are treating you well."

"They are spoiling me. That's never good for a soul, but I am not about to complain. I'm settling into my new little house just fine." His mother looked to be bursting with the next question. "Introduce me to your lady friend."

Yes, of course that's what his sweet ma thought. No

amount of explanation would talk her out of it, either. He might as well face the music. "Joanna has come upon hard times and she and her kids are staying in the shanty for a spell."

"I see." Ma's eyes lit up even brighter. Judging by the look of her, she didn't understand at all.

"Oh, no, Mrs. McKaslin." Joanna came to his rescue. "I'm not his, well, his friend. It's a business arrangement. I'm working in exchange for rent."

"Can't be much rent he's charging you. Or he'd best not be. You are being fair to her, aren't you, Aiden?"

He rolled his eyes. "Yes. Ma, does Thad know you ran off? He's probably looking for you."

"Joanna." Ma was hardly paying him any mind. She was setting her sights on Joanna. Probably measuring her up as future daughter-in-law material. "Your last name is Nelson, isn't it? I've seen you around, but I don't think we've ever been introduced. Your father, rest his soul, was never on speaking terms with our family."

"I understand that half of Angel County was not on speaking terms with my pa." Joanna, with a child in each hand, smiled kindly toward the fragile older woman. "It's mighty nice to meet you, ma'am. You have a fine son in Aiden. You must be very proud of him."

"I surely am not." Her twinkling eyes said otherwise. "I am about to take him to task for not telling me all about you before this."

"I'm only here for a short time, then I'll be moving along." Joanna shot him a look as if to say, *I'm trying to make her understand.*

"Don't worry, Joanna. My ma is a hopeless case. She's overly optimistic, and it's my opinion that is not good for a person." He gave his mother a severe look, but it apparently bounced right off of her.

"Come, Joanna." Ma reached right past him as if he didn't exist. "Your little family must join ours. Aiden, I take it Finn will be along?"

"That's my understanding." He watched, helpless to stop it, as his mother drew Joanna into a quick embrace, and fell in stride with her and her children. They were talking about the little ones. The boy smiled up at her. The girl skipped at Ma's side.

"She's already wondering if one day they will be her grandchildren," a voice quipped behind him.

Aiden didn't need to look over his shoulder to know his brother wore that irritating know-it-all grin. "You aren't helping matters, Thad. You broke down and got married, and now Ma will think I'm likely to be next. Good day, Noelle."

"Hello, Aiden." Thad's pretty new bride clung to his arm, as lovely as could be. Her emerald eyes sparkled up at him with happiness, although she could not see him, as she was blind. "I'm eager to meet your new lady friend. I would like to invite her to join my sewing circle."

"I'm not courting her." He had to make that clear. They were just a few paces ahead now. The wide brim of Joanna's sunbonnet hid most of her face from him, but he could see the delicate angle of her jaw, and the corner of her mouth was drawn up in a smile.

She was being kind to his mother. His chest muscles twinged and his knees felt a little watery. Maybe it was gratitude. He was even more grateful when the wind carried a snippet of Joanna's voice. "No, ma'am, I am not sweet on your son."

"Well, you might not see it, dear, but I can." Ma sounded pleased.

Yes, he thought, it was just as he feared. "Ma, do go easy on Joanna. A pretty woman like her isn't looking to get tied down with a dour old man like me."

"That's exactly right." Joanna's tone was very serious.

He couldn't say why that gave him a pang, seeing as the last thing he wanted was a woman's affections. He drew himself up, ignored the smarting of his pride—at least he wanted to believe it was his pride hurting him. Then she glanced over her shoulder at him, and her soft smile said more than words and simple assurances could.

He wished he could thank her. He wished he knew how to express what was fighting to life within him. But they were hardly alone, and as they approached the front steps, even more people were around. Besides, if he reached out to her, it would take him one step closer to her, the last place he wanted to be.

That didn't mean he wasn't grateful to her.

At the bottom of the steps, Joanna turned to him. "I'm sorry, Aiden. I'm doing my best."

"Not to worry. I fear it's a lost cause."

She smiled up at him, with both children in hand. For a moment, the sunlight framed her with gentle golden light, burnishing her blond hair and lighting her up, as if from within. Air caught in his lungs. Stunned, he could only stare at her, lost in her smile. In that instant, the pain of the hopelessness inside him eased.

Joanna turned away and followed the line of churchgoers into the building. She swished forward with a twist of her skirts, her children quiet and wide-eyed at her side. Aiden's feet felt rooted to the earth as he watched her disappear into the serene shadows of the church. She seemed to take the sunshine with her.

Aiden was a genuine blessing in disguise. Joanna could see him at the end of the pew, on the other side of his sister-in-law, faithfully singing the closing hymn. He seemed like a hard man, standing so straight and severe, brooding with a keep-away look.

But she saw a different man now. Because of him, she had a little more faith in humanity than she'd had a few days ago. That had made it easier to sit through the service and feel included in the minister's sermon. God had felt so far away for so long. He still did. But she no longer felt alone.

The hymn ended. The service was over. James took her hand solemnly, his gaze fastened not on her, but on the tall man at the end of the row.

"Ma." Daisy clung to her skirts. "I'm awful thirsty."

"Me, too, baby. We'll get you some water before we start home." She lifted her daughter into her arms and tugged Daisy's little sunbonnet back into place. She needed to get a hat for James. She smoothed his hair absently as she inched down the row, where Aiden stood like a sentry, waiting for her.

He was as severe as ever, but his eyes warmed when she came closer. "Ma has invited all of us to Sunday dinner. Including you. Will you come?"

"I suppose so, seeing as how you have the horse and wagon."

"Then you're at my mercy."

"Yes. That has not been a hardship." She wasn't certain, but thought he almost smiled. He waited for her to step into the aisle before he followed her. With every step she took, there he was, at her back. She could feel the faint flutter of his breath against her nape and his significant presence like a shadow.

"Who is that woman with Aiden McKaslin?" A sharp whisper cut through the rustle and muttered conversations of the other worshippers heading for the exit.

She heard nothing more, but her face heated. Had Aiden heard? She could not tell. His step didn't falter. He remained silent, as if nothing had happened. She knew without asking him that the last time he'd brought a young woman with him to church, it had been his wife.

"If he's looking for a woman, he could do much better than her." The whisper was louder this time, sharper.

He had to have heard that. Joanna winced. Her face burned. She was glad that her children could not understand. She wanted to turn around and tell whoever was speaking the truth, but perhaps that would make a bigger scene. Already the line was moving on. She could only hope the rest of the McKaslin family, who were in front of her in the aisle, had not heard. She glanced down at her plain dress, patched discreetly in places, and at her son and daughter, who were good and sweet, and told herself it didn't matter what others thought.

Aiden's hand settled on her shoulder and stayed there. What a comfort to have him behind her, his unspoken act unmistakable. She swallowed hard against the emotion balling up hot and thick in her throat.

Yes, Aiden McKaslin was a fine man. Far too fine a man for a plain woman like her, but that didn't stop her from admiring him. It was the sudden glare of the sun that had her blinking hard as she followed Ida down the steps and into the churchyard—nothing more.

"I'll get the children water," Aiden said before he withdrew from her, leaving her alone.

She had no time to thank him or to go with him. She glanced behind her to see a young woman in a lovely blue dress and fashionable hoops, with her hair done up in stylish ringlets, watching her through narrowed eyes. The whisperer, no doubt. Joanna lifted her chin. She had nothing to be ashamed of. She watched as the woman in blue sauntered past with a dismissive look.

"I heard Aiden invite you to supper." Ida turned to Joanna, after chatting with Noelle and Thad. "I'm so pleased you and your children will be joining us."

"It's kind of you to have us." She kept James at her side and Daisy on her hip, waiting for Aiden to return. The church crowd was thinning as people hurried home. She spotted him approaching holding a big dipper, which he handed to her.

"Sorry, there was a line." He said nothing more, but waited, staring off down the road, while the children each took a turn sipping from the cold, fresh well water.

"I'll take it back. You go on ahead to the wagon. Get the kids out of the sun. I'll be along in a few shakes. Don't drive off without me."

"Maybe I will. Maybe not. You'll just have to find out."

"What?" He couldn't have heard her right. Perhaps it was the hustle of other folk around him in the churchyard or the noise of the road traffic. He saw amusement melting the strain on her pretty face. Was she joking with him? Well, he could kid, too. "Sure. Horse stealing is still a hanging offense in this part of the country. I'd be careful if I were you, ma'am."

"Oh, I'm not worried one bit. Your bark is worse than your bite, Aiden McKaslin. I *might* stop the wagon for you. I might not. It depends."

"On what?"

"How fast you can run after us." She turned with a flick of her skirts.

A chuckle rolled through him. Who would have thought the serious widow could make a man like him laugh? He shook his head, watching her walk away. There was something stunning about her, but he couldn't put his thumb on it.

The dress she wore was simply cut and sewn, without anything more than a modest ruffle at the hem, and none of the hoops and frills and lacy things females added to fancy up their dresses. Joanna was enough without all that. Her walk was a sensible, no-nonsense gait that was still feminine and dainty. With a child on her either side, she could not be mistaken for a captivating woman.

Yet she drew him all the same. How about that? He spun on his heels and marched back to the well. Only a few people remained gathered in the yard, and he nodded a greeting to the minister, who was in a deep discussion with a man in a dark shirt and trousers. That was his new neighbor, Aiden realized as he dropped the dipper into the pail with a splash. He didn't know them like he should, but he gave another nod as he went past the minister and Franklin—that was the man's surname.

Joanna. He couldn't get over her quip, if it had been a quip. He might not know her well, but he had a suspicion she had been half-serious. He strained to look around the copse of cottonwoods and up the road. There she was, graceful and wholesome in her red calico, as she held a water bucket for Clyde. She made a pretty picture standing willow straight, chatting first with the horses and then with her kids, who sat safely inside the wagon.

"Aiden!" someone called out. Footfalls padded behind him.

The minister. Aiden came to a halt, noting the man's urgency. Oh, this was about Finn. "My brother missed church, unless he came and I didn't see him."

"No, Aiden. I didn't see him, either." Pastor Hadly seemed very grave. Concern was etched into his grandfatherly face, but it was his eyes, full of sadness, that startled Aiden.

"You know something about my brother." He hated saying those words. Once, he had been protective of his littlest brother, and defensive, insisting that Finn would grow out of his rebelliousness. That the boy was simply spirited.

But manhood had not mellowed Finn or put sense in his head. Not even the second chance Aiden was giving the boy. Finn was going to find himself back in the territorial prison if he didn't smarten up. Aiden braced himself for whatever hard news the minister had brought. "Do you know where Finn is?"

"No, I don't. This is about you, Aiden."

"Me?" Not again. Now and then the kindly minister felt he had to offer help. Some folks saw Aiden's self-imposed isolation as grief. No, grief had come and gone. It was what was left in its wake that was the problem, and what could be the solution for that? Aiden turned away. There was Joanna, holding the bucket for Dale. Dependable, that's what she was. A reasonable, sensible woman who knew what mattered. "Now's not the time, Pastor. Sorry."

"There is a season for everything, Aiden. Come stand in the shade and speak with me."

"Finn is heading down a path that will lead him straight to trouble, and I can't stop him. I can only pray that you can."

"I'll speak to Finn, don't you fear." Pastor Hadly took refuge from the blazing sun in the shade of the trees, and his expression grew grave. "What is this I hear of a woman living with you?"

"With me?" That was like a slap on his face. He recoiled and shook his head. Was that what people were thinking? And didn't they have anything better to do than talk? "No, I assure you that is not true. Joanna Nelson had no place to go. She was living in her wagon in my back fields, so I offered her the shanty."

"But the shanty is on your land. Rather close to your house, as I remember it."

"A couple acres away, I guess. Far enough to make us neighbors not sharing the same house. *This* is what you want to talk to me about?" Anger beat at him. He wasn't mad at Hadly; the man was just doing what he saw as his duty. "Joanna is a widow with two small children. I'm not the sort of man who takes advantage of that."

"Easy, now. I'm only saying the look of it isn't right."

"I don't care about the look of things."

"Aiden, I'm telling you this for your own good. Maybe there is no need for concern yet, but temptation being what it is—"

"Perhaps for some people, but not for me." He rubbed the back of his neck, turning to watch Joanna replace the bucket in the watering trough up the road. He tamped down his anger, knowing the minister had a fatherly concern for him. Always had. "You of all people should know how strong my faith is, Mel."

"I do. Kate's death and your son's loss strengthened your faith. There aren't many who can say that."

Heat built in his chest, but it was no longer anger.

Aiden drew in air to try to chase it away, but it remained hard and hot like a fist. He turned his back to the minister, fighting for control of emotions best left unfelt. Joanna had climbed up into the wagon box, tender with her children, who were talking rapidly and vying for her affection.

She really was a beautiful woman. Maybe more beautiful for the love he saw on her face as she gazed at her little ones.

The pieces inside him felt raw-edged and throbbed like a broken bone unable to heal. Yes, he had to believe that this was all part of God's plan. That he'd done right in having Joanna stay. That this wasn't the start of one big mistake. He'd had enough heartache in his life. He wasn't looking for more.

"If anyone questions my integrity, Pastor, then you point 'em to me." Aiden meant it; his soul resonated with the words. "The day that helping a fellow Christian down on her luck is wrong because of how it looks to some people, well, that is a sad day for heaven."

"Aiden, I have Joanna's concern at heart, too—"

"Sure. I know." He was already walking away, wondering how many people knew she'd been living with her children out of the back of her wagon. Wondering how many of those who knew had not offered help of any kind, not a handout, not a meal, not a job, not even kindness.

He was halfway to the wagon before he realized he'd stalked away from his minister, who was a good man. Suddenly, there was Joanna, her laughter, light and sweet, falling around him like dappled sunshine. A hot breeze puffed through the trees, and he'd never seen a sky as blue.

"It was tempting to leave you behind," she told him as he hiked himself up onto the high seat. "But I've developed a surprising respect for you, so I didn't want to make you walk all the way to dinner in this heat."

As if she would have stolen his horses. He smiled, really smiled. "That was mighty kind of you, considering I don't believe you one whit."

"Yes, but it made you smile. You looked unhappy, Aiden. I just thought..." She shrugged a slim shoulder, looking like pure goodness itself with the sun kissing her and the breeze tangling the delicate tendrils of her perfectly gold hair.

He did not know what it was about her, but he felt more like himself than he had in a long while.

He unknotted the reins and released the brake. The horses plodded to life, drawing them past the church, where Pastor Hadly stood, watching with grave eyes.

Chapter Seven

Noelle's kitchen was bright and sunny. The windows and doors were open to the breeze off the falls and displayed a view of the wild mustang herd in the far pasture. It was the perfect place to whip together the ingredients for a pie. Even more perfect to get better acquainted with Aiden's ma and sister-in-law.

"My mother's rule," Joanna explained as she brushed milk over the top crust. "I've never tasted a better strawberry pie. I always sprinkle sugar and cinnamon on it, too. You wouldn't happen to have fresh cream in the cellar, would you?"

Noelle, seated at the table, smiled. Her fingers were busy crocheting a delicate lace tablecloth. She was a beautiful lady with bright green eyes and a cheerful manner. "I'm sure we do. You have my mouth watering, Joanna, and the pie isn't even in the oven. Which reminds me, Ida, what about the roast?"

"We have a few more minutes to go, but it smells

done, doesn't it?" Ida wandered over to peek in the oven. "It's nearly there. I think the men are hungry. Look at them, Joanna."

Joanna finished sprinkling the cinnamon and set the pie on the counter, ready to go in when the roast came out. The window framed Aiden and Thad as they talked together, standing side by side, hats shading their faces, their wide shoulders braced. You could tell they were brothers. Aiden was slightly taller, brawnier and more mature looking. But they shared the same posture, the same rugged, strong jaw and chiseled cheekbones. "They keep looking at the kitchen door, waiting to be called in."

"Talking about horses, no doubt." Noelle's needle paused as she stopped to count the tiny stitches with her sensitive fingers. "And trying to avoid talking about Finn."

"They *are* men, and that's what men tend to do." Fondness warmed Ida's voice. There was no mistaking her motherly love as she gazed on her two oldest sons. "They don't talk much about what matters, but that doesn't mean they can't feel it. Finn has a powerful temper on him. He was a good little boy, always polite and quiet. He never got over his pa's death."

Joanna found herself listening harder. Her hands stilled as she tidied up the workplace at the table. How had his father's death affected Aiden? she wondered, but hesitated to ask.

"That was a hard time for us," Ida said as she checked one of the pots boiling on the stove. "We were mortgaged up to our chins. There were even loans on the horses. We had five poor years of crops, followed by a complete drought one summer. We didn't have a single crop that year. My, that hurt. We were lucky to keep the garden alive and producing, and it was sparse at best."

"My last year on our farm, my husband's land," Joanna explained, "was like that. In Dakota Territory. It was a struggle just to scrape enough off the land to survive the winter."

"Then you know how it was for us." Ida set the pot lid into place. "Noelle, you were a schoolgirl at the time, living in town. I'm sure the weather brought no trouble to your family, and I'm grateful for that. But my man took off that autumn. Finn was too young to know. Thad only thirteen. Aiden was a big, strapping young man. I had hopes of him finishing up and graduating from the school in town. I wanted him to have a real fine education. He had the mind for it."

"I can see that," Joanna found herself saying.

"It was a sadness that he had to find a job instead. He has been working winters at that mill up north since he was sixteen, and growing wheat the rest of the year."

"He has a winter job, too?"

"Yes, dear. Didn't you know?"

She shook her head, her mind spinning. She could see clearly how Aiden had stepped up to take on the burden of his family. It did not surprise her. As she piled the measuring spoons and cups, the wooden spoon and knife into the mixing bowl for washing, she could see what had made Aiden the man he was. His mother's gentle love, his sense of duty and his faith, which kept him strong even in hard times.

She wished she could say the same about her belief.

"My Aiden worked long hours six days a week. We had fuel and food enough through the winter, thanks to him." Ida gave a soft sigh, a sound of love and gratitude. "He and Thad worked beside me in the fields come spring, and we drew in a crop that harvest. It took all of us working, but Aiden made the difference. He is a good man, Joanna."

Oh, the point of the conversation. She carried the bowl to the counter. "You don't need to convince me, Ida. My opinion of Aiden is already sky-high."

"He's a rare one, just like my Thad." Noelle chimed in, rising from her chair, using her fingertips to guide her along the table's edge. "Aiden tells me you are available for hiring. Is this true?"

"Yes. I sound too eager. I'm sorry." Joanna's knees had turned watery and she leaned on the counter to steady herself. Work. She had stopped praying long ago for a job. A woman could get her hopes only so high before she realized they would just come crashing to the ground. And yet here it was, the hope she had been afraid to feel. "What kind of work?"

"Didn't Aiden tell you? Oh, isn't that just like a man." Friendly and so wonderfully gentle, Noelle came over to the counter as if she saw just fine. "I have been looking for someone to clean and do laundry for me. Maybe help Ida out in the garden, since I am a hopeless gardener, not being able to see one plant from another."

"That makes it very hard to garden, dear." Ida's merriment was lovingly meant. "I think Joanna would be just right for us. I would be happy to keep an eye on your children. What treasures they are."

"I would love that." She had a job. Her worries about her children's care were solved. Their future had changed. Just like that.

Thank-you seemed too small of a word for what Noelle and Ida were offering her. Gratitude built within Joanna like a rising dam. This was because of Aiden. Because of him, she no longer felt alone.

"We're starving out here." Aiden filled the doorway, wry humor in his half grin. "How much longer is it going to be?"

"We're setting the table now," Noelle said cheerfully as she counted out dinner plates from her glass-fronted cabinets. "You go back outside, wash up and take the kids with you. You men may as well make yourselves useful."

"Yes, ma'am." Aiden saluted her, then his gaze swept right past her.

Joanna felt the impact of his eyes, but it was a welcome thing. Here, with his family, he seemed happier, as if a little more life had crept into him. As if the hopelessness he was drowning in had ebbed away for now. Her heart filled with admiration for him.

In truth, maybe it was a little more than admiration she felt for him. A smidgeon more than respect.

"I'll make sure the little ones are washed and ready for dinner," he told her over the kitchen noise, his gaze meeting hers and shrinking the distance between them.

Her pulse stopped; her world stilled. The sounds of Ida taking the roast out of the oven and the clink as Noelle set the table faded into silence. There was only the man tipping his hat to her, only Aiden, his dark blue eyes holding hers a moment too long.

It was like eternity. Like hope found. Her unprotected heart tumbled a notch. She gripped the counter more tightly, afraid her feelings showed on her face. Afraid that he would look at her and know. Because she was certain now that this *was* more than plain admiration she had for him, more than simple respect.

"Ma!" Daisy squeezed past his knee and tumbled into the kitchen, breathless, with daisy petals clinging to her little pink pinafore. She held up her hands, full of wildflowers. "I got enough for a necklace!"

Aware of Aiden watching her, Joanna gulped hard and struggled to sound normal. "Come here, honey, and give them to me. It's time for dinner. We'll make your necklace after we eat."

She knelt, feeling Aiden's gaze like an unspoken question. She did not know what he was thinking, but whatever it was, the rare humor had faded from his face. His eyes were shielded, his mouth a hard, unyielding line. Her hands trembled as she collected Daisy's prize of picked flowers.

"Ma!" Her baby's eyes went wide. "Is that real butter for the potatoes?"

"Yes, sweetie." Real butter had been a rarity before and nonexistent lately.

"Goody." The little girl sparkled with excitement.

"Go with Mr. McKaslin and get washed up." Joanna swallowed down the lump in her throat. "Tell James, too."

"Okay." Good girl that she was, Daisy pranced off, shoes tapping on the wood floor, and raced out the open door.

Aiden was gone. He hadn't heard the butter comment. Joanna rose on her shaky knees, relieved that she didn't have to see that look of pity on his face or, worse, one of understanding. He knew what hardship was. Perhaps that was why she liked him so much. He understood that you could do your best, do everything right, and it could still go wrong. At least she didn't have to look at him and wonder what he'd read on her face.

"What a precious child," Noelle was saying. "And your little boy is adorable. I heard him pretending to round up wild horses outside the door. We should tell Thad. He and I have a new herd of mustangs that were captured on the prairie. Perhaps he would like to look at them, although they are not tame, I'm afraid. The stallion is very protective of his herd."

"I'm sure he would love seeing them. We have already met Sunny."

"Sunny is exceptional. He loves children. He's been Thad's horse for many years."

Joanna adored this woman—practically a stranger—for her kindness. She had forgotten there were such people in the world. She had forgotten what a difference kindness could make.

She would never let herself forget this moment,

these people. Just as she would not forget what she saw when she looked out the open door: the image of Aiden watching over her children at the pump. He held the soap for them and handed James the towel. He was a caring man, despite his gruffness and distance.

Kindness was one thing she could give him. She circled around Ida and slipped the pie into the oven. She owed Aiden McKaslin more kindness than she could possibly repay, but that wasn't going to stop her from trying.

"She sure bakes a tasty pie," Thad said as he clipped the lead rope on his mustang's halter. Sunny, a palomino paint, tossed his head and looked over the fence rail at the little kids on the other side. The horse gave a snort as if scenting the air, trying to make up his mind about the children.

He was a gentle fellow. Aiden ran his hand down the mustang's neck. Thad was trying to get more information about Joanna. He was fishing around, suspecting more was going on than appeared at the surface, just as their mother did.

Frustrated, Aiden shook his head. "That's why I hired her. She makes the best biscuits I've ever tasted and her pancakes are better than Ma's. It took one bite to know I would be a fool if I didn't hire her."

"And she just happens to move into the shanty a stone's throw away from you." Thad tossed him a smile over the top of Sunny's mane. "That's mighty generous of you."

"She and her kids have been living out of their wagon since her pa died."

"Back in June?"

"Yep. Good thing it's summer. A few more months and then what would they have done?" Aiden opened the gate into the training corral he'd helped Thad build a few weeks before. "I know what you're thinking, and stop it. The minister has already let me know how this looks."

"What? I was only thinking I'm glad you found someone to cook for you. I was feeling mighty guilty taking Ma off your hands."

"Noelle needs her help, we both know that, and it's been good for Ma, too. You know how she likes to be needed." He glanced toward the small rise where the new house stood, windows open to the warm breezes. He searched until he found Joanna in the kitchen, washing dishes and handing them to Noelle to dry. She was talking away like women were wont to do.

Joanna seemed relaxed and happy, the exhaustion gone from her face, replaced by a healthy glow to her pretty complexion. She looked good—more than good. Funny what a handful of nights with worry-free sleep and plentiful meals, would do.

He was doing the right thing, whatever anyone else thought, even his trusted minister. Pastor Hadly had helped him get through his grief, but nothing—not even his stout faith—could begin to help Aiden cope with what had come after the grief. Life hadn't been the same. It would never be the same.

Not until this moment, watching the pretty woman as she hefted the dishpan and disappeared from the window, did he feel life calling to him once again. Like the murmur of the nearby waterfall, he could hear the whisper in his soul. It grew stronger when she appeared on the back porch, marched down the steps and tossed the dishwater far out into the grass. When she turned, she smiled at him.

He found himself smiling back.

I have Joanna's concern at heart, too. The minister's words came back to him, stirring the anger like a hard fist in his chest. Already people were talking. He should have considered this before he asked her to stay. What would be the consequences for her?

"Ma!" The boy's call rose on the wind, echoing on the vast prairie. "Look what I get to do! I get to ride a real mustang."

"Me, too, Ma!" the little girl shouted.

Aiden did his best not to look at them, so small and vulnerable, with no man to protect and provide for them. He closed off his feelings, knowing full well that he was a man prepared to protect and provide—with no wife and children to look after. It was hardly fair to either of them.

"Are you being trouble to Mr. McKaslin?" Joanna set the dishpan off to the side of the walkway and hiked through the knee-high grass. "Thad, you oughtn't to feel obliged to let them ride your horse."

"I don't mind, Joanna." Thad seemed to hold back a lot of amusement.

Aiden frowned. Sure, his brother might say he understood, but he was understanding the wrong thing. Now what was Aiden going to do? Even Thad believed he was sweet on the widow.

Aiden steeled himself as she swept closer. The sunlight seemed to find her and follow her, and she was pure golden goodness as she swept the little girl into her arms and onto her hip.

"You two be sure and do exactly what Mr. McKaslin says when you're up there on that horse." She straightened her daughter's flower necklace. "And remember to stay away from the wild horse pasture. And to thank Thad kindly when you're through."

"Yes, Ma." James climbed up onto the bottom rail, excitement vibrating off him. "I want to thank you right up front, Mr. McKaslin."

He was a sweet, sincere boy. Aiden had to look away.

It was Thad who answered. "You're welcome, little buddy. You know how to approach a horse?"

"Yes, sir. You stick out your hand."

"Yep, so he can scent you. That's how he learns who you are. That's right, but put your hand the other way. Palm up."

Not to be left out, the girl leaned in her mother's arms to stick her hand over the fence. She was a darling thing, a lot like her ma. Light haired and wide eyed with a button face. So little and trusting.

Aiden tried to glance away, but Joanna held him captive with the love on her face. A softness came over her as she watched her children. She was tender-hearted and a sensible woman, not pining after frills and frippery. Content with the simple necessities of life—a shanty roof over her head, food on the table, security for her young ones.

He hadn't known too many women who were like that. Joanna was a rare one. She'd certainly made his life more comfortable, maintaining a clean and polished house from top to bottom, true to her word. She brought cold water to the field straight from the well, a luxury for a man who did not like to put down his work. Her cooking was some of the best he'd tasted. The garden was thriving. All of that, and he hardly knew she was there. She was making her presence in his house as easy for him as she could. She understood how tough the situation was for him, when not many people seemed to. His family included.

"I'd best get back to help out." Joanna set her daughter on the grass. "Do you want to come with me, baby, or stay here?"

"I wanna ride the pony, too, Ma."

"It's all right, Joanna." Aiden found himself reassuring her as he took the halter rope from Thad. He'd let his brother lift the children onto the horse and steady them. He'd do better leading the horse. "Sunny is as trustworthy as could be."

"I trust you." Her smile was for him alone, quiet and gentle as her soul. "You hold on tight, James."

"I will, Ma." The little boy clung to the fence. "Can I come in, sir?"

Aiden glanced down at Joanna's son. "Sure."

The broken bits of him hurt as he nodded to the boy and noticed his eagerness and his earnestness. The kid ducked between two rails and landed with both feet on the ground. His shoes were patched in the toes, Aiden realized, carefully done to allow more room, which meant they were too small. Joanna had been making do on very little for far too long.

This was such a hard world, he thought, watching her wait while Thad lifted her son onto Sunny's back. Such a hard world. Perhaps he ought to do what he could to change that.

"Ma! Look! I'm on a real wild horse."

"I see," Joanna said as she backed in the direction of the house, surrounded by the deep green of the field and the dotted brilliance of wildflowers. "You look like a wrangler to me."

"Yep."

The little boy brimmed with excitement. He filled his fists with the mustang's white mane, listening to Thad as he told of how he'd found Sunny as a colt on the wild plains. Joanna's son was clearly awestruck. The little girl was swung up behind her brother.

Aiden looked away, quieting his feelings. Best not to think of what might have been.

"All right, our wranglers are mounted." Thad cut into his thoughts. "Aiden? You all right?"

"Sure." He almost believed it as he led the mustang forward. The boy gasped in delight; the little girl gave one excited shriek. Sunny calmly kept walking, quite aware, Aiden believed, of the value of what he carried on his back.

It was the sun making his eyes smart. He blinked hard and kept going. His gaze went to her, to Joanna, as she bent to lift the dishpan from the ground. With one last look in his direction, she spun with a flourish and skipped up the steps.

He could not know for sure, but he felt that she'd been watching him, just as he had been watching her.

Chapter Eight

"Are they asleep?"

Aiden's low question seemed to come out of the twilight. Joanna padded barefoot across the shanty's floor and stepped outside, drawing the door shut behind her. There he was, a shadow in the gathering darkness. She kept her voice at a whisper. "Their eyes were closed the second their heads touched the pillows. They haven't had such a nice day in a long while. I don't know how to thank you."

"No need. It was mainly Thad's doing."

"Yes, but your idea." She made her way toward him through the grass. The soft blades tickled her feet and rustled against the hem of her skirts. "James was so excited to have met a real wild horse that he couldn't stop talking."

"Yep, it was hard not to notice." Aiden's baritone rumbled with humor.

"Even as he was getting ready for bed. He fell

asleep midsentence." It had been such a good day. She glanced back at the shanty, dark and quiet, where her treasures slept. "Daisy is in love with your ma. It was kind of Ida to sit on the porch and play dolls with her."

"You seemed to get on well with Noelle. I hear she hired you."

"Three afternoons a week. You don't know what this means to me. I'll have real wages, money for my children. Because of you."

"No. Because of *you.* If Noelle didn't like you and didn't feel comfortable with you, she wouldn't have hired you."

What was she going to do with this man? He could not accept a compliment. The twilight was giving way to night, taking the shadows with it. Darkness wrapped around them both, making it hard to see him. "Has your brother made it back home yet?"

"Not yet. I imagine he'll roll in sometime tonight. All I can do is apologize for him. Finn has a powerful weakness for whiskey."

"My husband did, too."

"Then you understand."

"More than you know. There's nothing you can do to stop him. It's painful to watch him destroy his life one swallow at a time, and it's impossible to make him see what he's doing."

"Yep. That about sums it up. It didn't work with my pa and it's not working with Finn." Aiden turned toward the east, where the first stars were struggling to life. "I'm at a loss. I know Finn's gonna do what he's determined to do, but I keep thinking I've got to stop him or at least slow him down some."

"You love him. You feel a duty toward him."

"I've been looking after him since our pa took off. It wasn't a month later that he died. We don't talk about it much, but the truth is Pa died in a tavern brawl in a little no place town south of here. It's a shame to him. It's a shame to the family." He didn't know how to put it into words. "There's enough hardship in this life without making more for yourself on purpose."

"That's how it was with my husband, Tom." Her voice wavered. "I didn't know of his problem when we married. He hid it from me, and by the time I realized that he would never care for me the way he cared for his liquor, there was nothing but one problem after another."

"It's a hard way to live. I watched my ma go through it." Aiden could see how it had been for Joanna, too. Her hardships had begun long before he met her. "You were not happy in your marriage."

"No. I wanted to be, but life doesn't turn out the way you want it."

He thought of those two grave markers on the hill and gave thanks for the night that hid them. Somewhere a coyote howled, and the forlorn sound echoed across the prairie. "No. Life never turns out the way you want it. It is not our lives, but God's for us."

"How do you keep your faith with all that's happened to you?"

"I guess the question is, what kind of faith would it

be if I could not? Real faith isn't something you put on and take off like a boot."

"No, I suppose not."

Silence settled between them. Night had come to the high plains. The vast sky stretched out over them, rich with thousands of diamond-white stars. Starlight dusted the crests of the prairie rises and the glacial peaks of the Rocky Mountains. An owl glided on silent wings in front of them. Aiden tried to draw the peacefulness into himself, but no luck. The tight coil remained knotted up in his chest.

There were questions he had to ask. Things he had to say. Putting them off wasn't going to get the answers he needed. "How long ago did your husband die?"

"It was more than a year and a half ago that Tom finished a bottle of whiskey at the kitchen table, fell asleep and didn't wake up." She looked down at the ground. Her braids fell over her shoulder and her hair shone like platinum in the starlight.

It wasn't sadness she felt, and he understood. "You did not love him."

"I did or I never would have married him. I did not have the kind of marriage you had."

He squeezed his eyes shut. The darkness within him was complete. "I was blessed for a time. But I do not think something as fragile as love can last long in this world. My chance to love has passed."

"Mine, too."

"Is that why you haven't remarried?"

"Me? Remarry?" She wrapped her arms around her

middle. "Available bachelors are not lining up to court me. A woman with two small children? I have little to offer a man. No, I can't imagine that. Not unless he was admiring how hard I work, but I would not marry such a man."

"Then you plan to raise your children alone?"

"Somehow." The darkness continued, deepening its hold on the land, on the night. "I don't see what other choice I have. I know staying here is just a temporary solution, and I am so grateful. Your help is like a burden off my soul. Maybe now our fortunes will turn, and if they do, you are responsible. I will always be grateful for that."

"You give me too much credit, Joanna."

"You do not give yourself enough." She could make a long list of Aiden McKaslin's outstanding attributes, but then, she had grown a bit biased. Starlight brushed him with a silver glow, and her eyes had adjusted to see the proud lines of his face.

She liked him more than she should, she realized. Much more than she felt comfortable with. She wished that it was a black night with no stars to shine on her face and reveal the feelings she feared were too strong to hide.

"Joanna?" He shuffled closer, his focus on her now, the dark pools of his eyes unrelenting.

She shivered at the power of his glance. She wanted to lift her chin and keep that easily imposed distance between them, but where had it gone? And when? Suddenly she was intensely aware that they were alone, as if they were the only two people for miles with nothing but the stars as chaperones. The children were asleep; it was late. Her better sense told her she ought to say good-night and head back to the shanty—except for the tiny problem that she could not seem to make her feet move.

A little flurry of panic broke out behind her ribs. She trusted Aiden. She trusted herself. But something frightened her. Maybe it was because he'd taken another step closer, so that she could hear the faint rhythm of his breathing and smell the hay on his clothes, which lingered from his evening barn work for the horses.

"What if this is not a temporary solution?" He took her hand in his. His big, work-roughened, warm hand seemed to engulf hers.

His eyes were shadows, his face as shielded as granite. It was too dark to see what he meant, and not dark enough, because she felt exposed and vulnerable to him. "Wh-what do you mean?"

"You could stay here."

"No, I couldn't impose on you like that. It is one thing to accept a little help for my children's sake, but another entirely to take advantage of your generosity. I've got a paying job. Soon the fields will need harvesting and perhaps I can pay Ida to watch the children for me. If I work hard enough, I could have money for a new start."

"That wouldn't be much of a start. The farmers don't pay that well."

"Well enough for me."

"I admire your sense of duty." His baritone rumbled, deep and strangely intimate. "You are talking of long days, maybe sixteen hours or more, working in the cornfields in the hot sun, day after day until the crop is in. That won't be easy."

"I don't mind, Aiden. If you are concerned I might fail and you will be stuck with a woman and kids in your shanty all winter, I promise you that can't happen. I won't let it. I refuse to let my children down."

"I know that." His voice came warmer this time, deeper, and his hand wrapped around hers tightened gently.

Emotion kicked to life within her. A little flame of caring she could not stop warmed her heart. "You have my word, Aiden. I know what some people must think—your brother Finn, for instance. I see how he looks at me."

"And that woman at church?"

"Yes." She bowed her head and winced. "You heard that?"

"Hard not to."

She broke a little inside. Was this why he had been asking about her plans? About her not wanting to remarry? Did he suspect her motives? The night's hot wind wheezed over her, stirring the dust in the air and making her eyes smart. "I promise you that I do not have designs on you. I hope you don't think—"

"No." His answer came swift and sure, cutting her off. "I'm not worried about that, Joanna. It's easy to see the kind of woman you are."

The kind a man like Aiden would never be interested in. The kind of woman, Joanna thought, who did not inspire real love in a man. It hurt, sure, but at least he didn't believe the worst about her. That was some consolation. She brushed at her watery eyes. "I'd best turn in."

"It's late, but I have one more question."

As if she could take any more. "It's been a long day. Can it wait for tomorrow?"

"I'm not sure I will have the gumption tomorrow." He kept hold of her hand, so small and fragile within his big rough one. "I don't know how to go about this, so I'm just going to say it. You don't have to answer right away or even anytime soon. This is just something for you to mull over, and when you are sure of your answer, then let me know."

"I'm not sure I'm going to like this question." She gazed up at him with so much worry on her face.

It was easy to see her fears. She had gotten so used to one hardship after another that it was all she expected. He knew, because life had become that way for him, too.

"This isn't easy for me," he choked out, hating that the words were so hard to say. His pulse began to hammer. He felt as if he'd fallen into a fast and deep river and was about to be carried right over the crest of a deadly waterfall.

Just say the words, he told himself. He took one last breath and let the current carry him. "Marry me."

"M-marry you?" She jerked her hand from his.

He could see he'd surprised her. His hand felt empty. He felt sorely alone. How did he tell her that? "I haven't given it much thought yet, but I believe it is the right thing."

"How can it be right? I don't ever want to be beholden and bound to a man who doesn't love me. And I know you don't, Aiden. You can't."

"No, I don't love you. I can't. That's true." He fell silent, at a loss over how to say what he meant. He didn't even know. "Folks are going to start talking about you, and it could get ugly."

"I have nothing to be ashamed about." Her chin went up. She was so full of dignity, and yet so fragile. "Let people talk, Aiden. I would rather leave than cause you any shame. Maybe that is what I should do."

"We both know that's not wise. You need to stay for your children's sake."

"Yes, I do. But then what do I do about yours?"

He squeezed his eyes shut, not wanting to see the concern on her pretty face. Yet even with his eyes closed, he could still see her wide caring eyes.

"It would not be a real marriage," he found himself saying, snapping open his eyes, because he found he did not want to look within, either. The fields of wheat beyond the fence waved gently in the breeze, graced with starshine. "You and your children would have security and I would…"

No longer feel so alone. He hung his head, unable to say the words. Hoofbeats broke the stillness. Divine intervention. Grateful, Aiden moved away. "Just think on it some. Maybe you'll get used to the idea. If you do, then let me know. I'd best go face up to Finn. He and I have a few scores to settle. Good night, Joanna."

She didn't answer as he walked away. He knew he had surprised her, just as he'd surprised himself. When he glanced over his shoulder to check on her, she was still standing where he'd left her. He wanted to think it was surprise, anyway, and not shock at assuming she wouldn't mind marrying a worn-out, average man like himself who was missing more than his heart.

In retrospect, maybe he shouldn't have asked his question. He'd proposed to her. Maybe a measure of how frozen he'd become was that he didn't feel a thing about it. Not at all. In fact, every step he took away from her made him more like the night—full of shadows and without a speck of light.

At least he wasn't as far gone as Finn. He found his brother in the barn. All he had to do was to follow the noise, the muttering and the smell of cheap whiskey. Finn had lit a lantern at the end of the main aisle, and he didn't look up as he knelt in the shadows loosening the cinch. The horses, in their stalls for the night, were agitated. Clyde's skin was twitching.

Aiden halted at his gate. "Easy, old fella. You know you're safe here."

The gentle giant nickered low in his throat and leaned over the bars of his gate, seeking reassurance. Aiden rubbed the horse's nose and ears while he watched his youngest brother heft the saddle from his horse's back. A little rough, in his opinion. "Remember

I bought that gelding. I see you treating him like that again, and you'll be walking back and forth to town."

"Yeah? Go ahead and do it." Finn tossed the saddle and blanket on the ground, his stance aggressive, his jaw jutting stubbornly. When he stood like that, he resembled Pa. "I'd like to see you try. I'm younger and I'm stronger."

"I wouldn't be too sure about that. I have sixty pounds on you and three inches. Add the fact that I'm not drunk, and I'm sure to be the winner."

Now that Clyde had settled, Aiden gave him a final pat and ambled down the aisle. "I told you how things were going to be if you wanted to live here. Staying away from the closest tavern would be one condition. Attending church every week would be another."

"So? Why should I go? I've been going since I was a kid. It's not like that old minister is going to say anything I haven't heard before. And neither are you." Finn tossed down the bridle. "I saw you with her in the field when I was riding up. You two looked mighty cozy. She's already got you holding her hand. Next thing you know, she'll be—"

"That's enough." Aiden didn't want to hear it, whatever it was. "You don't know what you're talking about."

"I saw plenty."

There was no reason for him to defend his behavior, and he wasn't going to try. Aiden bent to grab the match tin from where it had been tossed onto the floor, with the dead match on top. He didn't comment on that, either, mostly because he knew Finn well enough to know he had done it on purpose. He had a lot of anger about rules, even if they were only common sense.

Sorrowful, that's how he felt, for this boy in a man's form who refused to grow up. Well, he would have to learn sometime. Aiden put the tin on a nearby shelf, close enough now to see the glaze of alcohol on his brother's face and how clumsy he was as he fought with the latch and threw open the stall gate. It swung hard and banged against the wall. The noise startled the gelding and sent neighs of alarm through the barn.

Finn swore at the horse, but Aiden was quick. He laid his hand on the old fellow's jaw and cheek and talked him back into the stall. The gelding just needed a reassuring word and touch, and he was relieved to be back home in his stall. Aiden kept Finn in his sight as he closed and latched the gate. He saw the grimace his brother gave him before he lumbered drunkenly down the aisle.

"Hey, Finn. Where are you going?"

"To bed. I'm not in the mood for any of your grief, either. I don't need a lecture."

That was a matter of opinion. Aiden crossed his arms over his chest. "You aren't sleeping in my house."

"It's my house, too."

"No it's not." He hated to do it. It killed him to do it. "I warned you, Finn. If you came home drunk, then you are off this property."

"You wouldn't toss me off this place. Where am I going to sleep?"

"That's not my lookout. It's yours." Aiden gulped down enough air to force the next words out. "You're a grown man. It's time you started acting like one. Ma and Thad and I have done everything we can to help you get back on your feet after spending two years in prison."

"It wasn't my fault." Finn lashed out, just as he always did. "I didn't know what I was doing. Even the judge agreed I didn't know I took the blasted wrong horse from the hitching post. C'mon, Aiden—"

Typical Finn. Arguing a point that had nothing to do with the real issue. "You were drunk then, and you're drunk now. I won't have it. If you want to throw away your life, then you do it somewhere that I can't watch. I won't be responsible for helping you do it."

"Fine. I'll just take my horse—"

"*My* horse. And anything you have in my house is what I bought you. That makes it mine." Aiden wished his brother would see reason. He wished Finn would turn his life around. But he had to be tough about this. Finn's future was at stake. He took a ragged breath; he dreaded what he had to say. "Start walking. You take nothing but the clothes on your back, same as when you got here."

"But what about—"

"Don't care." He cut his brother off, tired of excuses, tired of everything. "I've got a ranch to run, crops to bring in and Ma to help support. You are not my responsibility. Now, go."

"I could fight you for the horse."

"You could, but let's be clear. I won't let you steal

this horse. I have to think of his welfare, too. You won't take good care of him. You don't deserve him."

"I should have expected this from you." Finn's temper flared, predictably, turning now to blame whoever he could. "It's that woman. You don't want me around because—"

"Go." Aiden couldn't stomach it. He took Finn by the shoulder and gave him a calculated shove. Not too hard, because Finn was much drunker than he thought, and he might fall and hurt himself, but hard enough to get him out of the barn. Aiden shut the door tight. "I want you gone, Finn. Don't come back unless you will follow my rules."

"Don't worry, I won't be back." Rage now, and it was ugly. Aiden tried not to remember when Pa was like that, blaming Ma for bringing him down and his sons for being a burden to him. "It's a sorry day when a man chooses a woman like her over his own brother."

Aiden clamped his jaw hard so he wouldn't rise to Finn's bait. Anger beat at him while he huffed in one breath after another, trying to keep control. He hated how his brother was living. He wished he could shake some sense into him. Prayer hadn't helped. Talks with Pastor Hadly hadn't helped. Not even Ma's pleas to Finn had made a bit of difference in the end. Aiden had done all he could for the boy ever since he had come home last February. There was nothing more he could do.

Now Finn was disparaging Joanna, getting in what licks he could as he staggered away. Aiden felt tired, deeply tired. Her words came back to him as softly as the night breeze. *Maybe now our fortunes will turn, and if it does, you are responsible. I will always be grateful for that.*

There was a difference he could make, if Joanna would let him.

He followed the roll of the prairie past his house toward the shanty. Its small peaked roof was topped by the stars' lush glow, and he thought of Joanna there. She was no longer in the field, at least that he could see. Was she thinking about him, too? Wondering about his proposal? Or was she not interested in marrying a washed-up man like him?

He opened the barn door to give the horses the benefit of the breeze, sure now that Finn was gone. He was only a faint blur of movement far down the road. Another blink, and he'd disappeared.

Watch over him, Lord. Wearily, Aiden headed back to the house through the grass, feeling as if the light could not touch him. It was as if night had fallen inside him, too.

Chapter Nine

"Ma! Look!" Daisy's high sweet voice rose above the music of the wind and the whirring sound of the cutter. She held up a handful of cornflowers. "I want a purple necklace, please?"

"All right. We can make it after we deliver this to Mr. McKaslin." Wearily, Joanna checked over her shoulder. It had been a long, sleepless night and a hard morning of work. There was James, bringing up the rear, packing the ceramic water jug, which he had insisted on carrying. "Are you sure that isn't too heavy for you?"

"I'm sure, Ma." James's chin stuck out and he frowned with intense focus. He clutched the jug with both hands. "I'm gonna be a rancher one day with lots of mustangs. I'll have to carry a lot of water. I'll get to cut hay, too. There he is, Ma! It's Mr. McKaslin!"

Yes, it certainly was. He was up ahead, walking beside the horses as they pulled a mowing machine. He had the reins knotted loosely around his neck, and although his hat hid most of his face, his strong jaw was squared with concentration. Bits of grass floated in the air and clung to him like dust. Why did that only make him more handsome to her?

She had no answer to that. Last night's question had unsettled her. She'd had the good luck of avoiding him at breakfast, and had left his and Finn's food in the warmer. He and his brother must have eaten quickly and headed out to their work in the fields, because when she came in later to clean up the kitchen, the tea had gone cold. All morning she had been safely in the house, cleaning away, but now there was no avoiding him. Her feet seemed to drag with every step she took through the sweet prairie grasses.

How was she going to face him? She would have to look him in the eye and know that he'd offered to marry her out of charity. Pity. A sense of duty. And that made her feel two inches tall.

If only there was a way to leave the basket without meeting up with him. With any luck he would keep right on working and miss seeing her entirely. She could leave the food on the fence post and leave. They wouldn't have to talk.

Luck wasn't with her. Aiden spotted her. Even across the expanse of the field, she could feel the impact of his gaze. Not full of pity for her, as she expected, but as stoic as the ground at her feet.

He chirruped and the big horses stopped. The cutter's blades went silent. Her pulse began to thrum in her ears and she went hollow with dread. She watched the capable way he unwound the reins and patted the horses before he ambled through the fallen stalks of mown hay.

All night she'd been up, her mind whirling. What if she turned down Aiden's offer? Did that mean it would be best if she left sooner rather than later? Even if she had some wages in hand, would the money last long enough for her to find another job? And if she did, what would it be? Without a doubt, she would be cooking or cleaning for someone else. And if that were the case, then why not stay? Staying might be better for the children.

If only that was all she had to consider. She remembered how Aiden had caught the eye of several women in church on Sunday. Not that she blamed them one bit for being sweet on him. No, she thought as he stalked toward her. He was more than simply good-looking. When he walked, he radiated strength. When he studied her, as he came to a stop before her, he radiated kindness. What a combination.

"That basket is a welcome sight." He broke the silence between them. The way he rubbed the back of his neck might be a sign he was as uncomfortable as she was. "Seems I've worked up quite an appetite."

"Then it's a good thing I brought lunch early, because I need to head over to Noelle's." She stared down at the basket. It was safer looking at the wicker top than at his guarded eyes. "I assumed you and Finn would be together. If he's working in another field, I could take his share out to him."

"Finn is gone." He looked past her toward the house, and then out at the western horizon, where a few lazy clouds were gathering. "He left last night."

"Left?" So that was why there had been a lot of breakfast leftovers. She had assumed Finn might have been feeling poorly this morning. "But he'll be coming back?"

"That's up to him." Aiden swept off his hat and pulled his handkerchief out of his back pocket to wipe the grit from his face. He said nothing more, standing like a giant with the sun at his back and the deep blue sky stretched over him like a dream.

"I brought your water, sir." James had finally caught up and lugged the container to Aiden. He held it out carefully with both hands. "It's still real cold."

The man hesitated, studying the boy quietly before he took the jug. "That's real fine. Thank you."

"You're welcome. Can I go pet the horses?" So much need in those pleading eyes. So much more in those words than the question.

The poor boy, wanting approval from the man. Looking for a father. Joanna felt her anxiety slip away. And poor Aiden, trying not to think of the son he'd lost as he set eyes on the boy. Sadness tugged at her soul, making her helpless to do more than put her hand on James's small shoulder. "Come, let's you and I go look at the horses together while Aiden cools down. Daisy, are you coming?"

"Yes. And my flowers, Ma."

"I haven't forgotten, baby." Every fiber of Joanna's being was aware of Aiden. Last night stood between them as unmistakably as the sun-baked earth at their feet. She felt small—very small—as she set the basket into the soft grass and walked away from him. If only she could walk away from the memory of his proposal as easily, but, no, it loomed like a weight on her shoulders.

Did he think she was the type of woman who ingratiated herself to a man, cooking and cleaning for him, making strawberry pie for his family, so that he might see how handy a wife she would make him?

You know that's not what he thinks, Joanna. She kept her back to him, walking steadily after James toward the standing horses.

"Ma! He likes me. See?"

Joanna blinked, pulled from her thoughts. There was James, alive with excitement, while the gray-whiskered giant fondly nibbled his hair. James laughed, simply, easily, without a care. He was like a whole different boy. He held out his hand, still laughing, as the horse stopped nibbling and snorted into his palm.

"Me, too!" Daisy raced up, her bare feet pounding on the hard earth.

Joanna reached out for the Clydesdale's bridle bits, but he placidly turned in his collar to give the little girl a snort, too, so Joanna settled for patting his velvety neck. The second horse was as gently tempered. The two were gruff and imposing looking, just like their master, with hearts of gold.

Boots crackled in the grass behind her. "You needn't have any worries around these fellas. We've had them since I was a boy, and I've never seen either of them startle or work up a temper about anything. Not even a rattler, once, that came out of the grass at them. Clyde just tossed him out of the way and kept on pulling the plow. He didn't hurt him, either, just stunned that snake so that he was too afraid to move. A good part of an hour passed before he slinked away."

"That is a good horse," Joanna praised, glad to know it. "They seem to like kids."

"They watched the three of us grow up. Finn was just about as little as your girl there. Clyde took to watching over him like a papa. No need to worry if Finn was off getting into trouble. The horse would give a sharp whinny, stomp out of the field and go after him."

She couldn't think of a thing to say to that. She had so many thoughts bubbling below the surface, she didn't know where to start. She had to turn down his offer. She had learned the hard way she had to rely on herself. That sooner or later a man let you down. She'd seen it happen to her ma, and her own marriage had been one heartbroken disappointment after another.

No, it was best she stand on her own feet. Joanna drew herself up, her decision made. And yet there he was, like the salt of the earth. When she looked at him with her heart, she saw more than his goodness. She could see her dreams: a stable life for her children. Security for them. They would never have to live out of a wagon again.

How could she not accept his offer? Worse, how could she?

"Here, I want you to take this." He pulled a handful of coins from his pocket and shook them around to count them. Five dollars. "You'll be driving through town. On your way back through, I would like you to stop and do some shopping. That money is just in case. I'll try to drop by and put your name on my account, but I can't say for sure if I'll make it before you do. I plan on stopping by the church to chat with the minister later today, and there's no judging how long that'll take."

"About your brother?"

His throat worked and he looked away.

He was more upset than he was letting on, she realized, and that came as no surprise to her. Was he regretting last night? Did he wish he could take back his offer? Her stomach coiled up into a worried ball. Was it his question last night that had changed things between them? Or was it her silence that answered his question?

"I'll be glad to stop by Lawson's store and do your shopping." She had time enough to make a list before she left for Noelle's. "What do you need?"

"Just regular groceries. Whatever you want for the kitchen for the week." He fisted his hand around the coins. "Wouldn't mind if you got some pie-making ingredients."

"You like strawberry pie?" The coins tumbled onto her palm.

"I would like anything as long as you baked it."

"Was that the real reason behind last night's question?" The words were out before she could take them back. In her mind they'd been light, but spoken, they hung in the air between them like a swirling tornado.

"Possibly." Aiden grinned slightly, but his eyes remained sad. "There are other reasons I asked what I did, you know."

"I'm a passable cook."

"A mighty fine one in my opinion. But there are more reasons, too." He glanced at the kids and said nothing more.

She heard what he didn't say. Daisy had taken to hugging Clyde's front leg. The other horse held his head low enough so that James could pet his ears. Her children were happy and giggling.

They were what mattered most.

Aiden was still at the center of her thoughts at day's end. She was driving toward town. Her first day working for Noelle had been the best job she'd ever had. She had helped Ida in the garden and spent another pleasant hour washing down Noelle's lovely new kitchen. Ida was glad to keep an eye on the children, who wore themselves out running in the wild grasses. Joanna was looking forward to returning on Wednesday afternoon to help with the weekly baking.

"Ma, why are you doing that?" Daisy bounced closer on the wagon seat. "How come, Ma?"

"It's a hem," James said from Daisy's other side. "From church."

"A hymn," Joanna gently corrected him. "I guess I was humming, Daisy."

"I can, too." Daisy clamped her lips together and gave it an off-key try.

James covered his ears. "Oh, brother. Do I gotta listen to that, too?"

"Yes, you do." Sympathy filled Joanna. She had been the oldest, as well. She knew how hard it was to always be patient.

As she turned into town, she couldn't help but notice one of the local saloons. Aiden had tried not to seem affected, but she knew him better than that. He had to have taken his brother's leaving very hard, which was why she had quietly mentioned Finn's departure to Thad. Maybe this was one heartache Aiden wouldn't have to shoulder alone.

She pulled the horses to a stop outside the mercantile. It had been a good month since they had all been inside the store. She had bought beans, cornmeal and flour, counting coins out of the bottom of her reticule to pay for them. "I want you both to remember to mind your manners."

"Yes, Ma," James said seriously.

Daisy's head bobbed in agreement.

Joanna thought of the few extra coins she had now as she climbed down from the wagon. Her little ones were so dear, sitting there as neatly as could be. Daisy's twin braids were tidy and her little pink calico dress made her look adorable. James had a grass stain on the knee of his denims, but that aside, he was a little gentleman. Her heart swelled with love for her babies. She held up her hands to lift Daisy from the seat.

She set her daughter on the ground and let James hop down on his own, as he insisted. But she kept a hand out to catch him just in case. He landed with a two-footed thud in the dusty street. She looped the reins around the hitching post and let James lead the way onto the boardwalk.

"Do you know what I have for each of you?" she asked just outside the door. "A penny. After we get all of Mr. McKaslin's groceries, then you each can pick out candy of your own."

"Really, Ma? Honest?" James's smile lit up his face.

"I want the striped kind," Daisy decided at once.

Together they went into the store, hand in hand. The pungent brine of the pickle barrel, made stronger by the day's heat, wafted toward them the instant they stepped through the door. It wasn't busy. Most folks had probably already done their shopping in the cooler part of the day. Joanna dug through her reticule for the list she'd made before leaving Aiden's house.

Mrs. Lawson had her back turned, kneeling to sort through a few low shelves behind the long front counter. She seemed terribly busy. Joanna lifted a small sack of white sugar from the stack against the wall and chose a can of baking powder from a nearby shelf. She felt a tug on her skirt.

"Are you done yet, Ma?" Daisy whispered.

"Not yet, baby. We just need a few more things." Like a sack of beans, a tin of tea and a few bars of lye soap, which she carried to the front counter.

Mrs. Lawson didn't seem to notice her. Joanna

waited, realizing she might be filling someone's order. She slipped her list back into her reticule.

"Now, Ma?" James asked politely.

"You may look." She hadn't gotten the words out before both kids were off, rushing across the floor toward the glass display of candy next to the door.

"Don't touch," she reminded them just as Daisy's fingers were about to reach out and smudge the spotless glass.

"I'll watch her, Ma." James, resigned to his fate, took guard over his little sister.

He was such a good boy. She was thankful for the new job because now she had a few pennies to spare. Now, if only Mrs. Lawson would be free to fill the rest of her order, they could have their candy and be on their way home. Home. A rush of relief swelled through her at that single word. Already that little shanty had become a safe place all their own.

"They have the striped ones." Daisy's whisper to her brother carried in the still hot air.

"And the lemon ones." James held his sister's hands to keep her from reaching out.

It seemed as if they had been waiting awhile, and no other customers were in the store. "Mrs. Lawson?"

"I'm busy, Joanna." The woman's tone was sharp and her hand faltered. A bobbin of thread tumbled to the floor.

"I know, and I hate to bother you, but I need a few more things. A pound of bacon and a large sack of flour."

Mrs. Lawson snatched the thread off the floor. Her

gaze was as hard as her frown. "You'll have to take your business elsewhere."

"Excuse me? I thought you closed at five o'clock."

"Oh, we're still open."

"But—"

"I don't need your kind in here. Women like you." Mrs. Lawson nodded toward the door. "Good day."

Joanna felt her jaw drop. *Your kind,* she'd said. What kind was she talking about? Oh, maybe it was because of last time she'd been in. She had to count pennies and put back two items before she could afford her groceries. She felt every stitch on every patch of her dress. Shame bit her hard, and she lowered her voice. She tugged open her reticule. "I can pay for this. It's for Mr. McKaslin. He gave me enough for—"

"Whatever he gave you is none of my concern, I can assure you." Mrs. Lawson sounded scandalized. Worse was the harsh judgment on her face. She lifted her lip as if she smelled something foul. "Your money is no good here. Please leave."

"But—" Shock washed over her. She stared down at Aiden's silver dollars at the bottom of her reticule. *Please leave.* Those words echoed in her brain over and over. *Your money is no good here.*

"Try the general store over on Eighth Street. Right next to Steiner's Saloon." Mrs. Lawson marched around the end of the counter. The strike of her shoes sounded like a gavel of judgment.

"But that's a bad part of town."

"Exactly." Mrs. Lawson seemed perfectly aware of

that as she yanked open the front door. "They serve your kind there. Take your children and leave. Now."

What kind of person did Mrs. Lawson think she was? Bewildered, Joanna left the groceries on the counter and forced her feet forward. She could feel the shopkeeper's disdain, as if she were little more than those unfortunate women who worked on Eighth Street. Was that what folks were thinking? That she was— No, she couldn't even think the words. Her mind closed off, her heartbeat lurched to a stop and she took each child by the hand.

"Come," she said quietly, struggling to keep her voice steady, although it did wobble a little. "We need to go to another store."

James hung his head, as if to hide his disappointment. He took one last long glance at the lemon drops. "Yes, Ma."

It broke her. James came along at her side, as if resigned, but his hurt seemed to hang in the air. He did not deserve this. Her eyes blurred and she blinked hard to keep control of her emotions. "Come, Daisy."

"But, Ma." Big blue eyes filled with tears. "I got my pieces all picked out."

"I know, honey." Joanna ignored the store owner's gaze boring into her back, and knelt down to kiss her baby's cheek. "Come, we have to go."

Daisy sniffled. "You said, Ma. You said we could."

"I was wrong. I'm sorry." Anger beat at her, because it wasn't right, denying her children. They might not have much, but they were good and honest. She mustered all the dignity she could and led her family out of that shop, shielding them the best she could from Mrs. Lawson's bare disdain, and started blindly down the boardwalk. She couldn't seem to think what to do next.

There. Her vision cleared enough to spot the dry-goods store at the end of the block. "We'll try in there. I know they have a good selection of candy."

"It don't matter, Ma." James fought to be brave, although the choked sound of his voice gave him away. "I don't want any candy. We can't afford it."

At least her children were spared the understanding of what had happened. How could Mrs. Lawson think such a thing? Joanna glanced around at the busy boardwalk, realizing that a woman she recognized from church was giving her a wide berth as she passed. No nod of greeting, no smile, nothing. Mrs. Collins deliberately looked the other way.

Apparently Mrs. Lawson was not alone in her judgments. Joanna withered inside, not at all sure what to do. What if she was turned away from the dry-goods store and the other stores on the good side of town?

She told herself that she didn't care what others thought; she knew the truth. But as another woman she didn't even know purposefully avoided her on the boardwalk, shame washed over her.

She stopped in the shadow of the barbershop's awning and dug two pennies out of her reticule. They shone coppery in the sunlight, winking like a promise. She handed one to each child. "Now don't drop yours,

Daisy. Hold on tight. We'll go in and you can buy your own candy."

She wasn't sure it would work, but it was worth a try.

Chapter Ten

Joanna was like a godsend in his life. Aiden led the way out of the minister's office and into the sweltering sunshine, glad for the drum of footfalls following him. He wasn't alone, because Joanna had mentioned his meeting to Thad. Thad had come, dutiful Thad, and he was going to take over the reins.

Aiden knuckled back his hat to take a long look at the sky. Storm clouds were gathering in the west, blocking out the lowering sun. He judged it to be near four o'clock, maybe a few minutes later. Those thunderheads might hold some rain, he figured, but it would take until dark before they would see any. It would blow on northeasterly, was his guess, and the hay drying in his field would be safe.

"I wish I could come along," he told Thad.

"Me, too, but something tells me Finn might take one look at you and lose his temper." Thad glanced over his shoulder, waiting for the minister to join him.

"We'll stop and get Hadly's son to help out. There are only four saloons in town. Finn is likely to be in one of them. Don't worry, I'll take care of him if I can."

"That's a load of worry off my chest." Aiden had hardly slept last night, torn between standing his ground and riding to town to search for him. He feared what choices his youngest brother was making—his baby brother. "You'll send word if you find him?"

"I will." Thad's seriousness eased a fraction. "No one could have done as much as you, Aiden. Finn has to know that somewhere deep down. This will right itself in the end, I know it. Now, go find that woman of yours—"

"She's not my woman."

"Sure, fine." Thad didn't look as if he believed it. "You go have a nice evening. Maybe she'll bake you another one of those pies. Best dessert I've ever tasted."

"You and me both." Aiden loosened Clyde's reins from the post. Dust scudded in whirlwinds down the street. He figured he had a chance of making it to the mercantile before Joanna did. "There's something you ought to know. I suppose you could call it news."

"That's no surprise, considering. Glad you're getting around to telling me." He gathered Sunny's reins and mounted up with a squeak of the saddle. "Are you going to marry that woman?"

"I asked her." Aiden slipped his foot into the stirrup and swung into his own saddle. "How did you know?"

"I figure that's why you wanted us to meet Joanna."

Aiden didn't correct him. His throat clenched up

tight. He'd brought Kate home to meet his family right before he'd got down on his knees and given her his ring. He couldn't seem to find the strength to say it was different this time. This wasn't love. This wasn't foolishness. It was practicality. He wanted to say he was doing the right thing for Joanna, but his proposal wasn't that selfless. He would be getting something out of the deal. Not his heart, that was for certain, but maybe his soul.

"I got to tell you, Aiden, I didn't think this day would ever happen." Thad drew Sunny around. The gladness on his face was easy to see.

Aiden struggled to breathe. Tangled pieces of too many broken feelings seemed to jam up, leaving his voice strained. "Don't say anything. She hasn't said yes."

"I can see why she might hesitate. She's a sweet-seeming woman, and you are no catch, big brother."

So now the teasing was going to start. Aiden rolled his eyes and guided Clyde into the street. "I guess that makes me a lucky man that she didn't say no right out. I'll try to catch up with her at the mercantile."

"Guess even the tough fall in love." Thad winked, and there was no hiding the grin on his face. He was enjoying this.

Aiden cringed, remembering how adamantly he had insisted he would never marry again. He supposed he deserved the brotherly ribbing. "Speak for yourself, Thad. I hope you can talk some sense into Finn. Good luck."

"Thanks. I'm going to need it and a whole lot of

divine intervention. There's the minister." Thad rode off toward the narrow alley next to the church so he could join Hadly on his white mare.

Aiden was mighty grateful to have their pastor's help on this. It was a perilous road Finn was walking, and if he didn't make a real change, then Aiden hated to think what would become of his littlest brother. He disliked feeling helpless. He wished there was something more he could do to change things. The failure ate at him.

There was Joanna's horse and wagon right in front of the mercantile. Looked like he'd lucked out. The prospect of seeing her again put a little spring into his step as he left Clyde at the hitching post.

His eyes were already searching for her through the wide front window. His ears were straining for the gentle music of her voice. When he heard it, his hand was on the door handle. Something was wrong; he could feel it like a cool breeze skittering down the back of his neck.

"But I wanted the candy, Ma." The daughter's face was streaked with tears.

"I know, baby. I did my best." Joanna scooped the child up into her arms, balancing her on her slim hip. She kissed away her tears. The boy was looking down at the cracks between the boards, his shoulders slumped.

What was going on?

"Joanna?" Aiden was halfway to her before he realized it. A few more steps and he was close enough to see the tight control around her mouth and the hurt in her eyes. It was all he could see—that hurt. He drew himself up tall, hands fisting, stunned by the overwhelming impulse to protect her at any cost. "What's wrong?"

"Aiden." She gazed up at him with regret—it could only be regret—as if she didn't want to be seen with him. Her face was pink from emotion and her delicate jaw set like steel. "I—I was just trying to get groceries."

"At the dry-goods store?" That didn't make any sense. He looked at her arms, empty of packages. He glanced toward the back of the wagon and didn't see a single sack of staples. Why did she look ashamed? "Come with me into Lawson's."

"No." She stopped, bracing both feet. "I don't want to upset the children. I'm sorry, Aiden, but I can't do your shopping. The only store that will probably serve me is one I don't want to go in."

This still did not make a lick of sense. "Why won't they serve you?"

"It doesn't matter, Aiden. I'll take care of it later."

"No. We'll take care of it now." He drew himself up taller, all might. All fight. "This better not be what I think it is."

"They don't serve my kind, according to Mrs. Lawson." Joanna wouldn't meet his gaze. She kissed another tear from her daughter's cheek and smoothed the boy's windblown hair with her free hand.

"Your kind?"

"That's what she said." Shame ate at Joanna. What more could she say? She could see Mrs. Lawson watching through the front window, tsking as she shook her head slowly from side to side. *We don't do business with your kind,* she'd said. *Women like you.*

"Ma?" James asked. "Are we gonna go home?"

"Yes, baby, we are." Humiliation had turned her mouth bitter, and her face felt sunburn-hot. She fought hard to keep her voice calm and her upset locked up tight, for her little ones' sakes. "Let's go to the wagon now."

"Okay, but you should have my penny." James held it out, trying so hard to be good, her dear little boy. "I don't need any candy."

"I do," Daisy hiccuped.

Joanna's heart just kept breaking off in pieces. "Baby, you keep the penny."

She didn't see it as much as felt it, the way Aiden seemed to swell up even taller, like a bear ready to fight.

"Stay here," he told her, already stalking toward the mercantile door. "I'll be right back."

"No, it's not—" *worth it.* She didn't have time to finish, for he'd already jerked open the door and disappeared inside. There he went, a big bear of a man, hunting down Mrs. Lawson.

"Is he getting my candy?" Daisy asked.

"I don't know." The last thing Joanna wanted was a scene. It was only going to make people like Mrs. Lawson think whatever they knew about her was right. That would only affect her children more. All she wanted was to go home. She would fix dinner—Aiden had enough on his pantry shelves for her to make supper—and she would come back and try again tomorrow. Maybe Ida could watch the children again.

"Come." She took James by the hand. "Let's get into the wagon."

A man came out of the barbershop, gave her a friendly look that lasted a bit too long and wasn't nice at all.

She cringed. The shame inside her doubled, and she jerked her gaze to her feet, studying the tips of her shoes as he sauntered past. She had never in her life wanted to disappear more than at this moment.

She helped James climb onto the high wagon seat, and hefted Daisy up after him.

"Hey, Ma." James settled onto the edge of the seat. "Mr. McKaslin looks awful mad."

He did. She could see him clearly through the glass. She had never seen a man look more intimidating or more controlled. He towered over the counter, tensed as if for a fight, but there was no threatening gesturing or temper. That was a surprise, since that was her experience with angry men. Aiden was merely speaking with Mrs. Lawson with a quiet firmness. Mr. Lawson came out of the back of the store to the counter and joined the discussion.

Aiden was going to make this right. Wonderful Aiden. He was standing up for her. No man had ever done that before. Places in her heart warmed—places she didn't know she had. The sunshine seemed brighter and the air more sweet. The backs of her eyes smarted as she watched Mrs. Lawson pull items from the shelves. Mr. Lawson went to the candy case and put several pieces into a brown paper bag.

"He got some lemon ones," James announced.

"How about the striped ones?" Daisy asked.

"Yep."

Aiden strode out of the store with a big brown package in his arms—the wrapped groceries. Mr. Lawson followed with two bigger sacks.

"Ma'am." He nodded cordially as he passed, and set the flour and beans into the wagon bed.

Joanna couldn't speak, so she bobbed her head, her pulse pounding nervously as he went back to his store. There had been no more judgmental looks. Nothing uncomfortable.

"I got things set right," Aiden told her as he put the package in the wagon bed. He held out the sack of candy. "For your little ones."

Joanna heard two excited gasps behind her on the seat. She took the bag. Her heart began to melt just a little. Maybe it was the way the sunlight graced his broad shoulders and the brim of his hat, but he seemed bigger to her. In her eyes, there was no one better. Caring swelled through her in the sweetest way.

"Thank you." Again, the words were far too small for the great kindness he had done for her and for her children.

"It was no trouble at all. You go on and climb up." He took her elbow to help her.

Her heart took another slide. It was no longer gratitude she felt, no longer simple respect. Her feelings for him had multiplied, taking on depth and layers. She let him boost her up, and she settled into the seat. Silence filled her as she waited while he untied the horses and handed her the reins. She cared for him very much.

Too much. She took the reins from his gloved hands, avoiding his gaze. There was too much swirling around inside her that she didn't want him to see. Too many emotions she was afraid to examine closely.

"I'll see you at home?" he asked, but the question in his eyes asked more.

That was a question she could not yet answer. Look how this afternoon had turned out, and what folks already thought. She might not care, as long as it didn't harm her children, but those opinions also painted Aiden in a poor light. How could she allow such a thing? As long as she was in his life like this, those rumors were not going to stop. Simply accepting his proposal might not make them stop entirely. Maybe it would be best for Aiden if she packed up the kids and rode out of his life.

"I'll be right behind you," she told him, instead of the yes he was waiting for. "You go on ahead."

"All right." He winced a little, as if disappointed.

She hated that. Guilt crept into her. She straightened the reins and released the brake, waiting as Aiden ambled to his horse and mounted up. His movements were sure and controlled. Maybe it was the shadows making him look so weary. Maybe it was her imagination, what she wished she would see.

The truth was, she was troubled by these rumors. She didn't want to leave; she felt she needed to stay. Because if she did, then she could do everything possible to make his hard life easier. She wanted to repay his kindness. She longed to have her children know security and stability and the care of a strong man who would not let them down.

"Ma?"

"Yes, James?" Then she realized she was still clutching the bag of candy. How on earth had she forgotten? She transferred the right rein to her left hand and held the sack out. "One apiece so you don't ruin your supper."

After James had chosen a lemon drop and Daisy a striped peppermint ball, Joanna tucked the sack into her skirt pocket. She gave the reins a firm snap. The horse plodded forward and the wagon wheels creaked. There was one more truth rising up from her heart, a truth she could no longer ignore.

She was a little sweet on Aiden. It was hard not to be.

Storm clouds had turned the northeastern sky coal-black and sent a cool wind skittering through the fields.

Aiden pulled up the horses, let the welcome breeze blow against him, and gave thanks for it. That felt good, for he was blistering hot. He'd been pressing hard since he'd gotten back from town, mostly because he had twice the work to do now that Finn was no longer here to pitch in. But the truth was, as long as he was working hard, he didn't have to think about what had happened in town today. He didn't want to speculate about how those rumors got started in the first place. He feared that Finn had been drinking and talking up a good story at one of the saloons. Aiden shook his head, remembering the hurt look on Joanna's face.

Yep, just thinking about it got his guts knotted up and put his chest in a tangle. Too many emotions blew through him and he fought them down. He didn't like feeling this much. He dragged in a long breath, took off his hat to let the breeze cool his head. Joanna and her kids were coming his way, bringing his supper.

The family was a pretty sight. The little girl was skipping ahead to collect wildflowers. The boy trailed after Joanna, carrying the big water jug. It looked to be pretty heavy for a kid that size, but his jaw was set with determination. In that way the boy was a lot like his ma.

Then Aiden looked at her. At Joanna. With her sunbonnet down and her braids uncoiled from her proper topknot, she was a sight to behold. The wind danced through loose wisps of blond hair that had escaped, and she could have been a ray of sunshine come down to earth for all her innocent beauty.

It wasn't a puzzle to figure out why she might not want to tie herself to a man like him. He felt like the dark side of sunset as she lifted a hand from the basket handle and waved in greeting.

His hand was up and waving in return before he thought about it. There was that tangle in his chest again, the one he'd do best to ignore. He left the horses to rest and headed toward the creek. By the time he had washed most of the grime off his face and neck, Joanna was there, handing him a small towel from inside the basket.

"I brought pie for dessert, just as you asked." She hardly looked at him.

"Did you now?" He dried his face with the soft cloth, feeling her distance and his. "I'm real partial to apple pie, too."

"I'll keep that in mind. I noticed the apples in the orchard are starting to ripen."

"I'd be mighty obliged." He folded the towel. "What else do you have in that hamper?"

"Sit down and find out." She shook out a blanket and let it settle on the creek bank, keeping her back to him as she smoothed away the wrinkles.

Yessir, he reckoned he had her answer to his proposal. He'd seen it in her hurt eyes in town as she sat on that wagon seat, holding the bag of candy out to her children. Being associated with him had brought harm to her reputation. There was no way she was going to accept him now. Why that hurt like a blow, he couldn't rightly say. He only knew his life was better with her near.

It was her cooking. At least that was the simplest explanation and the only one he would allow himself to think about. He knelt on one corner of the blanket, his mouth watering at the scents coming from the tin containers Joanna was opening. Buttered carrots; must be the first from the garden, since they were so small. Butter melting off the tops of fluffy buttermilk biscuits.

He couldn't believe all that she had done. "Is that chicken and dumplings?"

"Your ma made a point of telling me all your favorites." She placed the largest container in front of him, full to the brim. Joanna didn't look up or acknowledge him as she kept working, setting out the delicious food. "Ida wasn't even ashamed of herself, as if my cooking would be enough to, well, you know."

"Hook me?"

She hung her head. "I made something I knew you would like, because of what you did for us today in town. To thank you."

"I understand." He wanted her to be clear on that. He didn't want her to think he believed any part of such nonsense. "You won't have any more problems at the mercantile. I've made sure of that."

"I know." She turned pink, as if she was still ashamed.

"It's a hard thing having folks think the worst of you, I know." He paused when the little boy made his way up to the blanket, sweat dampening his flyaway hair.

"Here." Joanna's son set the jug on the ground. "I reckon you gotta be mighty thirsty."

"I reckon so." Aiden couldn't look at the boy. He wanted to; he just couldn't. "Thank you kindly."

"Here." Now that his hands were free, the kid reached into his trouser pocket and held out something on the flat of his palm. It winked in the sun.

A copper penny. "What's that for?"

"For the candy." Such a solemn little boy. "Thank you, sir."

"You're welcome, but you keep the penny."

"Nah." The kid shook his head. "Ma always says you gotta pay for what you get or it's the same as stealing."

What does a man say to that? "You have a wise ma. Then will you give your penny to your ma for me?"

"Yes, sir." The boy ambled off to hand over the bit of copper to his mother.

Nice boy. Aiden had to glance away. Joanna's daughter was at the creek's edge, reaching out to dip her fingers into the clear, shallow water. It was easy to see that Joanna had an eye on her as she took out a napkin, a fork and the final tin—no doubt holding the fresh piece of pie.

"Looks like a storm is blowing in." She handed him the knife and fork rolled up in a napkin.

It was hard facing her. Resolutely, Aiden steeled his spine. Last night the darkness had been a safe haven, but in the unforgiving light of this day, she had been able to get a real close look at him. At this man who had offered marriage to her—not a real union, true, but a marriage nonetheless. Last night he had been fairly hopeful, but he knew now that she was going to reject him. After what happened at Lawson's store, she was going to pack up her things and leave him.

He unrolled the silverware, hoping she couldn't see—that she would never guess—how lonesome he was going to feel without her.

"I think just north of here is likely to get a hard blow. Maybe some hail," he said practically. He was, after all, a deeply practical man. "My hay should be safe for tonight."

"And your wheat, too. You have a fair-size crop."

"Enough that it'll be a tussle getting it harvested in a day." He stared off at the horizon and thought about that storm gathering strength. About the lightning ready to strike. "Finn could have helped with that, but it's no matter. I've got neighbors, and Thad will come help me."

"You have a good brother in him."

"That I do." Thad was good to the core. Dependable. Aiden was blessed to have a brother like him, and he knew it. "I don't suppose he dropped by word about Finn?"

"No, I would have told you."

"Yeah, I knew that. I had to ask."

She nodded with understanding, rising lightly to her feet. "Where did you put the pitchfork?"

"Uh, over against the corner post. Why? What do you need me to do?" He was already rising, but she waved him back.

"No, you stay and eat. You can help me by keeping an eye on the children." She was already walking away, a pretty willow of a woman in a patched, pink calico dress. "You can join me when you're done."

"Done, what?" She was the most puzzling woman. "Joanna, what are you going to do?"

"I'm going to start turning the hay."

"Whoa, there." Why should she do such a thing? What had given her such a notion? He got to his feet. "The work is too hard for you. Besides, I don't take to a woman helping me in the fields."

"Too bad. You will have to get used to it, as these

will also be my fields very soon." She tossed him a small smile as lovely as the wildflowers nodding in the wind. "I've decided to marry you."

Chapter Eleven

"Are they asleep?" Hours later, Aiden's voice floated out of the darkness.

"Finally." Joanna left the shanty door open to the breeze and padded barefoot in his direction. Her muscles ached from the difficult work of turning the mown hay over so it could dry for stacking. She didn't mind hard labor and she hadn't minded the company, either.

Grasses tapped against her skirt hem as she made her way through the night shadows. "You were right. The storm is staying north of us."

"Good thing, or we'd be getting wet about now. It's a pretty sight from here, though."

"Yes." She followed the sound of his voice.

There he was, hunkered on the porch step, as still as the shadows. She eased down beside him. The thick clouds blotted out the sky and glowed with the sparks of lightning. Like black opals, they shone with a dark incandescence.

"I love watching storms," she confessed, "as long as they are a goodly distance away."

"Me, too. The lightning has just started." He nodded toward the far north, where a jagged trail of blue-white light snaked and crackled across the angry clouds. "Have you always like watching storms, or is it a recent inclination?"

"It goes as far back as I can remember. When I was a little girl, my ma would wake me and we would go watch the lightning together."

"Kind of like this?"

"Exactly like this." Her voice softened at the memory. Her ma had been a good woman, loving, hardworking and endlessly kind. "When I was James's age I would rush from one window to another trying to see the next lightning strike through the downpour streaking the glass."

"I would head out to the barn."

"I can't imagine your ma letting her little boy outside in a lightning storm."

"I wasn't so small, I guess. Twelve or so, and older. I still do it. I climb up and sit in the haymow. I can see the whole of Angel Valley from up there."

"And a lot of lightning."

"A few twisters," he added. The wind gusted through the grass like an ocean wave. He waited while another streak of light crackled through the clouds in one long bolt. That was quite a sight. And judging by Joanna's rapt attention, she thought so, too.

His eyes had adjusted to the dark so he could see

her against the glow of the clouds. She had a sweet profile with a cute slope of a nose and a daintily cut mouth and chin. The tangle of her golden hair curled over her forehead and framed her face. He remembered how hard she had worked in the field beside him, tirelessly and without one complaint. She had kept one eye on her children while she flipped shank after shank of cut hay, and expertly, too.

"You helped me more in one evening than Finn ever has." It had taken a chunk of his pride to allow her to work. No, he wasn't one of those men who believed a woman had her place, but he didn't think a woman ought to work that hard.

As a boy, he had watched how hard his ma had worked in the fields when Pa had been passed out. She had ruined her health, working herself to the bone. He had helped all he could and that made a difference as he had gotten older. He thanked the Lord he was built for hard labor. By the time he was twelve, he was doing a man's work in the fields so his ma didn't have to.

It had been difficult to keep quiet this evening, but he'd done it. Joanna had agreed to marry him. And he hadn't wanted to give her a reason to change her mind.

"Then your offer still stands?"

"You know it does." He smiled some. She was humble, and it was endearing. "After that supper and dessert, no man in his right mind would turn you down."

"At least I have something to offer you in our arrangement. It feels one-sided to me."

"It's not, believe me. But your cooking is not why

I proposed." He paused, gathering up his courage. It was hard for him to talk about the things that mattered. "I hope you know I don't look at you and see all the work you could do around here."

"Yes, I know that, or I wouldn't have agreed to marry you." She sounded young, suddenly, and vulnerable.

He bowed his head. It wasn't that she was so very young; it was that hardship had worn on him. His existence, numb as the frozen ground at winter, had aged him more than he liked to admit. Hopelessness could do that to a man.

Joanna seemed to understand what he couldn't say. "I know you need help around the house, and that's only sensible, as you work hard all day to make a living off this land. But your proposal is a practical solution, too. As are my reasons for accepting."

"Yes." He cleared his throat, glad that they had this understanding. "You know I'm not about to follow Finn to the saloon and leave you to bring in the crops."

"I do. My children are children again. I can't tell you what it means. James is no longer so worried. Daisy isn't as clingy." Joanna looked away, blinking fast.

She was trying not to cry, he realized. "I have an inkling. If the good Lord would have seen fit to make me a pa, I would have moved mountains if I had to if it meant my son would be safe and secure."

"You mean, those mountains?" She gestured to the west, where the great Rocky Mountains rose up like a fortress out of the prairie floor.

He nodded. Love was a tricky thing. All these

years had not diminished what he'd felt for the son he'd never met.

"I believe you, Aiden." Her understanding mattered. "You would move the entire continental divide rock by rock if you had to."

"I'm not alone in that kind of determination." It was why he admired her, not that he was able to tell her that. Joanna had a good heart, and in this world that had to be protected. That was his opinion, at least. "I've been thinking some tonight when we were working. That shanty is awful small for the three of you."

"Aside from my pa's farmhouse, a shanty is all my children have ever known. We're snug in there and I'm grateful, Aiden. More than you know."

"Winter will be here and the shanty won't be as snug. The main house will be warmer for you and the little ones."

"I'm not sure our moving into your house is a good idea." She swiped at the stray curls the wind was blowing into her face. "I figured we would keep things the way they are. I'm satisfied with that."

"I see." He nodded as if he understood. "You're afraid that I'll be upstairs in that house with you."

No, I'm afraid for you. She remembered how he had stood in the kitchen that first morning when she had made him breakfast. In her mind's eye she could still see him with his wide shoulders slumped and his face in his hands. She hurt for him. "This has to be hard for you, Aiden."

"I will be all right." His words were firm, but his voice sounded lost.

He would always do right, she realized. It was good to see that some men were really like that. Her spirit ached with hope in all the sad places life had created. "You have done so much for my children. The last thing I want is to cause you pain."

"Pain is part of living. It lets you know you're alive. I suppose that's a good thing." He rubbed the back of his neck, as if he was thinking, or trying to brush away what was past. "I told you this would be a practical solution, nothing more."

"That is why I'm agreeing to it." There were so many assurances she could give him, but she chose the most sensible one. "This is for my children."

"I know that, Joanna. I'll make certain they are always fed and sheltered and safe. You have my word on that."

"I already know that for sure." Gratitude filled her up until she brimmed with the burn of it. She blinked hard, fighting more than tears. What was she going to do about her feelings for this man? He had her endless devotion for his promise. He broke her heart with his vow, and she understood why. He had not been able to provide for his child, so he would provide for hers.

She swallowed, fighting to get the words out. When they came, they were shaky and thin with emotion. "You have my word that you will never regret marrying me. But I'm worried what certain people will say about you. When we wed, they will think those rumors are true."

"It's not my worry what others choose to fill their

minds with." Aiden shrugged away her doubts with a quick movement of his shoulders. "I know the truth. You know the truth. That's what matters."

"As long as you're sure."

"Absolutely." He did not pause. "When do you want to have the ceremony?"

"The sooner the better, but you are in the middle of haying." She stopped to watch another streak of light splinter the endless sky. "I don't think we should interrupt your work. What if the next storm comes this way? We might regret taking that time to get married."

"You're worrying about the hay?"

"I worry about a lot of things, Aiden. How about this? I'll be ready whenever it is best for you."

"You are a peculiar woman, Joanna." He chuckled, and it was a cozy sound, like a warm blanket on a cold winter's day.

"Peculiar? I don't like the implications of that. Is this the way it is going to be? You're going to change into a different man because we're married?"

"No, no. I'll always be the same, Joanna. Always have been, always will be." He shook his head, as if he couldn't win no matter what he did. "I meant to compliment you. There aren't many sensible women in this world."

"That's what a woman likes to hear from the man she's about to marry. That she's sensible."

"I mean that as a compliment, too. I loved Kate to the depths of my soul, but she was as impractical as the day was long. It took her a good part of five months to plan our wedding." He chuckled again. "And here you are, willing to get married around my haying schedule."

"You said this was a practical arrangement." She was laughing, too. "I could plan a big to-do, but I didn't suppose that would be fitting or a wise use of time or money."

"I'm a busy man and I don't have much money to spare. I appreciate your view, Joanna."

"Good, then it's settled." Soon, she would have the right to care for this man, to repay his kindness and his generosity. She had no wish to put that off. She intended to place him right up there with her children in terms of what she valued. "Are you sure you want me living in your house, Aiden?"

"I'm sure." And he sounded certain. "How about Sunday after church? We'll be in town anyhow, so it will save us a trip there."

"Sounds practical to me." Maybe it was far from romantic, but that set with her just fine. "I had such high expectations when I got married before. It was as if I was the lightning up there, glittering high above the earth."

"That's the problem with love. It's impractical, and it can't last."

"It devastates you when it's gone."

They sat in quiet agreement and understanding, the pain of their pasts between them as surely as the cool wind whipping by. Far in the distance the lightning flashed again, growing worse now, streaking the roiling black sky. White-blue cracks of light flared to life and faded.

"Did your work go all right for Noelle?"

"Very well." She said that with a sigh of relief, as if glad for the change of subject. "Noelle asked me to join her sewing circle."

"That's just like her." It didn't surprise him a bit. He remembered how his sister-in-law seemed to take to Joanna on Sunday. "You should go."

"I haven't made up my mind about it. There's so much to get done here."

"It will all get done eventually. You go." He watched the lightning instead of her. "There's something else I want you to do."

"For you? Name it."

"Tomorrow, head into town and go to Cora Sims's dress shop. Tell her you need something nice to get married in and to bill me."

"What? Oh, no, Aiden, I don't feel right about that."

He winced. She sounded sincere and stubborn. How did he tell her what he meant? He had no notion how to say it, so he made light of it. "Do you know how mad my ma is going to be at me if you get married in a patched calico work dress?"

"I have a Sunday best dress."

"I know, and it's calico, too. And patched."

"There's nothing wrong with that." Her chin went up.

"I'm not saying there is. I want you to have better, Joanna."

"You do?" Her throat tightened and she turned away.

"You have been struggling alone for a long time, but I want you to know that's over. You're not alone anymore." He meant that. "You go buy yourself a nice dress. It's what I want."

He didn't know how she was going to take to that order, or if she would give him her opinion, as he had already learned she was quick to do. But then he realized her silence was because of something else.

"Thank you, Aiden." Her voice was thin and vulnerable. She, too, watched the lightning in the distance, but he heard what she didn't say as a comfortable stillness settled between them.

He did not want a wife. He did not want to marry again. But helping her was the right decision. He could feel it with all the pieces of his soul.

Dread. Remembering her experience with the Lawsons at the mercantile, Joanna was not looking forward to pulling open the dress-shop door and facing another woman from town. But Aiden had asked her to. She couldn't let him down. When she stood up with him before God and his family, she did not want to embarrass him in her Sunday best calico dress. He was right—even that dress had been patched.

Thinking of him, she gripped the handle and pulled open the door. "Come in, you two, and remember to keep your hands to yourself, please."

"Yes, Ma," they said in unison, and followed her into the beautiful dress shop. James glanced around, already bored, but good boy that he was, he didn't say a thing. He squared his small shoulders like a little man, determined to make the best of the situation.

"Look!" Daisy let out a gasp of delight. "Ribbons, Ma. Look!"

"Yes, aren't they pretty?" She had never seen so many ribbons set out in a display, in so many beautiful colors, from sensible brown to candy pink.

It was a fine shop and far too fancy for her to ever afford. Perhaps Aiden did not know how much things were likely to cost in a place like this, especially the ready-made dresses she saw hanging along the back wall. She hated to think what those cost. Likely as not, they were far too fancy for her to feel comfortable in.

"Hello." A pleasant-looking woman in a finely tailored lawn dress rose from a chair at the farthest window and set her sewing aside. "I'm Cora Sims. Welcome to my shop. Are you Joanna, by chance?"

She noted the shop owner's earnest smile and took that as a good sign. Maybe not everyone in town had heard or believed those horrible rumors. What a relief. "Yes, I am. You have a beautiful store."

"Thank you. Ida McKaslin told me all about you at our church meeting this morning. It's lovely to meet you." She lifted a small basket on the front counter and smiled at the children. "You may each have one piece. Well, as it's a slow morning, perhaps two."

Bless Cora Sims. Predictably, James chose two lemon drops and Daisy two peppermint balls.

"Thank you, ma'am," her son said politely.

"Thank you!" Daisy practically hopped in place, her platinum-blond ponytails bouncing.

"You're welcome. What good children you are,"

Cora praised. She was truly kind. "Now, Joanna, can I offer you something cool to drink? It's a scorcher out there, isn't it?"

"That's kind of you, but I'm fine. I've come for a dress." Here was where things got tricky. "Aiden wanted me to have you bill him."

"Ah, I see. Of course." Cora's smile deepened. "You need a dress for your wedding."

"How did you know?"

"You would be surprised. I am one of the first people to know when a couple is going to be married. When is the big day?"

"Sunday." Joanna braced herself for that welcoming smile to fade. She knew how it must look. "They say marry in haste, repent in leisure, but we need to be practical. Harvest season is coming soon."

"Yes, and then Aiden will be too busy to even think about getting married." Cora didn't seem at all surprised by this. "My parents were farmers, too. I know how demanding it can be. You will need a ready-made dress. I believe I have several that ought to be about your size. Come in the back and see."

Joanna herded her little ones ahead of her, around a colorful table of embroidery threads and past racks with thick bolts of rich fabrics.

"Ma! Look!" Daisy stopped licking her peppermint piece long enough to exclaim, "Look at those buttons!"

"I see." She was amazed by that glass display case of hundreds of buttons on little paper plackets. Mother-of-pearl buttons, carved buttons and ones in shapes like roses, a teddy bear or a castle. "You may go look and not touch, if James will watch you."

While Daisy gasped gleefully, James gave a sigh of resignation. Dutifully, he trudged toward the case. "C'mon, Daisy."

She raced to keep up.

"I also have some little girl dresses. Would you be interested in seeing those, too?" Cora chose a dear little butter-yellow frock from among the others hanging on the rod.

Joanna stared, awestruck. There were ribbons of lavender and blue accenting the puff sleeves and tiered skirt. A row of daisy-shaped buttons marched down the front of the bodice. She'd never imagined anything so fine for Daisy.

"I just finished this yesterday," Cora explained. "Of course, you may have something already in mind for your daughter to wear at the wedding, but with her coloring, I thought of this dress instantly. It would look adorable on her."

"Yes, it sure would." Joanna stared at the dress longingly. She knew without asking that the price was something she simply could not afford, and Aiden had said nothing about buying a dress for Daisy. Joanna had never wanted anything more than that beautiful frock. She tried to tell herself that it would make a good Sunday dress and would wear well, but it made no difference. No amount of reasoning could make up for the fact that she did not have the money for it. And she would not take advantage of Aiden's generous nature.

Cora slipped the lovely garment back onto the rod. "Did you have anything in mind for yourself?"

"I don't suppose you have anything calico." It would be sensible, something she could wear to church on Sunday, too.

"No, I'm sorry. If I had more time, I could make something for you." Cora turned to the women's dresses; there were several dozen of them, in all colors and sizes.

Joanna's heart sank. Every one looked far too frilly to suit her, with expensive details like silk ribbons and lace and embroidered embellishments. She had no need for such a gown.

"Here, what about this lawn?" Cora pulled a dress out from among the others. "It's perfect for this summer weather we're having. It's simple enough to be serviceable, and yet fine enough to be special. What do you think?"

Joanna simply stared at the finely woven ivory fabric dotted with tiny green leaves. The style was tailored, the lace edging the collar and sleeves was the nicest she had ever seen, and pearl buttons accented the bodice. It was a fragile, beautiful dress and she loved it.

"The look on your face is answer enough." Cora held the gown up. "I think it was meant for you."

Joanna's hands shook as she took the fine garment. She had never owned anything so nice. But it wasn't the dress she wanted most.

She glanced over at her daughter. Daisy was still absorbed in studying the buttons. Joanna feared she already knew the answer, but she had to ask, anyway.

"There wouldn't be a way to make payments on that child's dress, would there?"

"No, I don't take payments," Cora said gently. "Usually. But I'm sure we can work something out."

"Really? Oh, thank you. I'll take it." She hesitated. "And maybe some fabric suitable for a new shirt for James?"

"I'm sure we can find something. You'll need a few things to go with your new dress. How about a nice bonnet to match?" Cora wandered toward the shelves of beautiful hats. "I'm sure Aiden would want it for you. He'll expect you to be well appointed."

That was true. He would be sure to comment on her patched sunbonnet, if she showed up to marry him in one.

"You are getting a fine man for a husband." Cora was friendly as she led the way to the hats. "You must be so thrilled, getting married in, what, just five days?"

"Yes," she said simply, stopping to study a lovely ivory bonnet.

Thrilled? Only for her children's sake. She did not love Aiden McKaslin and could never let herself. He had been honest with her. He would never be able to love her, and she was not surprised by that. No amount of fine lace and silk ribbons or this nice dress would change who she was, inside and out. She was not the kind of woman who inspired love in a man.

Maybe it was better this way, she thought as she glanced over at her little ones. This union wasn't based on some false romantic notion that would only bring her mountain-size disappointments. No, this marriage would be based on what was real, what was most precious to her. While she was not marrying Aiden for love, she was marrying because of love.

That had to be better. Her heart brimmed as she watched Daisy telling James about the pony-shaped buttons, and they both knelt for a closer look. She wanted better for them. She would do her best for them. She prayed that the Lord was up there somewhere watching out for them all. This marriage was a big step she was taking—one built entirely upon hope and faith.

Aiden put down his pitchfork the moment the horses and wagon pulled into the yard. He knew Thad was going to notice how he had stopped work at just that moment, as if he'd been keeping an eye out for her. It was true, but probably not for the reason Thad might think.

"Look who's back." His brother grinned at him from the other side of the wagon bed. "Has she made up her mind about marrying you yet?"

"Apparently. I still can't believe she said yes." Aiden flipped off his hat and pulled his handkerchief from his back pocket. "It's happening this Sunday after church."

"Congratulations." Thad was grinning from ear to ear as he pitched a forkful of hay into the wagon. "I'm glad you could find someone again. I was afraid that wouldn't happen for you."

"Me, too." That at least was the truth. Years had passed and he'd never considered marrying again, but Joanna had changed all that.

The trip to town must have gone well. She smiled

as she lifted her daughter down from the wagon seat. He had to squint against the sun, but he could just make out a big package wrapped up under the seat beside a hatbox. He was glad about that. It looked as if Joanna had found what she needed.

Bless Miss Sims. He'd figured she would help Joanna, as she was too classy of a lady to listen to the terrible rumors Finn had started. Finn. Aiden took a deep breath, trying to squeeze out his sorrow. They knew this for a fact, now. Neither Thad nor the minister could lure him from the saloon or talk him out of his destructive choices.

"Maybe you ought to go check on her." Thad seemed mighty pleased with himself as he kept pitching. "I'll finish up filling the wagon, don't you worry. Go on."

He could see as plain as day what his brother was thinking. "This is an arrangement I have with Joanna, nothing more."

"An arrangement? I don't understand."

"I'm marrying her because she needs help." How clear did he have to be? "That's the only reason we are marrying."

"That's it?" Thad looked mighty perplexed. "You don't love her?"

"No, and she knows that." Aiden slid his pitchfork against the tailgate, feeling that he ought to be honest. Thad was thinking one thing about this marriage that wasn't true. "She's not in love with me, either."

"Then why are you getting married? Wait, I know." His brother shook his head. "Don't worry, Aiden. No one worth their salt believes any of those rumors. Besides, they are already dying down. I've done my best to make sure of it."

"I appreciate that." Aiden turned away, dreading what his brother was going to say next, no doubt something about love needing to be a part of marriage.

There was Joanna's son petting the horses, while she unbuckled them from the traces. It was hard looking at that boy. The kid was about to become his son, and Joanna his wife.

His wife. The emptiness within him hurt like a broken bone. No, he would do best not to think of her as that. He wiped the sweat from his face and neck, trying to figure out what to say. "Joanna needs help, and I'm helping her. That's all there is to this. She'll be moving into one of the upstairs bedrooms in the house, and I plan on sleeping in one of the downstairs rooms, or the shanty. I'm still deciding."

"The shanty? You're serious, aren't you?"

"Yep." His voice sounded strained and he knew it, but he was managing this the best that he could. "After what I lost, I don't have it in me to love again."

"C'mon, big brother. I don't believe that."

Aiden shrugged, at a loss. "It's just not there. I broke after I lost Kate and the baby. My heart, my soul, they're ashes now. There's nothing left."

"But—"

"There are no buts. There's nothing to argue about, Thad." He stepped away from his brother and the painful conversation.

Joanna was taking the horses to the barn now, with the girl on her hip and the little boy leading the way. She was as wholesome as could be in her pink calico dress and matching sunbonnet. The sun seemed to follow her and grace her, as if heaven were watching over this good woman.

"Aiden, I still don't understand. This could be a second chance for you," Thad argued.

He cleared his throat in order to say what he had to say. "Think of how deeply you love your wife. Now, think of your future without her."

As if struck, Thad bowed his head, silent, his wide shoulders slumped. He looked as if he'd been hit in the chest with an anvil. It was like the sun going down, Aiden knew, never to rise again.

Without the need to say more, he grabbed his hat. "I'll see if Joanna needs anything. I'll be back in a bit."

Thad still didn't say anything, as if he were unable to move.

Aiden found her in the barn, rubbing down the horses, although they were not in a sweat. She sure took good care of her animals.

He hefted the water bucket from the corner and hauled it over to the stalls. "How's his hoof looking?"

"Better, I think. He made the walk to and from town just fine." Joanna looked at Aiden over the horse's smooth rump. "I don't think it's tender at all."

"Good. He'll likely be just fine. I'm having the blacksmith out next week, and he'll take a look. New shoes might help, too."

She nodded, folding up the towel. "How much will that cost?"

"You and I haven't talked about what we are going to do about money after we marry." His lungs felt empty, as if he couldn't get in enough air. The boy was walking down the aisle, peering into the empty stalls, as if dreaming of horses. The girl was staring at something small she held in her hand. He did his best not to notice. "It will be like any marriage, Joanna. I'll pay for what you and your children need. The horses, too."

"But that's not fair to you." Her jaw tightened and her chin went up in the air. "That isn't why I'm marrying you, so you can pay my way. I plan to keep my job with Noelle and maybe pick up some other work in town. Cora Sims has need for an extra seamstress. I'm going to work off a few things I bought for the children."

"I don't think I can stand for that."

"You'll just have to." She had character, he had to give her that. She stood up to him and met his gaze as if she had no intention of backing down. And she didn't. He could see that.

He held up his hands. "Whoa, there. No need to get all mad at me."

"I think there's plenty of need. I'm not marrying you to take advantage of you, Aiden, and if that's what you think, then I'd rather not marry you."

Yes, this was what he remembered of being married. Women, he thought, shaking his head slowly, wishing he could understand them enough to know how to avoid this type of thing. "I only meant I don't want you to work so hard, Joanna. First the fields. Now working for pay. I'm not used to that, is all I'm saying. I never allowed my wife to work."

"And neither did my husband, at first, and look where that got me." There was hurt in Joanna's eyes, creeping in like shadows. "I will always be grateful to you for my children's sake, but I have to know that I'm making a difference for you, too. That I'm making your life a little easier."

His throat choked up. He could not bear to feel one single emotion struggling to life within him.

"It's up to you." Those were the hardest words he had said in a long time. Marriage was like that, too, he remembered. "I don't want you working so hard, Joanna. You need to take better care of your health for those children."

She nodded, avoiding him, too. Silence settled between them, heavy with all they were both unable to say.

He filled the water troughs with a few splashes of water, just enough to wet the horses' tongues until they were a mite cooler. "I'll finish up the work here."

"Then I'll get supper ready for you and Thad." She took Daisy by the hand. "C'mon, James."

The woman left him standing in the aisle, alone in the waning sunlight, still a little surprised. She was going to be his wife.

Chapter Twelve

She'd said yes. Aiden still couldn't believe it, not even standing in church before the minister and most of his family. He was looking right at her and the shock was still with him.

Maybe because there was so much shock, for so many different reasons. He'd never figured he would marry again. He couldn't believe a good woman like Joanna would want to be stuck with a man like him. But mostly he was shocked because the lady in ivory and gold at his side had been hiding her beauty from him.

She wore a simple dress by most standards, but the light color brightened her like a moonbeam. Her golden hair was knotted up primly and properly except for the stray tendrils that curled around her soft face like fine silk. She was luminous in the light of the sanctuary. Her hand held his tightly, and he could practically feel her hope.

Lord, don't let me fail You, he prayed silently. *I'm*

trusting You to lead me from here. Only God knew how hard this was for him.

The last time he had been standing in this church and slipping a ring on a woman's finger, he had been so in love his spirit had hurt with the power of it. Never would he have thought his life would bring him here, back to this place.

Pain had a sharp edge as he tried to swallow. He tried not to think back on what he'd lost. He saw instead what he had to gain. A helpmate for his life of hard work. A purpose for his existence. Hope, however small, that providing for Joanna and her children would somehow make up for the loss of his own. Nothing could bring his heart back, he knew, but maybe he could bring life back to hers.

"I now pronounce you man and wife." Hadly, who should have been somber, was grinning. "Aiden, you may now kiss your bride."

"Kiss her?" he repeated, not quite understanding. Kiss her? Why, he had forgotten this part entirely.

"It's all right," Joanna was hastily saying. "It's not required, is it?"

"There's no reason for you two to be shy." The minister closed his Bible, cradling it in his hands. "You're allowed to kiss."

"Oh, my." She turned toward him. "I was so nervous about the ceremony that I forgot we're expected to—"

"Yes, the ceremony's over now." He towered above her, moving a tiny bit closer, and whispered, "I think one kiss would be okay."

"You do?" She discovered she was leaning a tiny bit

nearer to him, too. Nerves skittered through her. She did not love Aiden. She did not want to kiss him. They were standing before God, their vows spoken, and his mother watched expectantly with happy tears in her eyes. Joanna felt the pressure of Ida's hopes as surely as the muggy air inside the church.

Should they kiss? No one here, including the minister, believed their quick marriage was anything less than love at first sight.

"I do." Aiden looked solemn as he cupped her face with his big hands. His eyes were as dark as that stormy night sky without the cracks of lightning in it as he leaned forward and kissed her cheek.

Sweetness filled her. In the distance, Ida sighed with happiness and told Noelle, who gasped with pleasure. But it was hard for Joanna to hear over the rush in her ears. The way he looked at her with a question, as if asking permission, made that rushing sound a little louder. The sweetness within her swelled until she felt near to bursting.

"Thank you," she whispered, so that only he would hear.

"You're welcome." He took his hands from her face, but the caring in his eyes remained. "Now neither of us is alone."

"Congratulations," the minister said, beaming. "I pray that you two will always know more happiness and less hardship. Look at poor Ida. She is overcome. Aiden, you made her proud today. I don't think she ever thought this day would come for you."

"It surprised me, too." He stood straight and manly, leaning down to accept his mother's tearful hug. No one would guess by the small smile he managed and his stately acceptance of well wishes from Thad and Noelle, that he was hurting inside.

Only Joanna knew.

She felt a tug on her skirt. Daisy, looking dear in her new dress, gazed up at her pleadingly. "Ma, I have to go."

"All right. We'd best hurry outside." She took her little girl by the hand and turned toward Aiden, but he was already nodding to her, acknowledging that she was leaving, letting her know he would wait for her to come back.

Another piece of hope dammed up the broken pieces of her heart, and Aiden was the reason.

"Welcome to the family, dear." Ida wrapped her in a big hug right in the middle of the front yard. "I can't tell you how pleased I am to have you for a daughter."

A mother-in-law. Joanna hadn't thought that while her marriage to Aiden might not be real in the romantic sense, her relationship with his family could be. "I don't think I could have a better mother-in-law."

"There is no in-law, you hear me, young lady?" Ida was pure loving warmth. "You will be like a daughter to me, the same way Noelle is. Tell her, Noelle, that you can't get rid of me."

"Yes, that is very true. Lucky me." Noelle climbed down from the wagon into her husband's arms. "Ida, you are like a mother to me, you know that. Joanna, prepare to be spoiled."

"That sounds good to me." It was hard to believe her good fortune. That suddenly, with a few vows, she was here, surrounded by family. She lifted Daisy onto her hip. "Please come in. I have dinner ready to warm up."

"As if I'm going to let the bride do all the work!" Ida, apple-cheeked and rosy, reached out to take Daisy into her arms. "Why don't we go into the kitchen? Noelle, did you remember the baskets?"

"Of course!" Noelle was a wonder, cheerfully feeling her way along the wagon sides, her fingers lightly skimming the boards. "Aiden, come help Thad lift all this stuff. We brought wedding presents."

"And cake." Ida gazed down at the little girl in her arms. "And presents for my grandchildren."

"I got a new button for my collection," Daisy told Ida. "I have eleven now, all of my very own. Do you want to come see?"

"Yes, I do." Ida positively beamed.

She was a born grandmother, Joanna decided, feeling overwhelmed. Maybe it was the scorching heat of the day or the muggy weather, but her knees felt weak and her bones like water. Her children had never known a grandmother's love; her mom had died before she had married Tom, and his mother had no interest.

James had perked up at the word *presents.* He watched the older woman closely, as if afraid of believing what he had just heard. Gifts had always been strictly Christmas and birthday events. Until now.

Ida held out her hand, James took it and the three of them disappeared into the house. A kind grandma. Now, that was more than a blessing, it was divine gift. The hot breeze swept around Joanna, twirling her skirts and skimming her face. The gentle lilt of Noelle's quiet alto and Thad's rumbling bass made a cozy duet as they talked low together at the far end of their wagon. They obviously had a happy marriage, another rare blessing.

Aiden was one of those, too. Not only a gift, but a once-in-a-lifetime kind of man. Joanna's heart swelled tenderly as she searched the yard for him. There he was, standing at the far side of the house with his feet braced on the land like some western myth, watching the white puffy thunderheads building in the southern sky.

He didn't turn as she approached, but began talking, so he obviously knew she was close. "We might get a hard blow. I've got yesterday's cut hay drying in the field."

He seemed distant and motionless, as if made of stone. Alone, as if he were always destined to be. She ached, wishing she knew how to ease his pain. "Do you need some time? Or should I start setting out the meal?"

"Go ahead and eat." His throat worked, the only sign that he was made of flesh and bone and not granite. "I'll come in when I can."

She thought of Ida fawning over her grandchildren. Of how happy his family was for him. It had to be a painful reminder of the time he'd brought his Kate home after their wedding, and of Ida's first grandchild, who hadn't lived.

Now neither of us are alone. His words in the church came back to Joanna and touched her anew. How alone he must have felt all these years. When she laid her hand on the steely curve of his shoulder, he let it linger for a moment before he turned away.

"I've got to take care of the horses," he said hollowly. "I need to keep an eye on the storm."

The ring on her finger was a reminder that she was more committed than before to making this man's life better. But how? She was at the end of her rope. She had done everything she knew to do.

Lord, show me. Please. It was on faith she prayed, for she had no one else to rely on. Not even herself. She did not know how to help him. She didn't know if anyone could.

"I'll be inside if you need anything, Aiden." It was hard to force her feet to carry her away from him. She had so many things to do: change into her work clothes and get the little ones out of their new things, put the meal on the table, make sure everyone was fed and comfortable and happy.

"Joanna, dear, there you are." Ida was on the kitchen steps. "Does Aiden think bad weather is on the way?"

"Yes." She glanced over her shoulder, nearly missing her footing. He still had his back turned, watching the storm clouds gathering. She longed to draw him away from that lonely field and take him into the house where his family waited for him. She knew she did not have that power.

"Then we'll leave him to his weather watching." If

Ida was troubled over her son, it didn't show except in the tight lines around her mouth. "He'll join us when he's able. Come see what present we brought for you."

"For me?"

"Why, yes. You are the bride, are you not?" Ida took her by the arm and led her through the lean-to into the kitchen. "Don't make the mistake of thinking that this is no big occasion, being a second marriage for both of you, because you would be wrong. Come into the parlor."

Joanna noticed the leaves had been put into the table and it was set for seven. The stove had been lit and pots were sitting on top, heating up. The dinner rolls she had baked yesterday were spread on a sheet, ready to go into the oven. Ida had already taken care of heating up the meal.

"Ma!" James jumped to his feet and came running across the parlor. Excitement sparkled in his eyes and he appeared happier than she could ever remember seeing him. "Look what Uncle Thad made me. A real mustang."

Joanna glanced at the carved wooden horse with mane and tail flowing. She had to blink hard to keep her eyes from burning. "He looks just like Sunny, doesn't he?"

"Yep. That's what I'm calling him. I got another one, too." He pointed to the second horse he had been playing with on the floor. "That's Sky. They are best friends."

"Did you thank your uncle?"

"Yep. About five times." James wrapped his arms around her in a quick hug.

There was Daisy, on the sofa next to Noelle. Together they were dressing her rag doll in new calico dresses. "Ma! Look! Anna has lots to wear. And a nightie, too!"

It was like Christmas morning. Joanna didn't need anything more than this, to see her little ones so happy. Material things were not what mattered; she knew that more than most. But the loving people around them, welcoming them as family, were worth everything. More than she had ever dreamed could be.

She had been on her own for so long, even in her first marriage, that she had forgotten the comfort of a caring smile against the cruel harshness that came to a person's life. She had forgotten the simple pleasure of having someone hold out a hand, wanting her to join in.

"Come over here with us and see," Noelle offered.

Joanna picked her way around the pasture James had made on the center of the floor and left him there to play. Thad had also carved fence posts and a gate. There were other little things for Daisy, Joanna saw as she settled down beside Noelle. A doll-size knitted blanket, a calico sunbonnet and a ruffled apron.

"Thank you," she told them all. "This is… unexpected but wonderful. Too much, but wonderful."

"I had the most fun crocheting and knitting up these wee things," Noelle confessed.

"So did I." Ida smiled in her infectious, beaming way. "Noelle, this is good practice for you. You may be making a lot of wee little things of your own one day. You never know."

"Wouldn't that be a blessing?" Thad's wife lit up at

the thought. "In the meantime, this was great fun. Joanna, we have something for you, too. You have no notion how Ida and I had to hurry to get this done in time."

"We weren't sure we would," Ida interjected. "It was nip and tuck. But we did it."

"Here, this is for you." Noelle lifted a wrapped bundle from the cushion at her side. "We are so happy for you and Aiden."

She said it with great conviction, as if she had no notion that this marriage was not genuine. Joanna's hands trembled as she tugged at the white ribbon holding the wrapping together. The tissue paper fell away and on top was a beautiful, snowy-white bedcovering, crocheted in a breathtaking pattern of rosebuds and leaves. Beneath that were folds of matching lace scarves for the bureau and bedside tables, and delicate curtains.

Tears swam in her eyes.

"We understand what Aiden told Thad," Noelle said gently. "That this was an arrangement between you. But it is my wish for you both that one day, along with great happiness, you will find great love. Ida and I put our hopes and prayers into every stitch."

A movement beyond the doorway caught Joanna's eye. It was Aiden, standing like a shadow. Then he stepped forward, into the light. There was pain etched in his face, but it was a different pain from what it had been there before. As if he were forcing himself into living again, he eyed the folds of soft, frothy lace and nodded once—just once.

"So, this is where everyone is," he quipped. "Can't a starving man get a meal around here?"

"Yeah," Thad agreed with a wink. "Where's the food? I'm looking forward to dessert. Ma made angel food cake."

"You'll get it when we're good and ready, you two," Ida quipped right back. "Mind your manners."

"Manners? I don't have any. It's my ma's fault. I was raised up terrible." Tiny smile lines creased the corners of Aiden's eyes.

The warm glow of caring Joanna was trying to ignore sparked a little more brightly. Like morning after a long hard night, that's what Aiden was for her. She gently refolded the exquisite lace. He could not know what she was beginning to feel. That the brand of caring she held in her heart was changing into something richer.

She rose, striving to hide her affection. Tucking away what she did not want seen, she slipped out of the room and followed Ida to the safety of the kitchen.

"You should have seen the looks on those boys' faces." Ma paused over her slice of cake to laugh with the memory. "There they were, swooping blueberries into their little pails as fast as they could go. Thad would shovel a handful into his mouth every once in a while. His mouth was stained blue."

"I'm sure it wasn't *that* much." The man was blushing, fidgeting in his chair at the table, looking sheepish.

"It was, too," Aiden insisted, pointing at him with

his fork. He remembered well all the faults of his brother. It was an older sibling's right, after all. "It wasn't just your mouth that would be blue, but your chin and the front of your shirt."

"I was seven years old." Thad laughed good-naturedly.

Ma continued to regale Joanna with the family story. "There I was, trying to keep an eye on Finn, but he was running everywhere, and faster than greased lightning to boot. I had one hand on my pail, the other stripping berries from the bush, all the while looking over my shoulder at my youngest. Then I look the other way to check on my older two boys and I see this big grizzly sitting up on his haunches, looking at them with the most puzzled expression you ever saw."

Aiden watched Joanna's jaw drop. "But weren't you terrified?" she asked.

"Worse than terrified." Ma delighted in telling a good family tale, and she sparkled with the fun of it. It was great to see her looking truly happy. "In my mind's eye I already saw that bear munching down Thad like one of those berries, and holding Aiden in the air with his enormous, dangerous paws."

"Since I'm here," Thad interjected, "you can tell the story ended fairly well."

"For you, maybe," Aiden took the last bite of his piece of cake.

That caught Joanna's interest, because she fixed her gaze on him. Those big blue eyes of hers seemed to reach out to him, so full of life. He felt dark and dour by comparison. He couldn't help feeling that she had gotten the short end of the stick in this marriage deal, but he was going to do his best to make it up to her.

"I think that bear had never seen little boys before," Ma continued, putting down her fork, leaning forward, getting into the spirit of the story. "He watched them, a little aghast, as if he was trying to figure out if they were a different kind of rabbit or something."

Joanna laughed, a light musical sound, and Aiden studied her. She looked so different from the sad-eyed woman he'd seen that day at her pa's wake. She was no longer so painfully thin, and color had come back to her complexion. The heat made her hair curl up around her pretty face, and there he went, feeling drawn to her again. He pushed back the chair and rose to his feet. Time to get another cup of tea.

"Then he must have realized that most of his berries were gone from his favorite bush," Ma was saying. "Why, I had grown ten feet, or so it felt like, and I don't even remember dropping my bucket or crossing those few yards of that hillside, but suddenly I was right in front of that bear. He was enormous, bigger than a man by far, and I remember looking down at him."

"You were fearsome, Ma," Thad stated in that easy-going way of his. "Joanna, I remember being too scared to move. I froze with a big handful of berries in my mouth. I was no help. Aiden, he grabbed a stick and went up to help Ma, but he was too late."

"I'm not sure what good that stick would have been against that bear if he had a mind to take offense at us."

Aiden lifted the cool pitcher from the counter. "I remember thinking that animal was going to hurt Ma."

"He wouldn't have dared." Ma pointed her finger, in the way of scolding mothers everywhere. "I shook my finger at him and I said, 'Now, you leave us alone. You go eat your berries somewhere else.' He looked me up and down, bowed his head and waddled off."

"He left? Just like that?" Joanna asked.

"Thank the Lord." Ma nodded. "I was shaking so hard afterward I sat down and couldn't move for a good twenty minutes. Aiden had to help me get back to the wagon."

He heard his brother answer, his sister-in-law comment, which made them all laugh again, but he wasn't really listening. Outside, the clouds were building fast and coming closer. He thought of the field of cut hay drying in the summer sun, and the forty acres of growing wheat. He prayed there was no rain in those clouds, or hard wind and hail that would damage his main crop. He had to make sure Joanna had the security she needed. It was the one thing he could give her. The only thing.

He took a long pull of tea from his cup before setting it down on the counter. "I'm going to head out and start bringing in the hay."

"But, Aiden, it's your wedding day," Ma protested. "And it would be breaking the Sabbath."

"God will understand my need to save my hay. Is this all right with you, Joanna?"

"Yes. You now have two more horses to feed for the

winter." She pushed away from the table and stood. "You might need all the hay you can bring in."

"Exactly. There's no telling how long or hard the winter will be. I'm glad you understand that." He was already grabbing his hat off the hook by the door. "See, Thad? She's a sensible woman."

"A real catch." Thad winked at her as he ambled on past and hooked his own hat off the wall. "The question is, if she's that sensible, why did she marry you?"

"That, brother, is a mystery." The men's voices faded as they strode off across the yard.

Not such a mystery, Joanna knew, as she watched her husband go. The gathering clouds were like giant anvils bumping up against one another in the southern sky. But as big as they were and as enormous the sky, they did not diminish the man walking beneath them.

No, not such a mystery at all. Tenderness hit with such force she had to turn away. Letting herself fall in love with Aiden would be the worst mistake.

She closed the screen door, stepped around James, who was on the floor playing with his new horses, and dropped a kiss on Daisy's head as she dressed her doll. Joanna then began clearing the dessert plates from the table.

Chapter Thirteen

Exhaustion had burrowed deep and he felt as if he could never get it out of his bones, but he and Thad had beat the storm, first at home and then at his brother's place. Aiden reined in Clyde at the barn as the first fat drops of rain fell. Good for the land, but not necessarily good for his wheat. He dismounted, knowing there was nothing he could do about that.

"You were a good horse today." He led the draft horse by the ends of the reins, going slow. It had been a long day for the horses, too.

A surprise waited for him in the barn. One of the wagons was empty of hay. It just stood there, as if the wind had blown every scrap from it and left the other wagon untouched. The only telltale sign was the lantern carefully hung from the end aisle post, flickering low.

The rain began pounding like lead bullets on the roof and a shadow raced through the back door and into the pool of light. Dotted with rain and her hair in one long braid, Joanna held his pitchfork in her hand. "That's really coming down. I got the last stack finished just in time."

"The last stack?" Aiden hadn't realized he'd left Clyde standing in the middle of the aisle. All he knew was that he was already at her side, tight with concern. "It's late. That rain is cold. You aren't telling me that you stacked the hay."

"I told you I'm pretty good at it. I thought, why not? The kids fell asleep early, they had such a busy day. I can see the shanty from here, and I wanted to help out."

She amazed him. He shook his head, flummoxed, feeling a few raindrops drip off his hat brim. "What am I going to do with you? You are supposed to be in the main house, making ruffles or embroidering or something. Not this."

"Are you going to tell me you don't approve of women stacking hay?" Her rosebud mouth quirked up in the corner, and there was no mistaking her challenge.

Yep, she surely amazed him. She was like no woman he'd ever known. He liked her for it. Lord help him, he liked her. "I'm going to allow you to stack hay if that's what you want."

"Allow me?" There it was, the indignation on her face. The quirk of her brows, the rise of her chin. He was glad for the humor sparking in her eyes that told him she knew he was funning her.

He shrugged, removing his hat to shake off the rain spatters. "Am I the man around here?"

A handful of hay hit him square in the face.

"Take that, Aiden McKaslin. That's for that big fib you just told."

"I deserved it." He was laughing. Unbelievable, but it felt good. "I couldn't help it. You're a mighty pretty woman when you get all worked up."

Pink swept across her face. "Now, that's two fibs. What am I going to do with you? I hope this isn't a sign of things to come."

"I wasn't fibbing." Even with her hair wet and plastered to her, she was beautiful. More so every time he looked at her. He reached out, hardly aware of it, his fingers brushing a strand of curls away from her eyes so he could see them better. "My family loves you and your kids. All evening long that's all I heard. I couldn't get away from it."

"I'm sorry. They have hopes for you."

"I know." His fingers lingered at her temple. For some reason, he couldn't pull away. Being this near to her felt soothing to him, when he had hurt for so long. "I heard what they said in the parlor. About the gift."

"You have to know I don't feel the way they do. I know you don't love me. I don't expect that you would." Her forehead creased, and she looked down.

But she didn't move away. The empty places within him stirred like ashes in a winter wind. As if something was there, after all. "My family is hopeful for me, but you have to know something of what I am. You have children, a son. What if that had happened to you?"

Her face crumpled. Her gaze shot toward the barn

wall, in the direction of the shanty. "I could not have come back after that."

"No, I can't see as there is a way to be whole. Some things, once broken, can never be put back together again."

"Yes, I think you are right. Not when it's real love." She gazed up at him, seeing a man more substance than shadow. "I loved my husband in the beginning with all my heart. But the way he behaved and how he treated me wore at my love until it faded away. My heartbreak wasn't sudden like yours. It came one step at a time, like losing little pieces until the polish and beauty of that love was gone."

"I imagine it hurts the same in the end."

"For different reasons." She could see that Aiden had loved deeply and his love had been returned. Hers had not. That was a hard lesson to her. "You are safe with me, Aiden. I don't have your family's expectations."

"You mean, for me to love you eventually?"

"Yes." Sadness filled her, and no small amount of hurt. She caught his hand with hers, remembering how he had kissed her in the church. Tenderness twinkled like a new star in her heart. "I know you can't love me. I don't think it would be good for either of us to think it might be possible. I have my children to raise, and you have this land. We can help each other. That's good enough for me."

He closed his eyes briefly, and she had to guess that it was relief showing on his hard face. "I would give you more if I could," he murmured.

His hand trembled beneath hers, so she let go and stepped away from him. Her skin felt chilled without his touch, and she was aware of the inches separating them. It may as well have been the expanse of the entire western prairie. "It's all right, Aiden. No man could give me more. I'm not the kind of woman a man can love."

"Why do you say that?"

He seemed puzzled, as if he had no notion, and the caring in her heart for him flared more brightly. It was no longer anything resembling caring. No, not at all. She swallowed hard, trying to deny the truth even to herself. "Being loved is impossible for me. Look at me. All my husband really wanted me for was to ease his burdens in life. He saw me as a maid more than anything."

"When you had loved him."

She spun on her heel so she wouldn't have to see Aiden's face. Would it show pity? Or understanding? Either way, the truth remained. She did not possess great beauty or poise or city polish. What she could do was stack hay to shed even the hardest rain. That rain struck her now as she went to check on her handiwork. Her bare feet squished in the dusty dirt that had been quick to turn to mud. There were her half-dozen stacks, standing as tall and round and whole as the dozens Aiden had already built. She let the wind blow through her, wanting the cool gusts to scatter the emotions inside her. It didn't work. Her love for him clung stubbornly to her heart.

I love him. She swiped the rain from her face and stared out at the dark storm. Once again she had fallen in love with a man who did not love her. She was heading for heartbreak all over again. What was she going to do now?

Deny it, of course. She lifted her face to the sky, welcoming the wonderful wetness. It washed away the sting of tears that could not fall, and the disappointment in herself. It's different this time, she told herself. Better. At least she wouldn't wonder why, in this marriage. She knew.

His hand settled on her shoulder, comforting. His touch could make her spirit lift like birds at dawn.

"I couldn't have built haystacks any better." He moved away to circle the stacks, and nodded once he saw how well they were shedding rain. "Who taught you?"

"My ma. When I was a little girl, I used to help her with the work."

"I'm not surprised by that, as I knew your pa."

"He was not a hardworking sort." She held her hands out, palms up, as if welcoming the rain. It sluiced down her face and dripped off her skirt hem. "I've always liked working outside in the fresh air."

"Have you always liked standing in the rain?"

"You say that as if now you think I don't have a lick of sense. What about you? You are out here, too."

"Well, I'm going in." The haystacks were more than fine, and that was a compliment to her. There was a real knack to it, and he knew plenty of men who couldn't do as well. "Clyde's waiting for me to bed him down."

Rain drummed between them, a thousand drops

pinging and pounding all around like a symphony. Funny how he hadn't noticed all the rich notes of the winds in a long time. He hiked into the barn, glad for the shelter. "I'm sorry about this afternoon. I didn't know Ma and Noelle would want to come visit and bring gifts. I can't imagine how fast the two of them had to crochet to get all that made."

"I suspect they already had a start on the project and finished it for me instead of, perhaps, for one of their bedrooms. Noelle told me her house is only a few months old."

"Yes, they got married in late spring." Aiden remembered the hope in his ma's voice. *It is my wish for you both that one day, along with great happiness, you will find great love.*

He grimaced. His ma was a dreamer, always had been and would always be. "I had meant to move you and the kids into the house this afternoon."

"If the mud stays in the field, tomorrow will work out fine. We can move without interfering with your haying." She swiped the rain off her face. "I thought the children and I could share the room at the top of the stairs. It's big and roomy, with plenty of sunshine."

"It's a sensible solution." He held his heart still. "I've decided to move to the downstairs room. It was meant to be something else, but it would serve as a bedroom well enough."

"You had intended it to be a children's playroom for the winter," she guessed.

He nodded, swallowed hard and stripped off

Clyde's bridle. "That way you have the upstairs all to yourselves. I won't wake you all when I get up at four-thirty to start the chores."

"You know I get up to start mine."

He knew. There were more reasons, which he couldn't see fit to tell her. "Good night, Joanna. Thank you for all you did for me and my family today."

"They are my family now, Aiden." She padded past him in her bare feet, a perfect picture of a country woman in calico and grace. "You are my family, too. Good night."

What felt like ashes within him, in his heart, in his soul, stirred toward life. He wished he could feel something for her. He wished he had something left inside of him besides the ashes of his heart and the pieces of his soul.

He planned to avoid her in this big house of his, Joanna had guessed, so she wasn't surprised that his chores were done and he was out in the fields before dawn. While the children played on the doorstep, she whipped up a batch of pancakes, fried eggs and bacon. Because he didn't come to the table, she packed up the meal with a small jug of tea, and with James and Daisy trailing with her, headed out to the wheat fields.

The earth was moist and muddy in spots, the air fresh from the storm. A flawless sapphire sky glinted overhead, so blue it hurt the eye. She followed the trail along the fence line until she found Aiden in the middle of a field of wheat, chopping down fallen stalks. The stalks of wheat were tall and nearly ripe this time of year. Most waved softly golden in the temperate breezes. There were acres upon acres lost to wind damage. She saw great swaths of downed stalks, stretching from south to north. A grim sight, to be sure. She was thankful for the crop that still stood.

"We'll stay here," she told the children, who were ready to walk into the field. "We don't want to disturb the wheat."

"Oh." James hitched his arms over a rail and watched Aiden in the field, the man who was his stepfather now. "He looks awful busy."

"You know right before harvest is one of the busiest times for a farmer." She settled the basket on the ground.

"Yep. I know." He sighed anyway.

Aiden must have spotted her. He set aside his scythe, straightened his hat and began heading her way through the knee-high grain. The gentle sunshine seemed to follow him, making him bigger and brighter than she had ever seen him. Maybe, she realized, that was because she was looking at him with her heart. With a new love that had not been there before.

She lowered her gaze, as if that could lessen her feelings for him, and fumbled with the basket lid. Why her fingers were so clumsy, she couldn't say. She had to grab the tin cup twice and suddenly Aiden was there, his deep voice rumbling.

"Let me."

Her heart plummeted to the earth. This was a mistake, she told herself, as she uncapped the pitcher and poured a shaky stream of tea into the cup. She knew too much to fall in love again. But with this man, how could she help it? It was as natural as breathing.

"You are a welcome sight," he said simply as he took a long sip. "That's good after an early start."

"How long have you been out here?"

"It was still dark. I didn't look at the clock. Worrying about the crop, I didn't get a whole lot of sleep. So I got up and made myself useful."

He was tired. She could see the bruises beneath his eyes and the worry etched into his forehead. She unwrapped the clean cloth she'd folded around the food. "We are lucky half the crop was spared."

"I like to think it was more than luck." He took off his hat and hung it on the fence post.

She was beginning to think that, too. It was easier to believe when she was with Aiden, rock-solid in his faith. It made what she was beginning to see much clearer. "Do you think Thad and Noelle's ranch has this damage, too?"

"Hard to say. I've done almost all I can until the fields dry up some, so later on, I'll ride over and see." He took the plate she offered and bowed his head for a quick blessing.

There was a cowlick at the crown of his head. Why she noticed that, she couldn't rightly say. There was so much she didn't know about this man, so many things that she wanted to know and to cherish.

"This looks mighty good," he said when he was done. "Thank you, Joanna."

"You're more than welcome. Is there anything I can do here to help you?"

"No. You come out here and you'll likely get as muddy as me." She was a great cook; he had to give her that. The pancakes melted on his tongue. "This hits the spot."

"I'm glad." She was already packing up, ready to leave him with that gentle smile she always had on her face these days. "I don't suppose you had a chance to check the orchard?"

"Nope. I can only hope there's plenty of fruit left on the trees, as I'm looking forward to fresh pies later this summer."

"Only if you're good." There it was, that flash of mischief in her eyes.

"What does that mean?"

"Just wait. You'll see." She settled the basket on her arm, and with the breeze teasing the golden wisps of her hair and the brim of her pink sunbonnet, she could have been a wild summer rose come into bloom. So vibrant, fragile and alive, she pulled at the shadows within him. Made him feel every emptiness and every broken place.

"The three of us will have the upstairs room clean and waiting, whenever you're ready." She gave her bonnet brim a tug against the low rays of the rising sun. "I plan to go to Noelle's this afternoon."

"We'll do it before you leave then." He winced a little. "And I'll ride over with you."

"It's a good plan." She held out her free hand to Daisy. "I'll come for the dishes later."

"Not to bother. I'll bring them in with me in a bit. I can't do much more out here."

"All right." She wanted to stay and keep him company, but she could see that he was having a hard time. She hated that. She wished she knew what to do for him. "We don't have to move in with you, Aiden."

"My wife won't be living in a shanty if I can provide better." He pinned her with a firm gaze.

He meant it in the best possible way. Joanna could see that plain as day. That still didn't mean it was easy for him. What a blessed woman his Kate was, to have been loved like that. What an exceptional man Aiden was, to have loved with all he had, down to his soul. Joanna could see the pieces of what was left in him. Her heart swelled even more with affection best kept hidden.

"All right," she said quietly, ready to go. Her son hadn't moved an inch. He watched Aiden with more than interest, for surely the boy was old enough to have figured out what yesterday's ceremony had meant. "Come, James. We need to go."

There was a question in his eyes. Such a sweet boy he was. She knew what he was too shy to ask. He wanted to stay in the fields and help Aiden, although he was much too little for that. Aiden would have been the kind of father who would take his son with him just to spend time with him, and teach him by his example and kindness.

If only, she thought wistfully. She had no notion if Aiden would ever come to the place where he could be close to his stepson, so she held out her other hand. "Come, James."

"All right." He hopped down and ran her way, all little-boy energy. He waited until they were a ways off before he leaned close to whisper, "He's our pa now, right?"

"He's your stepfather. Remember I said he and I were married now." She had explained that when she'd tucked them into bed last night.

Daisy seemed unconcerned, but James pursed his lips, thinking hard. "That's like a pa."

"Yes. He's like having a second father."

James seemed satisfied. "Then are we going to stay in his house and not leave?"

"Yes, that's why I married him. So we have a home we never have to leave."

"That's sure good. Cuz I don't want to go back to the wagon."

"I know, pumpkin." She didn't want that for her little ones, either. "We're here to stay."

"I like Grandma," Daisy said, as if that settled it. "She gave me one of her buttons."

Joanna felt an odd tingle at the back of her neck. When she looked over her shoulder, she saw nothing but a meadowlark hopping onto the fence rail near where Aiden had been standing. She searched the meadow, to find him heading back to work, taking his plate and tea with him.

Even surrounded by the bright fields sprinkled with sunshine, and framed by the vivid blue sky, he somehow looked lost. The sunlight on her face was like a gentle touch, like reassurance, helping her to understand. For so long she had been sure that the Lord had forgotten her. Hardships had wedged their way into her faith, creating rifts that grew larger with every difficulty.

Looking back, maybe she could see the purpose behind every trial that had brought her to stay at her pa's house, and then the loss of that, too. God had been there all along, gently guiding her here. To Aiden.

Because he needed her.

Chapter Fourteen

"Where do you want this?" Aiden's voice boomed behind her. He stood in the doorway with the rocking chair hefted easily over his shoulder.

"By the window, please." She was fully aware that she was a sight. Her skirts were damp and strands of hair had come out of her braid, curling every which way.

She stepped aside to make room, but was hemmed in by the bedstead that had already been in the room, which she and Daisy would share. Then there was the smaller bed Aiden had moved in from one of the spare rooms, left over from when he and his brothers were young.

"Sure thing." Aiden passed by, brushing against the hem of her skirts as he went.

What a good husband he is, she thought wistfully, watching him as he carefully swung the chair down. He had a perfect profile, with the spill of his dark hair over his high, intelligent forehead, and a straight nose. His chin and jaw were a strong balance to his other chiseled features. Handsome, yes—she surely thought him so—but he was more. He was built of character, and she ached with admiration. With love.

What was she going to do about that? She could no longer hide from it. Love for him filled her as surely as light coming in the window filled the room.

"You could take one of the other rooms."

"I could," she agreed. It wasn't easy trying to hide how she felt. It wasn't easy knowing her abiding affection for him would cause both of them nothing but grief. She took a step toward the rocking chair, glad that it stood between them like a barrier, creating distance she desperately needed.

She forced herself to look out the window at her little ones playing in the shade of the house, James with his horses and Daisy with her doll.

"You don't have to all be cooped up in one room." He sounded gruff, but there were notes of concern there, too, and, as always, his rugged kindness. "That makes it about the same as the shanty."

"Trust me, this is not the same." Not with the light yellow wallpaper sprinkled with tiny cornflowers, a fireplace in the corner to warm the space on a cold winter's night, the polished wood floor and two big windows. "Was this your mother's room?"

"It was." Aiden faced the window, too, and seemed to be watching the children at play, although it was hard to tell. He was so distant, as if he were looking in and not out. "Maybe after you settle some and feel comfortable here, you'll want your children to have rooms of their own. There's enough for that. Finn won't be coming back."

"Maybe he'll realize the way he's living his life isn't right and won't bring him happiness. Then he will change. It could happen."

"It could, but I've been disappointed hoping in that before. I wish I could have him back. It's not that I don't want to."

"I know." Even a stranger, someone who didn't know Aiden at all, could see the anguish on his face. Love and life were such fragile things and could be lost in a blink. Aiden had lost Finn as surely as if he had buried him, too. She could see it plainly. "Maybe there's still hope for him."

"Maybe. Pastor Hadly is checking on him as much as he can, and Thad is, as well. Finn is still talking with Thad. That's something at least. Not that Finn wants to stop having fun, as he calls it."

Joanna could feel Aiden's pain. She longed to reach out and lay her hand on his shoulder and somehow absorb some of it. "I don't think even Finn thinks he's having fun. He's escaping from more than the responsibility of working and making a living on this land. He's escaping life."

"I won't argue with you." Aiden winced. "I know you're right."

"You've done so much for him. I wish he could see what I do."

"What's that?"

"How you want to make things right for him."

"Now, how do you know that?" He moved away from the window, away from her.

"It's what I know of you. What I see in you."

"You seem to know a lot about me." There were those tangled up feelings again, coiling tight in every empty space. "I guess I'm not so hard to figure out."

"No, not at all." There was a smile in her voice and a softness that made him want to turn toward her.

How he wished he could. He fisted his hands, sticking to what was safe, to what was right. "I'm trying to do all I can for him. It's my duty. It's what's right."

"You always do the right thing."

"I sure try. Heaven knows I've made my share of mistakes." He wished he could give Finn another chance, but he knew it wouldn't work. He had to stand firm. He had to let Finn figure out the consequences of his choices, the same as any man. It was the way the Lord intended. A man might have free will, but choosing the easy path was not easy at all. The harder road at first was the easier one in the long run. A man made a lot of mistakes on either path. There seemed to be no help for that other than faith and prayer.

One mistake he hadn't made was bringing Joanna here. At least he felt good about that. She was wearing her green calico dress today, and he was close enough to see all the careful patching she had done to the garment. Matching the pattern of the sprigged calico took great care. He knew, because his ma had done the same to all of their clothes once, when they were young and times were lean.

"You said you're doing piecework for Miss Sims?" he asked, his voice coming out more gruffly than he'd meant.

"I will stop by her shop on my way to Noelle's today, whether you object to my working or not."

He took in the flash of Joanna's grin and shook his head. No one had ever before disagreed with him so cheerfully. Or gotten around him quite so easily. He had no notion of how to keep her in check. He had a feeling he never would be able to. Joanna had spirit, one that hardship had not dimmed.

He headed to the door, smiling to himself. "Now, I never said I would object. I only meant to say you will get yourself some new clothes, and for your little ones, too. I won't be married to a woman with patched dresses."

"Oh, you won't?"

His smile stretched a little wider, surprising him. He hadn't smiled like this in more years than he could count. "I'm putting my foot down. I don't want to hear any arguments."

"What if I have plenty of arguments?"

"Too bad. You'll just have to suffer in silence." He reached the hall and glanced over his shoulder to make sure she understood what he could not say. "I mean it, Joanna. You'll do what I say."

"Oh, you have a lot to learn." She flipped her braid over her shoulder, as if trying to figure out what to do with a man like him. "Perhaps I'll do as you ask this once. The children are growing so fast."

It was a victory of sorts, and he was pleased with that. "There's something else. There ought to be a few boxes up in the attic. If you want to take the time later on, some of our old toys are crated up. Wooden horses and a barn my grandfather made. Your boy might like 'em."

"I'm sure he would."

He turned before he could see her sympathy, but he felt it while he hiked down the hall to his room. Here, he was alone, but no longer safe. He no longer felt as hollow. Without hesitation, he hefted the feather mattress off the bedstead and carried it down the hallway.

He was mighty glad to have that moving business done with. Aiden tightened the last of the buckles and gave Clyde a pat on the neck. "Good old fella."

The draft horse nickered and rubbed his head against Aiden's chest, knocking him back a foot. "Careful there, boy. You don't know your own strength."

Clyde gave a woof of expelled air and lifted his head. They had company. There was Joanna's son, standing just outside the barn door. His little shadow fell into the main aisle.

"Does your ma know you wandered away from the yard?"

"No, sir." The boy's voice sounded small and forlorn. "I haven't left the yard. I'm just standing in the dirt is all, instead of the grass."

"You know to keep within sight of the windows."

"Yessir." The boy paled but held his ground. "Ma can still see me."

Aiden took Clyde by the bits to lead him forward. "You know not to wander off, right?"

"Yep. I gotta stay close and watch my sister."

"That's right." Aiden was near enough to see past the narrow angle of the doorway to the span of yard toward the house. There was Joanna's daughter, sitting in the shade, changing her rag doll. "You know there are dangerous animals around. They don't come close to the houses, but I've seen them in the fields now and again."

"Yessir." The boy edged to the side to make room, his gaze and attention switching to the horse. "I reckon you know all the harnessing."

"Yep." Aiden steeled himself because he knew what was coming.

"I sure would like to learn that." The kid breathed that out in a sigh of longing, the question he was too afraid to ask lingering in the silence between them.

He hadn't shored himself up enough; the boy's wish hit him square in the chest. Aiden thought of all the reasons it would be better to ignore the boy and keep on going. All the reasons why it would hurt too much to stop.

His feet made the decision for him. He was handing over one strap of the reins before he had thought it through. "Can you lead Clyde over to the house?"

"I sure can, sir." Excitement snapped across his features. Hope sparkled. "I'll do a real good job, too."

"Walk him slow." He kept his hand on the horse's neck, but there was no need. Clyde gave a snort of pleasure and followed the boy, lipping his hair affectionately. The wagon wheels creaked, the boy giggled and the old Clydesdale plodded toward the house.

"Keep to the wagon tracks," Aiden cautioned, and noticed Joanna on the back doorstep. There was gratitude on her soft oval face and something else that made his pulse skid to an instant halt. Something that made him close his eyes. But the image remained on the back of his lids—the image of her lovely face watching him with adoration.

Maybe it was for the boy, he told himself. Of course she adored her son. That was it, he thought in a panic, opening his eyes and seeing the ground at his feet. Little patches of mud remained from the storm, but already the dust was returning, puffing up with each step he took. He concentrated on that, and when he looked at Joanna again it was to help her into the wagon.

She looked good, and when he took her hand, he felt his spirit stir, as if it was still there, after all, when he had thought that part of him was gone.

It felt right to help her up onto the front seat. "You'll sit up here with me," he told her, and since he now had enough experience with her to know what she might say to that, he added, "please."

That earned him her smile. He didn't think there was a more beautiful sight than Joanna at that moment, grinning down at him from the high wagon seat. The sun sat behind her like a jewel, framing her with gold. She was like a completely different woman. Gone were the lines of strain and worry. Fallen away was the worn-down look of hardship.

It felt good to think he had a hand in that. That his life amounted to something, after all. It was hard to believe an used up man with no life left could make a difference. Maybe God wasn't done with him yet.

She held out her arms and he turned to find the girl at his knee, clutching her doll.

"You're next, little girl." He hiked her up with no effort at all. She was no burden. She went to her mother's arms, leaving him to face the boy.

Aiden held his feelings still, tricking himself into thinking he didn't have any, but before he could offer help, the boy was climbing up on his own, nimbly and easily. Aiden couldn't say why he stood there, watching to make sure the little guy was safely over the rail, before he moved away. Joanna was watching over her son, too, making sure he settled safely onto the backseat. That's what Aiden respected about her most of all—that she knew what was precious in this world.

He gathered the reins together and hopped up next to her. It was strange having Joanna at his side. He gave the leather straps a gentle slap and Clyde ambled forward. Aiden couldn't rightly say why he felt as if a roll of barbed wire was lodged behind his ribs. All he knew was that Joanna was doing this to him, making him ache more with every breath.

"I didn't know where to put the lovely things your mother and Noelle made us." She turned to him, obviously unaware of her effect on him. "I didn't want to put them in my and the children's room."

"You should. It seems fitting."

"Sticky fingers," she explained, and there was that smile again. The soft, captivating look of fondness. "They might fare better in your room."

"I have no use for frilly lace. No offense."

There was her smile again, wide enough to reach her eyes and to touch his worn-out soul. He liked that he could make her smile like that. That meant he'd done the right thing, although judging by how he was feeling, it didn't seem that way.

"I simply wanted to know what to tell Ida and Noelle. Their gift was thoughtful and beautiful, and I wanted to be able to tell them where I intend to display their handiwork. How about the parlor?"

"Good solution." He pushed his hat back and guided Clyde onto the main road, although the big guy knew his way. It gave Aiden something to focus on beside the woman and her smile. Summer had bronzed the prairie. Everywhere he looked was the amber of ripening wheat, the russet of wild grasses and the yellow-gold of wildflowers nodding in the breeze. It would be harvest soon. "I didn't get a chance to look at the orchard."

"Nothing for you to worry about." Joanna glanced over her shoulder to check on her children, safe and quiet on the seat. "The apples were the hardest hit. We picked up what fell, didn't we?"

He kept his attention on the road, but knew the little ones were nodding. The girl's sweet, high voice filled the air and the boy's somber one added a comment or two. Aiden's chest tightened.

He eased Clyde as far to the right as he could go. A driver and wagon were headed their way. It was Stevens. Aiden nodded a greeting to his neighbor as they passed. Stevens waved back, tipping his hat at Joanna, a neighborly show of respect.

Aiden was glad for that. "I don't suppose you met him when you were living with your pa?"

"No. None of the neighbors took a liking to my father. He was a hard man."

"I can't argue with that. Stevens is one of the men I trade work with when threshing time comes. There'll be about six of us plus the hired help to feed. I suspect you know how it works."

"I do." She smoothed the folds of her skirts, as if she was working herself up to say something. "You don't have to worry, Aiden. I was married to a wheat farmer before. I know what's expected. I know the hard work you need done."

"I wasn't saying I needed you in the fields." One day he was going to have to learn how to say what he meant. "I was talking about the meals. Cooking for that many men."

"Me, too." She laughed, a gentle, welcoming sound, one that tugged at the lost places within him. That lured him like the sunlight, like the prairie, into noticing.

She drew him where he could not help following. He felt alive, as if he was breathing in air for the first time.

"For a minute there you had me worrying you planned to be out in the fields helping me." It felt right to laugh along with her. "The joke was on me, I guess."

"I have talked so much about working in the fields. What else were you to think?"

"I'm glad you don't have to work that hard, Joanna. I don't want you to. Do you understand?"

The laughter faded from her face, but not the smile. It remained, wide enough to reach her eyes and real enough to touch what remained of his soul. That felt right, too.

"You have done so much for me and my children, Aiden." Serious now, she laid her hand on his sleeve.

He swallowed at the connection, at the tug of emotion within him he did not want to feel. "I've only done the right thing is all."

"I wish I could do as much for you." Her fingers lingered on his sleeve, and in the heartbeat before she pulled away, there it was again. That fondness he'd spotted before.

For him this time. Clearly for him.

Joanna closed the worn book, quietly laid it on the bedside table and turned down the wick. The lamplight faded into darkness, leaving only the faint light from the sickle moon spilling in through the cracks between the curtains. It was enough to see the shadows of her little ones tucked into their beds. Daisy lay on her side, clutching her doll, looking like perfection, so still and sweet. James, on the other hand, stirred, fighting sleep.

"Sweet dreams," she whispered, and kissed his forehead, hoping that would settle him.

Instead his eyes popped wide-open. "Ma, I can't hardly sleep."

"Yes, but you must. Tomorrow is another good day."

"This sure is a great room." Even in the dark shadows, it was simple to see the contentment on his face and hear the gladness in his words. "I like this house the best. Mostly because we really get to stay here."

"That's right." No more worries for her children. No more want. She thought of the man who had avoided her since he'd helped her from the wagon at his brother's place. The strings of her heart knotted tight. "You get some sleep, now."

"I like my new pa." There was something else there exposed in his words and hidden by the dark. "He let me lead Clyde. Did you see?"

"I saw." She remembered the picture the three of them had made, the small boy, the big man and the giant horse together. "You did a real good job with him."

"I know. I like Clyde. He's a good old fella." James imitated Aiden's intonation.

So much need. How did she explain it to a boy who wanted a father? "It was nice of Aiden to take the time with you, but you know he's terrible busy this time of year."

"I know. That's why he didn't come home with us. Or to supper. He had to help Uncle Thad with his wheat. And tomorrow Uncle Thad is gonna come here and help with ours."

"That's right." She had to find the right words, the right way to handle this. She had to protect James from disappointment. She had to protect Aiden from James caring too much. Tonight, when she knelt down to pray, she would ask for the Lord's help. Just as he had led them here to Aiden, surely he was continuing to lead them.

She brushed James's bangs from his eyes. "We must be careful not to burden Aiden. He did a good deed taking us in. You sleep tight, sweetheart."

"Do you think he's home yet?"

"Not yet." She stood, full of love for her children and for the man who could never love her in return. "For the last time, go to sleep."

James gave a little giggle. "Okay, Ma. I'll try."

She closed the door quietly and padded downstairs. She had left the windows open to the night breezes, and the house was pleasant and smelled of ripening wheat and wildflowers. She went from window to window, closing up before she lit the lamps. There was no tidying left to do in the parlor, and the kitchen was spick-and-span, so she grabbed her sewing basket and sat down at the table to work.

A moth beat at the screen door as she threaded her needle. She planned to work on the fabric she had picked up for James before the wedding. She had not made as much progress on his trousers as she wanted. Ida had pointed out today that school started in town in a few weeks' time.

As she knotted the end of the thread and double-checked the pins on the side seams, she thought of her little boy. He looked up to Aiden. It was natural for him to want a father. Of course that's what he thought Aiden ought to be. He was too young to understand. It was his heart that was wanting what he had never had. Certainly not from Tom, when he'd been alive, and never even from her father in the year or more they had lived with him.

How could James understand, when she didn't understand herself? She didn't know why the heart yearned to love and be loved. It was simply the way God had made hearts. She could not say it felt wrong that a skyful of love swept through her every time she thought of Aiden, powerful enough to fill her world from horizon to horizon, and every place in between.

There was no hiding from it. No changing it. No way to go back in time and stop every step she'd taken that had brought her here. She slid the needle into the fabric, basting long, even stitches, working without thought. Her mind was on Aiden. On hearing the plod of a horse in the yard. Seeing his familiar profile as he rode one of Thad's horses through the shadowy darkness. She longed for the moment when he'd walk through the door. She couldn't wait to hear the rich timbre of his voice and simply to have the privilege of making his life easier.

She finished the seam quickly and set down her work. There was the supper she'd saved aside for him, in case he was hungry when he came home. It was a pleasure to set out the big slice of the pie she'd baked for him—apple pie.

There he was, striding through the darkness, outlined by the faint moon glow, more light than shadow. He pulled back the screen door and entered—her husband. He was the perfect image of everything good in a man, and she could not stop her heart from falling ever more in love with him.

When he saw her, he froze. He did not smile, but changed to granite before her very eyes. He let the door close with a hollow slap, and turned away from her. Something was wrong. Very wrong.

"I'm sorry, but I ate at Noelle's," he said, then went straight to his room.

Chapter Fifteen

She sat at the kitchen table, graced by lamplight. Washed and changed out of his work clothes, Aiden debated. Every instinct he had told him to keep his distance. And yet she was his wife now. She deserved more than that from him. Look at her, even at eight o'clock at night, working away with her head bent over her sewing, so intent that she didn't notice him standing in the doorway like a statue.

"Is that apple pie I smell?"

That got her attention. Her needle stilled in midstitch and her head whipped up. Instead of the censure he deserved, there was only a gentle look, more a question than anything. Those places within him began aching again—from the past, for the future…he didn't know.

"It sure is." She put her work aside and was already rising. Anxiety pinched the smooth skin around her eyes. "If you like it warm, it will take a few moments to heat. I just need to light the stove."

"Don't go to any trouble. I'll cut it, Joanna."

"I don't mind." She was already reaching up into the cupboards for a plate and a cup, quick to please. "I have tea cooled, or I can fetch cold water from the well."

He hung his head. This wasn't what he wanted. He wanted a sensible, working type of marriage. Not one that made every piece of him hurt whenever he looked at her. He couldn't miss the pain he'd put on her face. He felt as if a cinch were drawing tight around his chest and he couldn't breathe. Like a man suffocating, panic set in. The need to protect himself from an endless pain.

His hand trembled as he took a knife from the drawer. He steeled himself, heart and soul, before he moved closer to her. He wanted to tell her that he didn't need anyone. That he didn't need her to slide a spatula beneath the wedge of pie he'd cut, and put it on a plate for him. That he didn't need her fresh baked dessert or her kindness or the veiled look on her face that told him she was hiding her heart.

He didn't need love. He didn't want love. It had only brought him devastation. He was still holding the shards of that life, unable to let go, unable to move on. Being near Joanna with the soft fragrance of baking clinging to her clothes, and her flower-scented soap, was tearing him apart. He wished he could forget the radiance he'd witnessed in her and what he'd seen of her heart. He wished he had something left inside him still able to care. He wished the twisting coil of turmoil within him would stop, simply stop, and leave him be.

He drew a ragged breath, willing himself to walk calmly to the table and set down the plate. It took all of his might not to notice as Joanna swept close with a cup of tea. He felt as if he were breaking apart as he sat down at the table.

"You worked a long time at your brother's." She lingered a moment too long.

He could feel the emptiness within him like a sore tooth. He grabbed up the fork, trying to pretend everything was as it should be. But he was only fooling himself. "Thad's fields weren't as hard hit as ours. That was a blessing, at least. Still, it took the better part of seven hours to clean them up."

"It's a hardship for him." She swept away, taking all the air in the room with her.

It was the only explanation he could come up with for why he felt as if he was gasping for breath. "It's his first crop. I helped him break sod this past spring. The first yield is never good. He wasn't expecting a solid crop until next year."

"But you were counting on the crop here, weren't you?" Her voice was resonant with understanding, her concern rich with layers. "If things get hard for you…"

He couldn't look at her, but he heard her silence and the weight of questions she did not ask. They stood between them as solidly as the table. He could feel them. He winced. "I hope that's not what you think of me. That I'm a fair-weather man. That if times get rough, I'll break my vows to you."

"No, that's not what I think. Not at all." Her words

rang low and as sweet as the apple pie in front of him. Warmth crept into her voice, the kind that came with a deep caring. "I only meant that you weren't banking on having two extra horses to feed through the winter, and that's a cost to you. Now me and the children to feed and shelter, and that's a greater cost. If the crop isn't enough… Well, I'm already doing piecework for Cora Sims. I'm sure I could do more."

He squeezed his eyes shut. She had no notion of what she was doing to him with her generous compassion and willing heart. "Joanna, you do more than enough every day. We'll get by. I've got savings put aside. I had a good crop last year. You're not to worry."

"But with part of the wheat crop gone, I imagine we'll need to watch every penny."

"True."

"And my wages will help." She watched his reaction through her lashes. His jaw was granite, his gaze stony. "You don't think a woman ought to be concerned with making ends meet, is that it?"

"No, I was just thinking I'm not taking your wages." He cut into his pie with his fork, his voice flat. "I'm not a man who takes his wife's money. Now, before you start arguing—"

"How did you know I was going to argue?"

"You're a woman. And if there's one thing I've learned, a woman always has an opinion." His mouth crooked in the corners.

"Well, you are right about that, mister." She picked up her sewing and began stitching away. Poking the needle through the fabric gave her some satisfaction at least, as she could not accomplish as much with him as easily. "It's my opinion that I won't be a burden to you. I owe you, Aiden. More than you know."

"How did you come to that opinion?" His forehead creased as if he was puzzled. "You are a good wife, Joanna. You deserve all I can provide for you—more than I can do for you."

"You don't know what you're saying." She reached the end of the seam and knotted it swiftly. Her eyes were hot and she had to squint to see what she was doing. She tried hard not to think of those dark days of chaos and disappointment of her first marriage. Of trying so hard. "You appreciate everything I do. You compliment every meal I make. You see me, Aiden."

"It would be hard not to. All I have to do is open my eyes."

"You know what I mean." He could try to tempt her away from her feelings with that dry humor of his, but it wasn't going to work. Love bubbled like a well-spring in her soul, always running, always renewed.

She lowered her gaze, hoping that would hide any rogue feelings showing in her eyes. She bowed her head over her work, hoping the shadows would mask her. "You don't make me feel less than. I can't tell you what it means to me. Your kindness…"

She stopped there, willing her tongue to stop forming any more words that could give her away. She was in love with him. It would not be right to let him see that she had already broken a promise between them.

She blinked hard and knotted the thread again and a third time, before weaving the end thread through the fabric.

"My kindness is the least of what you deserve, Joanna." He looked lost again. "You had heartbreak in your first marriage as surely as I did in mine. In little bits at a time. I can see how it was. One disappointment after another until there was nothing left but pieces of your dreams."

"Yes." She was not surprised that he could see this in her so clearly. Aiden always had that knack. She prayed he could not see her as clearly now. She wrapped her love for him up and hoped it was hidden deeply enough that he would never see. "We're a pair, aren't we?"

"Yep." He paused to stare out past the pool of light to the window, where night and shadows beckoned. "How do you do it?"

"Do what?"

"You've had heartache and hardship in your life, and yet you've never closed your heart. How have you done it?"

"I did not have your losses, Aiden."

"No, but love lost is the same in the end." His chest hurt something fierce. He set down his fork, feeling trapped, needing to feel the breeze on his face and the expanse of the sky blowing on by. She reached across the table and laid her hand on his. The shards that had once been his soul stirred.

"I should not have been here, waiting for you tonight." It wasn't understanding or sympathy in her words, but love. Quiet as dawn coming and as sure as first light, that's how she sounded.

Did she know she was so transparent? She deserved better than a man like him, barren of heart and grasping for any embers that might remain. He was too tangled up to pray. Too unsettled to feel his way to that calm place of God. Aiden passed his hand over his face, torn up inside, feeling like a rope unraveling shank by braided shank.

Footsteps crossed the porch behind him. Finn, was his first guess, but the heavy gait was wrong. Just wishful thinking, Aiden supposed, wanting his youngest brother to come back to his senses. Wanting to save him, maybe because he could not save himself.

A soft knock sounded on the door frame. He was already on his feet, heading toward the door. He didn't recognize the man's shadow on the back step until he came closer and saw the faint glint of a silver star. The sheriff. This had happened before.

"Clint." He yanked open the screen door. "Don't tell me this is about Finn. I'm not in the mood."

"You know that's why I'm here." The lawman swept off his hat. "Now, I can leave or I can tell you the truth. Which way do you want it?"

"What did he do this time?" Aiden tensed, as if he were bracing himself. "Tell me he's sleeping it off in a cell."

"I would, but that's not the whole truth. He's in big trouble this time, Aiden."

"What kind of trouble?"

"He was taking part in a robbery."

"I knew he was going to get into trouble again. How bad is it?"

"Bad. I'm holding him in jail until the judge comes to town. He was armed, Aiden. I regret having to tell you that someone got hurt."

"I was afraid something like this might happen." Aiden's wide shoulders slumped.

"You can see him tomorrow if you want. Thought I'd swing by Thad's place and let him and your mother know."

"That's good of you, Clint." Aiden wedged one shoulder against the door frame, as if bracing himself. "I appreciate you coming out all this way."

"That's all right. I'm sorry to have to bring you news like this." The sheriff took a step back into the darkness. "I know you've been trying to keep him on a better path."

"Nothing I've done has worked."

"Sometimes that's the way it is, and it's a shame, too. I'll be seeing you, Aiden."

"Thanks, Sheriff." He didn't move from the doorway. He stood stock-still, maybe too stunned by the news. Maybe too discouraged.

"I didn't mean to overhear." Joana was across the room without realizing it, drawn as if a rope were pulling her. "I'm sorry."

"I am, too." He sounded hollow, as if all the life had been sucked right out of him. "I was afraid he would get into worse trouble than before. He's not a bad boy, but he loses all sense when he's in the bottom of a bottle."

"This isn't your fault, Aiden."

"I made him leave. Without money. Without a place to live. I tried to do the right thing by him. To make him think about what he was doing."

"That was his choice." Her hand settled on his shoulder. She could feel the agony vibrating through him. "Likely he wouldn't have stopped no matter what you did."

"I should have done more. What, I don't know. Now I've lost him, too."

"I know you, Aiden. You did everything you could for him. You gave him a new start. I know, because you did the same thing for me. You gave him a chance to improve his life. Believe me, that's quite a gift to hand someone."

"He's going back to jail for a long time."

"That was his choice, too."

"I feel as if I failed him." Aiden sounded tortured. He moved away from her touch, slowly, as if breaking away hurt him, too, and strode into the darkness. There was no moonlight to illuminate him, just faint stardust. It gilded him in the velvet blackness of the night like a dream. His shoulders were wide, feet braced apart and head bowed as if in prayer.

She closed the screen door quietly. Should she follow him? Did he need comfort? Or would he want to be alone? She longed to go to him. She had to be careful not to give herself away, she thought as she padded down the steps. It wasn't easy to pull back her affection and lock it in her heart. She gave thanks for the night that hid her face as completely as it hid his.

"Aiden?" She ached to soothe him with the right words. To reach out and let her hand settle on his shoulder again, so he could feel that he wasn't alone. "You didn't fail him."

"It sure feels that way."

"I'm guessing that you haven't failed anyone in your whole life. You are so strong. In faith. Of heart. Of character."

She squeezed her eyes shut, willing back the love inside her. She could not let it show.

When she opened them again, he was facing her. He had moved as silently as the night, and he seemed a part of it. Lost and bruised, with only the faintest light to guide him.

"You're wrong, Joanna. I am not that man. You see someone else. Someone you wish to see. Not me."

"I see how much you are hurting. From this news of Finn. From what you've lost. From seeing me sitting in your kitchen, and that's my fault. I let you talk me into moving in when I should have stayed in the shanty."

"You misunderstand." He sounded as if he was suffocating. She could only see the faint outline of his forehead and nose. He was pure shadow. "I feel. Before you came, there was nothing, only hard work and making a living off the land and keeping my distance. You changed that."

"I didn't mean to."

"I know, but it happened just the same."

She worked at the thin gold band on her fourth finger, the one he had put there with a vow and promises he would not break. She didn't know what to say. Love beat stronger within her, and yet it was not strong enough. "I wanted to make your life better, Aiden. To make your burdens easier, the way you did for me and my children."

"I know that." His palms cradled her face, rough with calluses and tender with care.

She brought her hands up to his, holding on to his strength, taking in his sweet tenderness. He cared for her. That was more than she expected. More than she had dreamed. She breathed in the silence, and the night did not seem as bleak. The gleam of starshine seemed to linger like hope.

"I wish I were like you." His baritone voice was raw, as if speaking brought him pain. "But I cannot do this."

"Do what?" Was he talking about Finn again? she wondered. Or her presence in his house?

"I know, Joanna. I see how you look at me."

She squeezed her eyes shut. But it was too late. She had not hidden her love for him as well as she'd thought. Heat swept across her face and regret into her heart. She tugged what defenses she could around her and steeled her spine. Whatever he said next, she knew it was going to hurt. There was no other way it could be. "I know you can't love me, Aiden. I'm not asking for that. You have to know."

"I do." He grimaced, and what little she could see of him was tortured. "Don't think I don't want to. I wish I could. Prayer hasn't helped. I can't find my heart. Sometimes you lose too much of yourself and you can't get it back."

"I'm not asking you for anything." She had to stop him, because there was only one way this could end. She told herself she wasn't hurting. That he couldn't be rejecting her if he never loved her in the first place.

But hearing that he wished he could love her was worse than any loss. Any pain. She saw him for the first time, a man broken beyond repair, struggling for life the way a drowning man fights for air. He was going down and there was nothing she could do to stop him. Nothing but try to fix what she could. She did not want to lose him.

She drew in a ragged breath and gathered up the bits of her dignity. "Nothing between us has to change. Everything is the same, Aiden."

"It's not the same." He choked on the words. "I'll move out into the shanty."

"No, you don't need to do that."

"It's what I want." He stood firm. Resolute. "I won't uproot the children again, and it makes no difference to me where I live. I'll move tonight."

"But it's l-late."

"It's only a mattress and my pillow. Not much to move."

"No, please I…I—"

"I'm sorry." Hearing the tremble in her voice was agony. He was cracking apart like a frozen river in spring, one sharp break after another. It was too much.

It was more than he could take. "This isn't what I want. I wish—"

He couldn't finish that, not with words, not even in thought. The presence of her hands on his destroyed him. She was soft as moonlight and as comforting as prayer and her hands were small. How could she do so much with them? She was powerful enough to tug at the embers of his heart.

"You wish that you had never married me." Her voice was thin and raw.

No, that wasn't true. But when he tried to tell her, his throat closed up tight. He leaned forward an inch, longing for what he could not let himself have. She tipped her face up. The starlight dusted the curves of her face, revealing her loving heart. She shone like a polished pearl, lovely from the inside out, and he yearned for her tenderness the way stars longed for the night.

He cared deeply about her. He wanted to deny it, to lie to himself, to hide from the truth. But it was like life in his veins, like the beat coming back to his heart. He was drowning, without air to breathe or ground to plant his feet on. If he took her into his arms and let her settle her cheek against his chest and held her tight, he would find what was lost. Letting himself fall in love with her would be like walking in the light again.

Panic made him step back. His vulnerabilities were exposed and the depth of his soul found.

It took all his strength to let go of her. To do the right

thing and protect them both. Life was too hard and love too uncertain.

"I'd best get settled." He left her standing there, graced by starshine and the rising moon, and holding his heart.

Chapter Sixteen

"That's a dear little dress you're making," Cora Sims commented days later, across the width of Noelle's comfortable parlor. "For your little girl?"

"Yes. From the fabric I bought at your store." Seated next to Noelle on the sofa, Joanna held up the calico frock. "I've made it a bit fancier than usual, with ruffles and satin ribbon trim."

"Adorable." Lanna Wolf, an old friend of Noelle's, put down the quilt patch she was sewing and leaned forward to admire the fine workmanship. "I love the backstitching you've done here. And the little embroidery work on the collar and cuffs."

"I'll have to have Ida remember this for when we start making baby clothes." Noelle paused, happiness lighting her lovely face as she waited expectantly for her hint to sink in.

"A baby? Really?" Matilda Worthington, Noelle's

cousin, gasped on Joanna's other side. "That's wonderful news."

"Don't you tell your mother yet. I'm planning on letting her know in person. She is not fond of surprises." Noelle stopped to count her stitches with her fingertips.

"Thad must be beyond the moon," Lanna said. "Your first child. Joe and I are still waiting."

"It can come when you least expect it," Joanna found herself saying. Why there was a lump in her throat, she couldn't rightly say. "I had been married two years before I found out I would be having James. He was worth waiting for."

"I guess God knows when the time is right." Noelle sparkled, radiant with joy. "I'm thankful for this little one on the way. Speaking of which, I think I hear the patter of small footsteps."

Sure enough, James bolted into the doorway and skidded to a stop. Grass seed clung to his shirt and a grass stain was at his knee. Luckily, he wasn't wearing his new trousers. "Ma. Can me and Daisy have more pie?"

"Not right now." She secured her needle and folded up the tiny dress. "It's about time for us to head home. How about an extra big piece after supper?"

He looked around at the women watching him and squared up his chin. "Okay, Ma. I'll get Daisy's toys so we can go."

"Thank you, baby." The lump in her throat remained, stubbornly stuck in place. She leaned forward to slip her things inside her sewing basket as his footsteps padded away.

"Oh, he's such a dear." Cora watched him go with longing. It was clear to see she was not a spinster by choice, and that she wanted children. "You have such well-behaved little ones."

"They are good." Joanna secured the lid on her basket. "They are my greatest blessings."

"Aiden seems good to them." Cora folded up her work, too. "At my age, I keep hoping I might find a handsome widower with children. I think there's nothing that says more about a man than being a good father."

"We'll have to see if we can't find you one of those," Lanna said, and the conversation turned to which handsome widower in the county might be right for Cora.

Joanna lifted her basket and went to get her things in the corner by the front door. It was a beautiful sight to see the golden wheat fields out beyond the large windows. The air puffing in through the screens smelled like bread baking. Harvest time was coming. A few more days, and she would be busy cooking and baking enough to feed the men. A few days later, she had agreed to do the same, with Ida's help, in Noelle's kitchen.

Aiden. Whenever she thought of him she had to lock up the feelings in her heart. She was too busy to waste a minute crying for what was never meant to be. She was too vulnerable to really think about what she had done. She had tipped her hand, and Aiden had not only guessed her feelings, he hadn't spoken to her since, beyond a few thank-you's, and letting her know the date the threshers were coming. She put his meals in the empty shanty, not knowing how warm the food would be when he finally wandered in from his work. It was her fault that they were both miserable—all her fault.

She would do anything she could to wind back time. To work harder at keeping her feelings hidden. Or, better yet, she should have nipped them in the bud when she first realized she was falling for him. Now, she did not have his friendship or his presence in her life. She was alone all over again, and missed him terribly.

She knelt to unpack the preserves she'd brought, and began setting out enough jars for everyone.

Cora had come to fetch her reticule, but stopped at the colorful sight. "Look at what Joanna brought. The prettiest jams I've ever seen."

"And hopefully the tastiest, too." Joanna couldn't help being pleased. She had worked from dawn until dark over a hot stove. Canning was next. "The orchard is brimming with more than we could possibly use. If anyone wants fresh fruit, just let me know."

"I love peaches. Oh, and plums." Cora sighed. "I miss having my own trees, living in town as I do."

"Me, too." Lanna spoke up, joining them. "I'll bring dessert next week. If Joanna will let me drop by for a bucket of peaches."

"Sounds like a treat," Joanna agreed, unable to remember the last time she'd had this much happiness in her life. Although she was still getting to know these women, she had the feeling they would be good friends for life. She could see her little ones out front on the porch with Ida. James had his wooden mustangs and

Daisy had her doll. Both children were well-fed and secure and happy.

The only thing wrong in her life was Aiden. She feared that was something that would never be right again.

Aiden forked fresh hay into the corral manger and watched the horses, tired from their fieldwork, amble over to get their supper. Over their sun-warmed backs, he could see Joanna coming toward the house from the shanty. It ripped him apart to watch her, but he could not seem to look away. No doubt she had delivered the evening meal, and her attention was riveted on the hillside between the houses where her children were playing.

He heard Thad come up behind him with the water bucket. "Why is she bringing our suppers to the shanty?"

Aiden winced, although he had been expecting the question. He set the pitchfork against the wall. "I told you this wasn't a real marriage. I gave Joanna the house, figured it was better for her and the kids, and I took the shanty."

"So you really are doing this? You're married to her but you're living apart from her." He upended the bucket into the water bin.

"That's right. Don't see as how it's any of your business." He tossed his brother a half grin. "Thanks for your help cleaning up, Thad. That storm left quite a mess."

Although, *he* was the one who'd felt like a mess that night, talking to Joanna. He flicked his gaze back to her. She was on the kitchen doorstep now, leaning down to speak softly to her son. The boy was looking at the barn and his face was squinted up, as if he was trying not to cry.

She had kept the children away from him; she probably thought he would be happy about that. He wasn't, but it was just as well. He blew out a sigh and kept to the shadows in the aisle. She soothed her hand over the boy's head. His nose was slightly pink from playing in the sun.

The boy needed a hat. Joanna ought to buy him one, and if there was a voice at the back of Aiden's mind saying that he could do it the next time he was in town, he ignored it. It was easier, sure, but sensible not to listen to that. The boy wanted a pa, that was plain to see. That could only spell trouble.

"I'm glad to help, you know that." Thad lowered the bucket, looking thoughtful. "I was going to head to town tomorrow and see Finn. You want to come?"

"I don't think he wants to see me." Aiden watched Joanna as she knelt to give her son a hug. It was a marvel how she radiated love. She was a vision in calico; somehow she was more beautiful to him every time he looked at her. And that tore at him, too.

Thad plodded closer. "I think you need to see him. And then there's the matter of getting him a lawyer."

"I don't see how we can afford to." Aiden braced himself against that pain, too. He'd let down too many people. "I don't see how we can afford not to."

"I talked to Noelle's friend Lanna. Her husband is a lawyer and he'll cut his fee for us. What do you think?"

"I can pay half if you can."

"We'll figure out a way." Thad led him down the aisle. "C'mon, I'm hungry enough to eat a bear."

"That's two of us, little brother." He hated that he wanted to drag his feet. Joanna was still in sight. She was lifting two five-gallon buckets, empty now, and swinging them as she walked. Thank heavens she was heading away from him. He wouldn't have to face her and remember the other night, when he had let her think that he regretted marrying her.

"Aiden, do you reckon she left us any pie?"

"There's a mighty good chance." There she was, about to round the far corner of the house. He drank in the sight of her, trying to harden his heart, fighting to keep from caring, but it came anyway. His feelings for her were sweet like spring. Two more steps, a swish of her pretty green skirt, and she was gone from his sight.

But the caring in his heart remained.

"Look at this place." Thad's voice brought him back to the moment.

They were standing in the shadow of the shanty. The amber prairie rolled out before them in a thousand shades of tan and yellow, but where did his eye go? Toward the far corner of the orchard that he could see. There was no sign of Joanna, but he knew she was there, picking fruit.

He ought to be out there helping her, but he couldn't make himself do it. So he followed his brother into the small house and went to wash his hands at the basin.

"I can't believe this is the same shanty." Thad

glanced around as he passed Aiden the soap. "She put up new curtains for you and everything."

She had made such a difference here.

All he had to do was look around to see the spotless and polished stove, the gleaming counters and shelves, the gingham curtains, clean and pressed and fluttering in the breeze from the screened window. A cloth lay over the table, where supper for two was set out and covered and two place settings awaited them.

"Peach cobbler," Thad exclaimed as he lifted one of the tins. "It's my lucky day. Tell me again why you're not in love with that woman?"

Aiden winced, and rinsed his hands in the basin, glad he could turn his back to his brother. He didn't want him to guess at the truth. He cleared his throat, wishing words alone were powerful enough to change his heart. "Love ought to be based on more than a well-baked dessert. But I don't want anything to do with love, anyway." He took the towel from the rack and ignored the subtle scent of sunshine and the soap Joanna used. "I'm not building my life on something that can be gone in a flash. It's foolish, plain and simple. It's not what life is about."

"I see."

It was the quiet way his brother said the words that made his lungs seize up. His hands fumbled as he hung the towel. "I'm glad you understand then."

"I do."

The way he said that made Aiden grimace. "You think I love her."

"Yep." Thad looked mighty sure of himself as he poured tea into the glasses that Joanna had left them. "I think she loves you back. Look at all she's done for you. This meal. She spent time on this. She put care into this. She could have spent half the effort and it would have been more than enough."

"She's a hard worker. It has nothing to do with me." He didn't believe it, but he wanted it to be the truth. More than anything. His hands shook as he pulled out the ladder-back chair at the table. There were comfortable cushions tied neatly to the chair seat and back. Joanna, again.

"You can say it all you want—" Thad stared as he settled across the table "—but that won't make it true. I know. I've been where you are. Letting yourself fall in love with a woman is a risk. There's no guarantee you won't get your heart broken in the end."

"You make too little of it." Pressure built in Aiden's chest, expanding against his ribs. He'd had enough of this talk. Instead of saying what he meant, he bowed his head for prayer. Since his throat was hurting, too, he growled, "You say the blessing."

"I'll say it when I'm good and ready, big brother." Thad looked to be in one of his stubborn moods. "You listen to me. You've got a mighty nice woman for a wife, and I think you're falling in love with her and it scares you to death."

"You don't think I haven't turned to my faith on this?" He leaned back in his chair, hurting, just hurting. Why wouldn't Thad leave it alone? "I've prayed for years on this. I've prayed until I've run out of prayers. I trust God knew what he was doing when he took Kate and my son from me. I don't know why, but everything God does for us is because he loves us. I accept that. But what I can't do is lay everything I am on the line again and lose what is most precious to me. I can't do it. I won't. I'm not strong enough."

There. He watched the realization dawn in his brother's expression, his brother who had always been someone he could count on, and he gave thanks, as he bowed his head, for Thad. "Are you going to say grace, or am I going to?"

"I'll say it." His brother bowed his head, beginning the prayer.

Aiden hardly heard it. What he heard was the rapid swish of his pulse in his ears and the truth in his heart.

The days had fallen into a rhythm, but although life was pleasant, Joanna couldn't say she was happy. Mornings were spent on chores around the house, and if she didn't work for Noelle or Cora, she squeezed in all the time she could working outside. Now, as she carefully twisted a peach from the branch of the reaching tree, she checked between the leaves for her little ones.

There was Daisy, sitting in a patch of small-faced sunflowers. She had a chain of them around her neck and was making what looked like a bracelet to go with it. James was not next to her. His wooden horses were there in the grass, but he was missing.

She laid the peach in the basket, slipped down the stepladder and scanned the orchard. Nothing. She didn't see him behind any of the trees or climbing in the branches. How had he scampered off? And why? He knew better. Then she saw Aiden talking to Thad in front of the barn, leading Clyde by the reins. The big draft horse was saddled and had his nose toward the ground, stretching out as if he was scenting something. Or somebody.

James. There he was, partly hidden by the dip of the rise, wandering close to the men and their horses. Thad's mustang gave a low nicker and turned, swishing his tail. Both horses watched the little boy hungrily, stretching out for the first fond caress.

She swept Daisy onto her hip and was already at the orchard gate when she saw Aiden focus in on the boy. With every step she took closer, she could more clearly see the strain on his face, the shadows in his eyes and the white lines around his tense mouth. Yet he was kind as he leaned down to speak to her son. James's shoulders slumped and he shook his head.

"…you oughtn't to run off on your ma like that." Aiden's low tones drifted toward her. "Here she comes. She's in a panic, if you ask me."

"I'm sorry, sir."

"You'd best tell that to her." Those words were kind, but she knew they cost him. All she had to do was look at how tight Aiden was holding himself to know.

She ached for him and for her son. Her soul felt near to cracking as she bundled the affection for him away, storing it down deep. With any luck, it would be deep enough not to show. She set Daisy on the ground. "I'm sorry, Aiden. He snuck off on me. Hello, Thad."

"Howdy, Joanna." He lifted his hat in greeting. If any man could stand next to Aiden and hold his own, it was Thad. They were clearly good men cut from the same cloth.

"I've got a crate of apples and peaches in the lean-to set aside for you. Maybe one of plums, if I can get to it." She took hold of her son's shoulder. "I'll have Aiden bring them in the wagon on Sunday."

"That's mighty kind of you." Thad mounted up. "We're going in to town to see Finn, although I reckon Aiden has probably already told you that."

No, he hadn't, but Joanna bit her lip. What Aiden chose to do with his time was surely not her concern. If it hurt that he hadn't turned to her and that he would not, she had to tuck that down deep inside, too. "I hope your visit goes well. I've been praying for Finn."

"That's gotta help." Thad tipped his hat to her before he wheeled his mustang around. "Come Sunday, I'll let you have another ride on Sunny. What do you think about that, James?"

"That would sure be swell." The boy drew his shoulders up, hope vibrating through him.

"I get to, too," Daisy called out, holding out her handful of flowers. Clyde took a couple out of her hand as he walked by.

There was Aiden, towering far above them on the back of the giant horse. He sat rigidly straight, as controlled as a soldier, as remote as the farthest horizon. His mighty shoulders were braced, as if he were carrying a world of burdens on them. He did not look at Joanna as he passed by, but she could see the cords bunch in his neck and the muscles in his jaw clench tight.

If only she could forget his words. *Don't think I don't want to. I wish I could. Prayer hasn't helped. I can't find my heart. Sometimes you lose too much of yourself and you can't get it back.*

She watched him ride away into the sinking sun with regret weighing heavily upon her. Regret for rushing into marrying him. Regret for being a reminder of what he had lost. Regret for the love alive and committed in her heart, this time for a man who wanted to love her but never could.

"Ma, can you tie this up for me?" Daisy's innocent request broke into her thoughts.

Again, she tucked both her love and her hurt away, and knelt to twist the last flower into place around her daughter's little wrist, completing the chain.

"Ma?" James stood with his hands at his sides, watching Aiden disappear around the distant bend. "When I grow up, I want to ride a black horse, too."

James's admiration was sky-high for the man he wanted to be his pa. Another arrow straight to her heart. Joanna winced at the inner pain. Was this the way it was going to go? James pining quietly for a father, and Aiden always riding away? She was no different, she realized, wanting what could not be.

What could never be.

She took each child by the hand and headed back to the orchard. Whether she was happy or not, there was work waiting. She would have plenty of time to rest on snowy winter afternoons and think of her mistakes then—and of the man who would be sitting alone in his shanty, always separate from her.

From them.

Chapter Seventeen

The next morning the hurt on Joanna's face still troubled him. Maybe because it was difficult thinking of his little brother locked up behind steel bars. Finn had refused to see him. Or maybe because his failures weighed heavy on his soul. Either way, he didn't feel prepared for how she watched the ground instead of the world around her as she came out of the house in her Sunday best.

Her daughter hopped down the steps in two-footed jumps, her white-blond braids bouncing. The son saw him and took off at a run, eager to see the horses. Clyde gave a snort of welcome and stretched against the harness collar, reaching his neck as far as it would go.

"'Mornin', sir. Thank you kindly for the hat!" The boy skidded to a stop in front of Clyde, who was calm enough not to bat an eye. The gentle giant gave a low nicker and lipped the boy's hat brim affectionately.

Aiden nodded. It was the best he could do. He'd left the Stetson on the kitchen table late last night, knowing it would be found this morning. He held his heart firm and prayed that Joanna would hurry up so they could get this over with.

Heaven didn't seem to be listening today. Joanna was taking her sweet time, locking the door, checking the lock, grasping her daughter's hand. Every step she took toward the wagon seemed slower than the last. He shuffled his polished boots in the chalky dust, trying not to see the dread on her face or the little boy giggling softly as he petted the horses.

"Thank you for James's cowboy hat. He loves it." Her gaze was fixed on the wagon instead of on Aiden.

"Sure." That one word seemed to stick in his throat. Maybe because the bonnet she wore made her eyes bluer than wildflowers. Delicate curls fell down to frame her gentle face, making him remember the night they had stood not far from here, and how he had held her face in his hands, her sweetness in his soul.

He hadn't wanted to admit that then, but for some reason it was easier now when there was a vast distance between them. A distance so wide there was no way to cross it. They both knew it. Even if he risked everything within him by telling her how he felt, it wouldn't matter. He had hurt her, and now she watched at him with dismay.

"We'd best get on the road," he said, holding out his hand to help her up.

She didn't take it. With a little hitch to her chin, she

swung her daughter into the back of the wagon. That smarted a bit. He told himself it was just as well. Taking her hand would only bring him closer to her. And being closer to her was the one place he could not be. He waited until she was safely over the top rail before he climbed up onto the high seat.

"James," Joanna called out. "Leave the horses, honey, and climb up."

Something moved at the edge of Aiden's vision. Something pink. "Mister, do you know what?"

He stared into the girl's blue eyes—like Joanna's—and swallowed hard.

"I made all this." She patted the pink carnations wreathed around her neck. "Do you know what? I made you somethin', too."

To his surprise she stuck a flower in his shirt pocket.

"There." She gave it a pat, so innocent and pure hearted. "Did you know God made all the flowers?"

"Y-yep." The word scraped like a serrated knife. He swallowed hard. He couldn't feel a thing. He wouldn't let himself.

"Daisy, come sit down," Joanna said in that patient, gentle way of hers. "Sorry about that, Aiden."

"It's no trouble." Her nearness rubbed the edges of his heart raw. His throat worked and he gathered the reins. He could no longer make himself cold or steely enough not to feel. Longing whipped through his soul, regret though his heart. He released the brake. "You ready back there?"

"We're all seated." She sounded calm, as if he had

never hurt her. As if they had never been anything more to one another than strangers.

He snapped the reins and the wagon lurched forward into the searing August sunlight. It was the brightness; surely that was the reason his eyes stung and why he found it hard to see.

"Why, look at you, children. You are simply charming." Ida knelt in the church aisle and welcomed the little ones with a grandmotherly hug, and then went on to tell Noelle how cute each child looked.

Joanna filled up with adoration. Ida was an absolute blessing. The older woman fondly praised Daisy's flowers and was delighted when the girl presented her with a carnation for her bonnet. Wearing the pink flower proudly, Ida hugged her again and complimented James's new hat. He put it on for a moment to show her, before taking it back off politely. Ida said he looked like a wrangler, and he happily settled next to her on the pew.

"I need to talk with Thad," Aiden said, a shadow at her back and nothing more, before striding off toward the far aisle.

Joanna caught her mother-in-law's curious gaze and shrugged. What could she say? She remembered the lovely lace Ida and Noelle had made for a wedding gift, stitching in all their hopes and prayers for Aiden. How did Joanna tell Ida that present was still wrapped up for safekeeping? That she and Aiden were like strangers again, and no amount of prayer, it seemed, would stop it?

She settled on the hard wooden bench, disheartened. There was Aiden standing at the back of the church, discussing something with his brother. He looked serious and so grim, his face a granite mask.

"How are you, dear?" Ida asked after the children were settled. "You look weary."

"It's a lot of work to keep up with the orchard. I suppose you know that, since it used to be yours."

"And glad I am that it's yours now. It was getting far too much for me to tend to at my age. I wouldn't mind lending a hand, if you would have me."

"And me," Noelle offered. "Although I'm not sure how much help I could be, but I'm excellent at moral support."

"You both are more than welcome." She had been alone for so long in the past, and now again in her marriage, that to have this friendly offer felt like a great treasure. Joanna hoped that she could offer them as much in the years to come. "How about after threshing day? I've been doing a fair amount to prepare for that, including enough baking for the both of us."

"You are a wonder, Joanna," Ida said as Daisy leaned against her for another snuggle. "And with all that is happening in your life, you get so much done. Now I have a question for you."

Uh-oh. She had a terrible feeling that her mother-in-law was going to ask about Aiden or their marriage. She sneaked a glance over her shoulder, and there he was, deep in conversation with Thad and another man.

"That's Joe Wolf," Ida told her. "He's a good lawyer,

from what we hear. Now, how was Aiden after he came home from trying to see Finn?"

From trying to see Finn? What had happened? Had Finn refused to see Aiden? She knew that had to be hard for him; Aiden loved his family. "He said nothing to me about it."

"I suppose it was late by the time the day's work was done." Ida nodded. "I remember how it is. There's never enough daylight to get everything done in, and it seems the work doesn't end. He looks troubled. What's happened to Finn is a heartache for all of us. His lawyer says they are going to make some kind of a plea, so he will get less jail time. He wouldn't even see me when I tried to visit him."

While Noelle soothed Ida with comforting words, Joanna sat there silently, dismayed. She did not turn around. Aiden was hurting; she was hurting. What was the solution? She had once asked for God's guidance in helping Aiden, and she thought she'd been heard. She really had.

She stared down at the battered Bible clutched in her hands, the one that had been her ma's and her grandma's before that, and had been held through decades of prayers. As she stood for the opening hymn and then the opening prayer, no answers came to her. She had felt this way so many times, in need and feeling forgotten. Lost. When the sermon began, she took Daisy onto her lap. The little girl settled against her, a sweet weight in Joanna's arms and in her heart.

"Today's sermon will be from Psalm 71. *'But I*

will hope continually, and will yet praise thee more and more.'"

Her soul stilled. How was that for an answer? Maybe she had forgotten to listen and to wait for Him—certainly God was worth waiting for. Humbled, she listened to the minister's words, realizing one thing. Faith, life and love were not easy. Sometimes you just had to hold on and—no matter what—believe.

She was still wearing her patched dresses, and it irked him no end. Aiden dumped a few cups of oats in the trough for Clyde and Dale. The old horses dug in, eager for their favorite treats. While they munched, he leaned to get a good look out Thad's stable door toward the front yard, where Joanna stood in the shade of the house talking with Ma and Noelle, a peach cobbler in hand. Faint snatches of conversation whipped by on the breeze, and he couldn't deny the way Joanna's gentle alto could bring him peace. Or how softer life was simply from being near her.

"How's the arrangement working out?" Thad asked wryly as he secured the lid on the grain barrel.

"Just fine, little brother. And keep in mind my marriage is none of your concern." He arched his brow, but judging by the grin on Thad's face, it didn't work.

"Let me know if you need help." Thad unhooked Sunny's lead from the wall. "I've got a fair bit of experience when it comes to marriage."

"Funny, as you've been married, what, four months?"

"I'm just offering, is all. Trying to be a good

brother." He ambled past and clipped the lead on the mustang's halter. "Here come your stepchildren."

Aiden gulped. He'd done all he could not to think of them that way. They weren't his; they were Joanna's children. Sure enough, they were bounding across the grass. The little girl was in the lead, braids bobbing. The boy stayed with her, keeping watch over her. They had both changed out of their Sunday clothes, and as they pounded closer, Thad's wild mustangs broke into a run in the nearby field, startled by the sound and the motion.

The kids started talking. Thad answered, leading Sunny out into the yard. The mustang swished his tail and lowered his head politely to accept their eager strokes. He clearly wasn't one to mind basking in the glow of adoration. Aiden gathered his strength, took a deep sustaining breath and followed his brother out into the yard.

"Sir!" James ran right up to him with a grin just like his ma's and an earnestness that was hard not to like. "I got denim riding pants just like yours. Ma just finished 'em!"

So that's what Joanna had been doing late last night. He had noticed the parlor lights on past midnight. He had wondered if she had been unable to sleep, too. Watching the night skies had always soothed him. Maybe sewing did the same for her.

The boy seemed to expect some sort of approval, so Aiden gave him a nod. A small twitch of pain made it through his defenses. He shored himself up more as the little boy ran back to Sunny, but the days of not feeling anything were past. Emotions slammed into Aiden like a summer storm, crashing with a physical pain against his ribs, and deeper, against his soul.

Joanna. She was coming toward him like a song, lightly, breezily, carrying a tray with a pitcher and cups, her skirt rippling in the wind. Those patched skirts. He clenched his hands, fighting the pain and something worse.

He wanted to be angry about those dresses she wore, and about why she hadn't gotten new ones as he had told her to. A voice of reason somewhere in the back of his brain told him that maybe she was too sensible to go spending a bunch of money on dresses all at once. That would be just like her, he reckoned. But maybe she hadn't done it because she did not want to rely on him. Her stubborn independence made him grind his teeth.

He wanted her to be closer. He wanted her to keep away. He wasn't making a lick of sense and he knew it.

That irked him, too.

"I thought you all might be thirsty. It was a hot, dusty ride out here from town." She set the tray down on the top of the feed barrel and faced him. "Aiden?"

He was not strong enough to look at her. If he did, he felt he might come apart. All his defense seemed to be nothing against her loving presence. He cleared his throat and studied his boots. "Sounds good."

The kids clattered up to her, pressing close to her skirts. He did his best to shut out their happy sounds, telling Joanna how they were going to go riding. He heard James say, "I get to learn to ride by myself today! *He's* gonna teach me how to rein!"

"You mean, Aiden?" Joanna sounded confused. "No, honey, I think you misunderstood."

"Nah, I heard just fine."

Thad's promises, Aiden knew. Thad was trying to help, that was all. Aiden realized his mistake. He had been trying to stay back from the children, so hadn't been able to keep watch over what Thad was telling them.

He swallowed hard against something fluttering in him—panic. He felt trapped. Suffocating again, unable to get air. Then suddenly there was Joanna, offering him a cup of lemonade. She was like rain in a drought. Everything he wanted beat within him like a deadly thunderhead.

"Your ma said this was your favorite."

Her smile was likely to undo him, and yet he could not look away. Her hand against his was the greatest comfort and the deepest agony. He would have moved but he was rooted like an oak to the ground.

"Dinner won't be more than a few minutes." She was compassion and hope and love. It was all there in the brush of her fingers against his, before she slipped away. She gathered up the tray and the empty pitcher. "We'll be eating on the porch due to the heat. Don't be long."

His soul seemed to follow her, and there it was, the love he could no longer hold back, cracking like a lightning bolt against his spirit. He stood as if paralyzed, a man unable to think, and too afraid to feel.

"Aiden, you okay?" Thad asked.

Somehow he managed to nod. He glanced around, realized Thad held a cup, too, and took another sip of his lemonade. The little ones had already gulped theirs and were standing next to Sunny, who was trying to get at the sweet-smelling cups they held. The children's giggles lifted his heart.

"You don't look okay." Thad ambled closer. "Maybe it's the heat. You want to go sit in the shade for a spell?"

He shook his head, not trusting his voice. What he wanted to do was be alone and stay real still until this pain died down. Until the turmoil settled.

"Then if it's not the heat, it's got to be Joanna, right?"

His throat worked. How could he admit to that? It was folly, that's what it was, to let himself care about her. No—that wasn't the truth. He didn't just care about her. *Caring* was too miniscule of a word to describe what he felt for her. From the bottom of his scarred soul to the top of his battered heart, he loved her. What was he going to do about that? How was he going to stop it?

Thad was still there, concerned. "You told me once that you trusted God to know what He's doing. Maybe bringing Joanna and these kids to you is God's doing, too. Have you considered that?"

"I've been trying not to."

"Well, consider it. That's all I'm saying." Thad paused as the dinner bell clanged from the porch.

Aiden bowed his head, refusing to look up to see Joanna ringing that bell, refusing to note the sympathy on his brother's face.

"Sir?" The boy sidled up, peering at him from beneath the brim of his hat. Those big, need-filled eyes brimmed with too many questions, every one of which was too big for Aiden to answer now.

"What is it, kid?"

"I wanna be just like you when I grow up." Joanna's son looked as if he'd been gathering up hope the way his little sister picked flowers. "I'm gonna be a wheat rancher with lots of horses."

Aiden hung his head. There was nothing he could say to that, fighting as he was not to feel.

Thad saved him. "James? I figure we can tie Sunny to the porch rail, and after dinner is done, you can ride him. You wanna lead him to the house for me?"

"Do I!" James rushed up to take sole possession of the rope. "C'mon, Sunny. Come along with me."

Aiden was barely aware of feet scampering off and Thad's voice, calm and friendly with the children, moving farther away. All that he had been holding back broke apart like a winter's thaw. The keen rush of emotion that rolled through him nearly brought him to his knees. Perhaps this pain was life coming back to him. Whatever it was, it hurt. He drew in the hot air and let the sun bake him, trying to fight it. Trying not to be ripped apart.

There was Joanna on the front porch, waltzing down the steps with a carrot, a treat for Sunny. James and Daisy swirled around her skirts, excited by the horses and by the family surrounding them. Thad joked with James and then with his wife. Ma reached for Daisy's hand. Noelle leaned in to kiss Daisy's cheek. They were a family again.

Aiden had done everything he could to keep this from happening. He'd held back his feelings. He'd refused to care for Joanna and her kids. He'd stayed away from them. He'd barely talked to them. Hardly acknowledged them, and still, it happened just the same.

He clenched his fists, moving without realizing where he was going, only knowing he needed to get somewhere quiet and pray. He had to take this to the Lord because he was not strong enough to do it on his own. He was sure he would never be strong enough.

Chapter Eighteen

Oh, Aiden. Joanna caught a glimpse of him through Noelle's kitchen window as she grabbed the pan of rolls to carry outside. He stood far out in the sun-scorched bunchgrass beyond the mustang pasture, with his back to her. He gazed off at the river and the reaching prairie, hands behind his back, feet braced, looking like a solitary pillar of strength. Aloneness radiated off him like sunlight off the dry earth.

So much was pulling at him right now. According to Thad, Finn was seeing a judge next week, and it did not look good for him. It was a heartbreak for all the family, she knew, but especially for Aiden, who had fought so hard for his little brother, whom he loved. That was Aiden. He was faithfulness and loyalty. Those were a few reasons why she loved him so much, why she longed to go out to him and hold him until he no longer felt sore and alone.

If only she could. She tucked away her wishes and

turned from the window. No matter what, she would not give up on him. She would not stop loving him. Love made a difference in this world, she firmly believed, and she would be Aiden's difference. She would wait and she would hope. Maybe all he needed was time. God had brought her here for a purpose—to love Aiden. She would not yield.

The breeze off the river was a pleasant relief after being in the hot house. Joanna pushed through the screen door, renewed at the sight of Daisy sitting next to Ida at the outdoor table. The little girl wiggled with happiness; it didn't look as if she could sit still.

"Ma!" Her grin was the widest ever. "Grandma Ida said we're gonna have ice cream!"

A rare treat. "We are?"

"Yes! To go with the cobbler we brought. I helped make it," she told her grandma, leaning toward her eagerly. "I sifted the flour and got to put the peaches in."

While Ida praised her as lavishly as any doting grandmother, Joanna slipped the pan of rolls onto the table and looked around. James's place was empty. Where was he?

"Joanna? Is that you?" Noelle was standing at the railing. "Thad went to look for James. He was right beside me on the bench when you went into the house. I felt him slip behind me, but he must have been moving fast. I called out to Thad, and he looked up just in time to see him dart around the corner of the house."

"He knows not to run off." Joanna fought down the panic. She tried not to immediately think of the long list of dangers to a small child on a working ranch—especially the wild mustangs. "I can't believe he's not right here. Noelle, will you watch Daisy?"

"Yes. Are you sure he didn't run off to the outhouse?"

"No." Thad's voice came from around the corner. "First place I checked. Then the barn." He strode into sight, worry and dust marking his face. "There's no sign of him in the corral. I'm going to check the mustangs' field next."

"He went to Aiden." Joanna was sure of it. She was already moving, hurrying around the wraparound deck to the back of the house. Panic beat with her footsteps, and she tried to stay clear and focused. She scanned the pastures and the stretch of field beyond, where Aiden was. No sign of a Stetson among the waving grass and wildflowers.

"James!" She hurried down the back steps. "James!"

No answer. She heard Thad and Ida calling out his name on the other side of the house.

She rushed through the fields, fighting panic, heading toward Aiden. Surely that's where James would go.

Maybe bringing Joanna and these kids to you is God's doing, too. If only he could get Thad's words out of his head. Aiden stared off at the river rushing below, churning, tumultuously, and realized that was just how he felt. As if he were in that dangerous current, being pulled under against his will. Life was like that river; a man had little control over it. He had to accept that the current was stronger, and let it take him where it would.

How do I do it, Lord? He truly had to know. Living hurt, and he couldn't remember the sky being so blue that it stung his eyes, or the sun a tangible heat on his skin. And the colors—they were everywhere, vibrant and shimmering. The thunder of the waterfall had never been louder, and a rainbow reaching from the cliff to the river below never brighter.

He was alive and whole and unable to trust. *Lord, how can I believe in love again?*

He couldn't; it was as simple as that. He could still feel the scars within him, wounds that could never heal. How could he take another chance on love? His entire being froze at the thought. Pain slammed through him. No, he could not lose like that again. He just couldn't. Love could be gone in a blink of an eye. Love was too risky. Love could take all a man was when it died. He did not want to risk like that again. He was simply not strong enough.

He hung his head, unable to believe, after all.

He jammed his hands in his pockets. He could not go back to the house, couldn't face the family he'd let come so close to his heart.

"Aiden!" Joanna's shout pierced his thoughts, high and shrill with panic. "Aiden!"

Instantly alert, he whipped around and there she was, racing through the field as fast as she could toward him. That's when he saw the mustangs running, too, and the stallion leading the pack, focused on something hidden in the grass. The top of a little Stetson. James.

Aiden was already moving. He climbed over the fence in one quick motion and hit the ground running. That stallion was closing in, ears laid back flat to his head. A sharp neigh of fury shattered the silence, but that animal's fury was nothing, nothing at all compared to Aiden's. All he could think about was James. There he was, just ahead, frozen in place, stiff with fear.

Aiden saw it in an instant: the stallion was going to get there first. He was vaguely aware of Joanna's cries, of Thad shouting, but he knew they were all too far away to do anything. Aiden had to protect James. It was up to him. He changed direction, running toward the horse, pushing himself with all his might. His legs ate up the ground, but it didn't seem fast enough. The distance between them was closing, and there was James, standing stock-still and whimpering.

Aiden launched himself at the horse and hit it, shoulder to shoulder. Pain shot up his arm, but it was distant, nothing at all. His feet went out from under him and he hit the ground. Pain slammed into his ribs and side; must have been a hoof that struck him. The air was driven out of his lungs, leaving him gasping.

Time slowed down. He squinted up to see the stallion, knocked off stride, recover and rear up against the brilliant blue sky. Aiden didn't like seeing the underside of those hooves flailing in the air, because they were going to come down upon him. Sadness filled him, because he was not ready to leave this earth. But at least James was safe.

James. He could see the boy at the corner of his

vision, standing with his jaw open, still frozen in fear. Regret filled Aiden at how he'd treated the lad, his stepson, and at the way he had spent his time here. But at least he'd accounted for something. James was unharmed, and he would stay that way. Thad was coming, and Joanna, too. That was a relief. As Aiden watched the horse rear above him, he felt at peace. At peace, because God had led him back to life. To what mattered most.

Something snaked across the blazing sky. A rope. Its noosed end sailed around the stallion's neck and pulled tight. Time snapped back, and Aiden heard the furious neigh, heard the rapid cadence of James's breathing and felt the pounding of footsteps beside him. The horse came crashing down, pulled a few feet away by Thad's strength. A shadow cut across the sun and fell over him like grace.

Joanna. His heart stopped when he saw at the stark concern on her face. His spirit stilled as she knelt over him, touching his cheek and then his chest with her fingertips.

"Aiden? Aiden, where are you hurt? I saw you go down, and I…" Tears pooled in her eyes, precious silvery tears just for him. "You've hurt yourself something bad, I can see it."

He gasped in air, but none of it seemed to reach his lungs. He couldn't rightly say she was wrong, but he didn't mind so much. Looking at her and drinking in her beauty and her goodness was enough to sustain him for this moment and for the rest of his life.

A tear plopped onto his chin. Her tear. His heart broke all over again with a great crash of love for her. It was a tide he could not hold back. A greatness he could not control. So he didn't even bother. God had put this love in his heart for a reason. It wasn't a matter of not being strong enough; all he had to do was trust God, come what may.

"I'm so mad at you for getting hurt." She sniffled and blinked hard, but those tears just kept coming, anyway.

He heard, loud and clear, what those tears said. "Sorry," he choked out.

"You should be." Fear, that's what he saw. And hurt. "Aiden, I know you don't want a real wife, but you are a real husband to me. I don't know if I could stand to lose you."

He'd put that hurt there. He winced and did his best to cowboy up. Loving someone with all you had was a frightening thing, but he was no longer afraid. He felt strong. Courageous. Because life was hard enough. Love didn't need to be, too.

"Thank you for this." She pressed a kiss to his cheek. "For saving my son."

Sweetness filled him right up. It sealed up every crack in his heart and every fissure in his soul. How about that? Air eked into his spasming lungs, and he hurt something fierce. But that was good, right? It let him know he was alive.

"No problem," he choked out, needing to correct her. "I saved *our* son."

"But…?" She shook her head, as if to tell him he

was wrong, but then it must have struck her what he meant. Tears spilled from her eyes again, and the love in them, why, it was the loveliest sight he'd ever seen.

Another shadow fell across him. Little James, his face screwed up in heartache. He gave a sniff, fighting a sob.

Pain streaked through Aiden's chest as he lifted his arm to catch the boy's small hand in his. "Don't cry, little buddy. I'm gonna be all right."

"But you l-left."

"Aw, I wasn't going anywhere." It hurt to see what James needed—and what Aiden hadn't given him. He felt ashamed, and vowed on his life that he would move mountains for this child if he had to—for his child—to make this up to him. "I guess I was to teach you to rein this afternoon. We might have to postpone that for a bit."

James nodded, sniffling.

There. That was one thing made right. Now, for his biggest offense. That hurt worse than all the broken ribs in his chest. "Joanna, I love you."

"What?" She was gazing at him in shock, as if she were the one with the broken ribs. "What did you say?"

"I love you with all my heart and soul. I want you to know the whole truth I've been hiding from you and from myself. You are like the sun coming up in my life every day."

"I love you, too." He loved her. She could see the measure of it right there in his heart. Joy overwhelmed her. She had never hoped for so much. Aiden's love was a dream come true. She smiled through her tears. "But then you already know that."

"I do, but it never hurts to hear." He smiled back, and there it was, the zing of a deeper, emotional connection between them. She could feel it in the hitch of her soul and the brightening of her spirit. It was love, abundant and abiding and true.

"You are a great gift to my life, Joanna." Aiden struggled up onto his elbows.

She settled beside him, supporting him, taking him gently into her arms, this man she loved more than her life. Because he could not save his son, he had saved hers. What a treasure he was.

"I want a real marriage, Joanna. I want to cherish you the right way." He coughed a little, gasping in pain, but that didn't stop him. "I want to be the man you need in all ways. I won't let you down again. I promise you."

"You never let me down, and you never will."

"Then that's a yes?"

"Absolutely, beyond all doubt." It was in the happiness lighting her face and in the brush of her lips on his cheek.

Footsteps drummed on the earth. Thad was coming; he must have gotten the stallion secured. "You're looking a bit pale, big brother. I suppose I should go fetch the doc."

"Suppose so."

"Aiden?" It was Ma, bringing Noelle and little Daisy with her. Their little girl sidled up against Joanna's skirts. Ma was all business. "Let me take a look at that wound. I can put a poultice on that until the doctor gets here. Thad, let's get him in the house."

Aiden hardly noticed the pain. He was surrounded by family, the people he loved the most. He was in Joanna's arms, his love, his bride, his everything. Elation left him dizzy.

"Just a minute, Ma. There's one thing I've failed to do. Joanna, are you ready?" He pulled her gently to him and kissed her for real this time, tender and sweet. Their first kiss as man and wife.

Epilogue

November, three months later

Those were Aiden's boots coming up behind her. Joanna let go of the scrub brush, leaned back on her heels at the foot of the stairs and swept her bangs out of her eyes. "I suppose you want something from our bedroom, don't you? Too bad. I'm afraid the floors are still wet."

"And you're not going to let me in with my boots?" He looked like a man who'd been working hard in the barn. Bits of hay and straw clung to his shirt and trousers, but that only seemed to make him more handsome. Perhaps it was because there were no more shadows. He was whole and alive and happy.

She couldn't resist teasing him, just a little. "Sorry. I'm not going to let you through. You'll just have to wait."

"Wait, huh? It might take a long time to dry. And

it's not yet time for me to drive to town to pick up James and Daisy from school. I'm not sure what I ought to do with this free time."

She plopped the brush into the bucket of sudsy water and rose, wiping her hands on her apron. "You could go back outside and bring in more wood for our fires."

"I could, but it's turning awfully cold out there. It might snow."

"That's a handy excuse." She let her fingertips run up the placket of his flannel shirt, thinking of those ribs he had broken that were now good and truly healed. "Am I supposed to believe that a big man like you doesn't want to go outside in the cold?"

"That's right." His baritone dipped warm and low.

"Excuses, excuses, Mr. McKaslin." Her fingertips reached the top button on his shirt and she couldn't resist laying the flat of her hand there over the reliable beat of his heart. His devoted, faithful heart. "I can think of only one more chore that's left on my list and this is an important one."

"Is that so?" His hand covered hers, affection alight in his eyes. "You can trust me. I won't let you down."

"I know." Happiness filled her as she went up on tiptoe. "You could kiss your wife."

"My wife?" His right hand cradled the side of her face. "I love calling you that. Almost as much as I love kissing you."

"Lucky me." Joanna closed her eyes, breathless, waiting for the brush of his lips to hers.

His kiss was sheer perfection. It was pure sweetness

and complete tenderness. It was like floating on clear blue sky without a storm in sight.

"So you only wanted one kiss?" he murmured against her lips.

"I suppose I could endure a second one."

"It will be tough, but I think I can, too." He brushed the tendrils out of her eyes. "I can endure anything as long as I am with you."

"Me, too." His lips claimed hers again, this time as reverent as a promise kept. As miraculous as grace. She gave thanks for this man's everlasting love. He loved her, honest and true, the way she loved him.

"I love you, Joanna, with all of my soul," he said, and kissed her forehead.

"As I love you." She was so happy, it was easy to see the future with her beloved. There would be more children filling this house one day, James graduating from school and taking over the ranch, and some day, far from now, Aiden would walk Daisy down the aisle. Joanna's dreams for her children were coming true.

But for her, there would always be Aiden, strong and true and loving. He was her shelter, her dream, her everything.

Lace curtains framed a snowy view at the parlor window directly behind them, a reminder of the power of love and faith. And of their great love.

"I have one more request." She stepped back to look into his eyes. "Take me to town with you."

"Sure. Let's go fetch our children home." He slipped his arm around her shoulder and they went off into the world together.

* * * * *

Don't miss Julian Hart's
next Inspirational romance,
HER PERFECT MAN,
available August 2008 from Love Inspired.

Dear Reader,

Thank you so much for choosing HIGH COUNTRY BRIDE. I hope you enjoyed Joanna and Aiden's journey toward love as much as I did writing it. I first met Aiden when I was writing his brother Thad's story (HOMESPUN BRIDE), and my heart ached for this man so closed off from the world but so unshakable in his faith. I wanted him to find love again, and Joanna seemed the perfect wife for him. I hope their story to hope, faith and love touches you.

Wishing you the best of blessings,

Jillian Hart

QUESTIONS FOR DISCUSSION

1. At the beginning of the story, when Aiden finds Joanna and her children living out of their wagon on his land, what is his first reaction? What emotions are beneath his anger? What does this say about his character?

2. Joanna is in difficult circumstances at the beginning of the book. How does she handle hardship throughout the story? What does this say about her character?

3. What is Aiden's initial behavior toward the children? What does this reveal about him?

4. Joanna has been let down by love. How has that affected her? What does that reveal about her faith and her values?

5. Joanna has lost track of her faith. She fears God has stopped listening to her. How does this change through the story? How does she come to an understanding? What role does Aiden play in this?

6. How important is the theme of second chances in this story?

7. Joanna believes she is not the kind of a woman to

inspire true devotion in a man. How does this change through the book? How does she come to believe that Aiden can truly love her?

8. How are the themes of compassion and duty developed throughout the story?

9. How does Aiden turn to the Lord in times of need? What does he discover about God and faith?

10. What do you think Joanna has learned about love?

11. What role does James play in the story? What impact does he have on Aiden? How does that change through the story?

12. What makes Aiden risk his heart again? What do you think he has learned about life?